MANUSCRIPT 512

RICK CHESLER

SEVERED PRESS
HOBART TASMANIA

MANUSCRIPT 512

ISBN: 978-1-925840-22-3

PROLOGUE

1925, Xingu region of the Brazilian Amazon Rainforest

Colonel Percy Fawcett grinned broadly despite the fact he was almost surely about to die. Along with his son and his son's best friend, he reminded himself. Together, the trio comprised his entire highly-publicized expedition. He snapped himself from his moment of self-congratulations at having achieved the goal that had consumed his life for so long: the Lost City of Z.

He had finally found it.

For over two decades he had undertaken dangerous expeditions into the Amazon to prove the city's existence, enduring professional ridicule as well as the hardships of the jungle along the way. A fool's errand, many archaeologists claimed, a fairy tale, a myth, a legend based on a document known only as "Manuscript 512," created almost two hundred years ago.

Glancing around at the golden spires towering above him, though, and at the solid gold road upon which he stood, he could hardly deny that it was real. Oh, how he longed to bring news of this incredible place back to the world at large...But as he heard the crackling noises again, louder this time, he knew that was not in the cards.

He had seen the creatures before. He was lucky enough to have eluded them then, but this time he knew they would not allow him—any of them—to escape.

Strange and yet familiar at the same time, they defied satisfactory description even to his experienced explorer's eye. The piles of denuded human flesh, left by the natives—themselves savage cannibals-as a sacrifice, did not, however. And yet, he had deliberately not heeded those warnings.

"They're coming back, father!" Fawcett's son, Jack, yelled. He and his best friend, Raleigh, both still boys really, at the tender age of twenty-one, would not be living out full lives. His son ran up to him, penetrating a tapestry of thick vines to do so.

"We're not going to make it, are we? We're going to die here!"

Fawcett grabbed his boy by the shoulders and stared into his eyes with unwavering intensity. It was true, of course, but as his father, responsible for bringing him into this world, he searched his mind for parting words to offer him. And to himself, he supposed.

He was going to utter something about how he had already seen more than most men had in their entire lifetimes, but then changed his mind. Had he even been with a woman yet? He didn't think so. He had not yet born his own children, at any rate. Yes, he had travelled the world more than any young man not serving in the military had a right to, but a full life could not be lived in so short a span of years.

"Son, listen to me: I saw a golden staircase leading down beneath the ground that way…" He turned and pointed emphatically to a thick clump of foliage some distance away. Not far, perhaps a sixty-second sprint. "Go! Take Raleigh with you!" His son's friend was currently overcome with fear, cowering beneath a bush and crying softly into his cupped hands.

Jack whipped his head toward the clump of bushes and then back to his father. "What about you?"

"I'll see if I can create a distraction and draw them off—over the waterfall—then I'll meet you down the stairs."

Percy chided himself that he was offering false hope to his son so that he wouldn't have to come up with some final words to say. A coward's way out, he told himself. And yet, even through this veil of dread, the feelings of triumph endured. As his son ran off, he gazed up at the gleaming spires of gold, camouflaged amongst the glorious jungle canopy trees that blotted out the afternoon sky. He had found it! He had been right all along!

I knew it…I knew it!

Oh, how he longed to spend vast amounts of time luxuriating in the splendor of it all, photographing and measuring and drawing and writing notes and articles and dispatches to break the news to the civilized world. But the rustling noises were impossible to ignore now, and he knew what they meant.

Death was at hand. A pain-ridden, slow, hideous death, unbecoming of a true gentlemen, but then he had never been fully part of civilized society, had he? Fawcett flashed on his wife and younger son alone back in England, how he had left them, and Jack as well, time and time again over the decades, to explore his precious jungle, to fight in World War I, and then to explore the rainforest some more. He could long since have retired to the lecture circuit, recounting tales of his larger-than-life exploits in posh cigar lounges around Europe for handsome fees, but the real call of the wild was too strong, too alluring.

A smile formed on his visage as he stood in place, listening to them surround him. Yes, he wished he had more time here, but there was no place he'd rather die. This was the fulfillment of his life's ambitions, his destiny. He dropped to his knees and held up his arms to the towers of gold, to the awe-inspiring power and timeless knowledge of the ages that they represented.

He did not avert his gaze from them as the living wave of all-consuming beasts overtook him. Instantly they began stripping away his flesh, like a time-lapse video of a corpse being dissolved in strong acid.

He parted his lips and screamed, a guttural, raging soundwave intended not to reach the heavens, but to wake the dead. His utterance ended only when his vocal cords were severed by grasping, clutching appendages.

Colonel Percy Fawcett had finally discovered what he sought.

CHAPTER ONE

Present Day, Rio de Janeiro, Brazil

"See you here in precisely one hour. Don't forget," Dr. Hunter Winslow said in Portuguese. He tipped the cab driver an amount he hoped would be enough to gain compliance, but not so high as to be unusually memorable. Winslow adjusted his beret—something he never wore—on his bald dome before stepping from the cab onto the busy street. He glanced quickly up at the edifice in front of him, the National Library of Brazil.

An impressive, multistory façade of beige bricks and red tile roof, the structure occupied an entire city square block, surrounded by trees. Winslow strode with purpose straight up the front steps and into the grand entrance hall of the building. He had been here before and knew where the elevator was to the fifth floor, where he would find the reason for his visit today. He smiled good-naturedly at the help desk staff as he passed by on the way to the elevator, where he was pleased to find an open car waiting.

Winslow stepped inside and pressed the button for Five. When it let out he stood in the hallway for a moment, relishing the quiet compared to the general hubbub of the first floor. Without glancing at the sign reading Special Collections, he turned right and strode down a hall lined with framed historical photographs of Brazil. He felt remarkably calm for what he was about to do, and yet he couldn't deny an undercurrent of energy, like some unseen force pervading his entire being, propelling him forward. *You're about to fulfill your destiny. This is it, you've earned it, now you only need to claim it…*

He repeated these thoughts like a mantra in his head while he walked to the end of the hall where two closed double doors marked the entrance to the Special Collections room. This was the domain of the library's rare documents, maps, books and works of art—items deemed too valuable and precious to be randomly handled by the public. They were never allowed to be removed from the premises, and could only be viewed, handled and examined on site, and then only by vetted appointment. One generally needed association with a recognized research university to be granted access.

As a faculty member at Brown University, Dr. Winslow would have no trouble meeting those prerequisites, and so he walked up to the help desk and introduced himself by his real name. No turning back now, he told himself after handing his legitimate credentials to the pretty young librarian. She told him she would be right back and retreated to a photocopy machine to reproduce his IDs, both driver license and university badge.

Winslow forced himself to stop tapping his foot. He didn't need to appear nervous. The calm demeanor he had possessed minutes earlier was begging to evaporate with the reality of the situation. Once he did this, there was no turning back. *It's not too late, you can still change your mind*, he told himself...*Right up until*...

His thoughts were interrupted by the librarian handing him his identification back. "Thank you, Dr. Winslow. Your pre-visit paperwork is all in order. I'll show you to your document. Manuscript 512 correct?"

"Yes, that's the one." *That's the one, all right. My destiny.*

"Right this way, please."

Winslow checked his wristwatch as he followed the employee across the room to the narrow stacks. His glance was meant to appear casual, but in reality was anything but. *Eight more minutes. Good.* He let the cuff of his tweed jacket cover the watch once again and continued walking behind his chaperone. He didn't want to seem off-putting for not holding conversation, to give her any reason to decide she didn't like him, for he would need all the access and room to operate he could get. So he made what he hoped seemed like normal conversation for someone requesting a rare document from a specialty collection.

"So I guess you don't get many people requesting 512—just bored intellectuals like myself?"

She laughed briefly before pointing left into a narrow aisle between shelves and heading in that direction. "Well, there aren't a whole lot of academics who ask to see it, to be honest, a handful a year, but it probably gets more rejected requests than anything else in the entire Special Collection unit."

"Really?" Winslow pretended to be genuinely surprised by this. She answered him while walking down the aisle at a brisk pace.

"Yes, treasure hunters the world over ask to see it. Ninety-nine percent of them are unqualified and so their requests are rejected, but I'd say not a week goes by where someone inquires about how to get their hands on it. Which is strange, since anyone can read the text of it online," she added, turning right down another aisle of stacks. Winslow stepped on a small spider that scurried out from beneath one of the shelves.

"Ah, but the original document itself holds so much information," he put forth, urging himself to be careful not to divulge too much.

"Of course," his guide said, turning around to look at him as she said it. "That's why we have a Special Collections Department of the library in the first place. Everything is digitized, but as you say, there is no substitute for holding the real thing in your hands. Okay, should be right up here..." She slowed her pace while consulting a handheld device. "Here it is."

Winslow felt a chill run up his spine as he watched her slide a key into the lock on a square drawer. He looked up and down the aisle to make sure they were alone before first looking back to the librarian to watch her slowly slide open the drawer. They were still alone. Then he eyeballed his watch once again. *Five more minutes. Right on schedule...*

"Okay, so the manuscript is contained in this tube, and I will now escort you to the climate-controlled room where you will be able to remove it from the container and examine it."

"Excellent, thank you so very much." Winslow bubbled over with gratuitous enthusiasm. The closer to his goal he got, the more excited he became. *Keep it together*, he told himself, it *won't be long now.*

Most men would be watching the derriere of the woman sashaying ahead in front of them, but as Winslow followed her, the only thing on his mind was curbing the instinct to check his watch yet again. *Everything's on schedule. Get to the viewing room and then you can check the time...*He knew from experience that while not technically private, often the viewing rooms afforded him with the chance to be alone with his document. And he would need some alone time today to pull off what he came here to do.

He made the rest of the steps to the viewing room in a functional trance, not realizing he was there until the librarian's voice snapped him out of it. "Here you are, Dr. Winslow. As I'm sure you remember, you are permitted to stay here as long as you like, until we close, but we do ask that if you leave the Special Collections area of the library, for example to go to lunch, that you leave the document you have checked out with our front desk, and it will be returned to you upon your return."

Winslow raised a hand in a dismissive gesture. "Yes, yes, I know the drill, darling. It's not my first rodeo, as it were."

"Very good, sir. I'll leave you to your studies. Let me know should you require any assistance."

Winslow bade the woman thanks and retreated into the inner sanctum of the Special Collections Department. He looked around the space, at the rows of spacious cubbyholes, and quietly rejoiced. He was alone! The possibility that someone else might be in here during this phase of the plan had kept him awake last night and many others, for it was completely beyond his control.

He moved to the farthest work station from the entrance door and set the tube containing the centuries-old manuscript down on the desk surface. Then he tugged his sleeve up his wrist and noted the time. *Two more minutes…right on schedule.*

Winslow pulled a pair of blue latex gloves from a dispenser mounted on the back wall of the cubicle and put them on, following procedure. He uncapped the storage tube and ever so carefully slipped the manuscript out of the tube. Though he had held this very document in his own hands before, though he already knew full well what its content was, and though he was about to engage in the single most risky and daring action of his entire life, the historian still felt a powerful rush on seeing the original manuscript in tangible form before him. Not a scanned image on a computer screen, but the real thing.

The only sound in the room other than the motion of his own hands to unroll the precious document was the hum of the fluorescent overhead lights and the whir of an air conditioner unit. Winslow grinned as he unrolled the manuscript and pinned it to the table with the provided paperweights. He stared at the familiar text, written in Portuguese around 1753, the spidery longhand beckoned Winslow yet again.

But he was not here to ponder the meaning of the words, hidden or otherwise. Yes, he was still more convinced than ever that the document held the key to the location of the fabled Lost City of Z, the mystical jungle fortress that legendary explorer Percy Fawcett spent much of his life searching for, and who, Winslow was well aware, had gone missing on a famous 1925 expedition in quest of it.

For all of Winslow's research into the meaning of Manuscript 512's words, the document continued to disappoint him. As the librarian had noted, hundreds, even thousands of would-be treasure seekers had pored over the physical text, as Winslow had, hoping it would lead them to the storied city of riches, to a mythical jungle fortress with streets paved of gold and buildings comprised entirely of the same. And yet, he, along with everyone else who had searched for Z, had always come up short. For many explorers, fatally so.

Winslow himself had undertaken only one previous expedition to the Amazon to have a look around. He had visited the last known and documented position of Percy Fawcett on his ill-fated expedition, a remote site known as Dead Horse Camp. It was so-named because that's where Fawcett had to shoot one of his horses that could no longer carry on.

And that was Fawcett's base camp, the place he started his serious exploring from.

Winslow had ventured a couple of days' worth of trekking from there, found nothing but overgrown and impenetrable jungle, and returned home, satisfied he had done enough to convince his deskbound colleagues at universities back home that he was a real explorer. But he had returned no closer to finding Z than he had been before. Despite all his research, he had to admit its location was not able to be deduced or inferred. Fawcett had been notoriously tight-lipped with information regarding his expeditions' itineraries, routes and coordinates, even going so far as to provide his wife with false routes in order to throw off his competitors. His own journal contained similar false information.

Now, as he stared down at the weathered document, he focused on the infamous damaged portions. The author of Manuscript 512 was an explorer named Barbosa, who penned it to inform the Viceroy of Brazil that an impressive city had been discovered deep inside the confines of the infamous "green hell." Those early expeditions had been funded in order to bring back gold and silver, but the domain of the jungle was known as a bastion of savages, therefore the discovery of an actual advanced civilization within its confines was a stunning revelation and worth documenting.

But if the author of Manuscript 512 knew where the lost city lay, why hadn't anyone else been able to find it, especially Percy Fawcett, who made the most serious and documented attempts in modern times? As Winslow stared at the weathered paper—at the partially rotted paper—he was sure he knew why.

Worms.

Parts of the manuscript, ranging in length from a word here and there to entire paragraphs—had been eaten away by a type of burrowing worm that nests in the heavy papyrus-type paper that the old manuscript was written on. Winslow felt that if those destroyed words were legible, they would divulge the missing information needed to gain a full understanding of the city's precise location.

Many explorers and historians pointed to the fact that, compared to Fawcett's day, the Amazon rainforest—an astoundingly dense, unbridled wilderness the size of the U.S. mainland—had been reduced in size by about twenty percent, due to logging and clearcutting for pasture lands.

Even with this denuding of the pristine old growth forest, no trace of Z had yet been found.

And Winslow was convinced it was because parts of the manuscript were unreadable. Numerous restoration experts had tried to make it so, including those under the auspices of the Brazil National Library itself, which had the longest running custody of 512 and had given it its "name." Yet none of them had been able to make any progress. The medium itself, the consensus was, had been irreparably damaged, the words not simply obscured, but actually erased, the ink itself no longer there.

Dr. Hunter Winslow had thought long and hard on this matter. His wife, decades ago when he last had one, that is, had called him obsessive-compulsive, frequently calling him out on habits she deemed to be "OCD." Most of them were trivial things, such as wanting his keys to hang on a particular hook of the key rack every time, insisting his ties hang in a certain order in the closet, that sort of thing, but secretly, Winslow knew that it carried over into his professional work as well. He simply had to do things a certain way or else he would get irritated, grumpy, and eventually all-out angry. Some of his colleagues referred to this type of behavior as "stubborn."

Part of it, too, was that he just liked to win. Winslow liked to be the best at whatever he did, which meant publishing well-received and widely read scholarly papers that were the envy of his colleagues. But as he grew older—he was in his early fifties now, as Percy Fawcett was when he undertook his fateful expedition—a younger, more aggressive crop of historians had entered the halls of academia, infiltrating the ivory towers with their information-age, hive-mind mentality.

One day, Winslow realized he was no longer the leading historian in his field; not only that, but he was not even *one* of the leading historians. The new bumper crop of academicians had usurped his reign using exotic new technologies (at least they seemed that way to his Luddite self) such as LiDAR, satellite imagery and various remote sensing tools. Some even called themselves "space archaeologists," which Winslow could only shake his head at and scoff. He had made his mark on the virtues of good old-fashioned library research and the occasional boots-on-the-ground expedition.

Lately, his colleagues had taken to doing things like examining the actual paper the documents were written on and analyzing them at the chemical level. The results of such analyses were written up in prestigious journals, while his traditional treatises were being increasingly ignored. So he had begun to take matters into his own hands, deciding that if the source material, at least at his very own university's Special Collections room wasn't available for his colleagues to examine, then he'd have a leg up.

The first document he stole was the original Constitution of the state of Oklahoma. Boring, really, nothing too attention-grabbing, and yet it was the type of thing that was the bread-and-butter staple of historians everywhere. If he was the only one who had it, his twisted, born-of-desperation reasoning went, then only he could benefit from it, at least at the hands-on, physical level where most of the groundbreaking research seemed to be happening. Sure, all these ancient manuscripts were available as scans and high-resolution images, but all the meaningful work that could be done at that basic content-level alone had already been done. The low hanging fruits had already been picked. So Winslow would become the guardian of those documents he could obtain.

And slowly but surely, it began to work. He targeted documents he knew his colleagues had an interest in, which was easy to do since they all loved to blab about their research interests, on their faculty web page, to their captive audience of students, to anyone who would listen, really. So Winslow plucked those documents from the Special Collections room, literally pulling the item from its storage place (he had the benefit of less supervision at his own institution), and then dropping it out of an open window to a clump of bushes below. Later that afternoon, he'd casually sauntered past the building, stopping beneath that very window as if to tie his shoe, and grabbing the manuscript and stashing it in his briefcase.

For a period of years, he repeated this procedure with only slight variation here and there. He probably never would have been caught had he not gotten greedy, had he not realized that he could not only withhold historic documents from his colleagues to make his own research acumen seem more competitive, but that he could make a nice little chunk of change—untaxable change, at that- on the side by selling said documents and manuscripts on the black market. It was this greed, ultimately, that proved his undoing, for unbeknownst to him, the local police had been monitoring the thefts as reported by the university library, and when they began to appear on the black market, it gave them something concrete to follow.

And that was how one crispy autumn day in New England, esteemed historian Dr. Hunter Winslow found himself staring at a uniformed policeman standing at the door of his cluttered but livable ivy league university office. Would he mind accompanying the officers down to the station to answer some questions about missing documents from the university's Special Collections Department? *Why yes, of course*, Winslow had muttered, dumbfounded that he had been caught. They were still civil to him now, and the cuffs weren't on yet, but he knew that if they were here, it meant they were onto him.

Unfortunately, he was right. It took a few weeks, but he was arraigned on charges of grand theft and convicted, accepting a plea deal that resulted in a misdemeanor charge with no jail time served in exchange for dropping a felony charge. He was still a free man, but his career was ruined.

That was one year ago. Oddly, he hadn't slipped into the post-termination funk many people faced when suddenly fired from a long-time career job. Financially, although not well-off, he was far from destitute and could even retire early if he planned a budget based around frugal living. But one piece of his past work still haunted him, still clutched at his imagination: Percy Fawcett's Lost City of Z.

Through his own research he had become convinced that it must be real, that it really existed somewhere in the Mato Grosso region of the Amazon rainforest. Now that he was pressed into forced retirement, he had to keep himself busy, he rationalized with himself. And perhaps make himself rich in the process, you know, boost that retirement lifestyle to what he had become accustomed to during his working years. The Lost City of Z would fund his retirement. To any normal person, it would sound beyond crazy. But Dr. Hunter Winslow was anything but normal.

For the first six months of his forced retirement he did nothing but pore over maps, charts, researcher journals, old letters, manifests, ship's logs and expedition notes, painstakingly cross-referencing and taking notes until he was confident he'd gleaned everything worthwhile.

He then became convinced that the city's location could not be pinpointed with the existing information alone. The closest one could reliably come—Fawcett's Dead Horse camp—still offered too many possibilities to branch out into. He had to have more to go on, and he was convinced that more resided in the worm-damaged sections of Manuscript 512 itself, the document that started the fervor for the lost Amazonian city.

Winslow had spent the next six months hatching his plan to steal the original Manuscript 512 from the National Library of Brazil, meticulously working through every possible detail, option and combination of outcomes, as if it was his full-time job, which in fact it had become.

Presently, Winslow heard a woman shouting from out in the main area of the Special Collections wing, drawing his eyes straight to his watch. He'd allowed himself to daydream a little too much, but no matter.

The plan was afoot.

And on schedule.

CHAPTER TWO

Rio de Janeiro, Brazil

The librarian's rapid-fire Portuguese reached Winslow's ears in the examination room. He knew the language well enough to get the gist of it from his trips down here over the years, as well as his research reading Portuguese documents. "Miss, I'm sorry, but I need to see your identification before you can check anything out. This is Special Collections, not the regular library."

"Oh fine, fine, I'll dig it out of my purse, hold on a minute, where can I put my sweater…"

The exchange would have been comical to Winslow were it not for the fact that he knew exactly why the woman was here. She was not simply a confused library-goer or irate patron. Winslow himself had hired her off the street of one of Rio's many *favelas,* for the express purpose of providing a distraction. He'd paid her twenty U.S. dollars, and for that he was pretty sure he could have gotten her to follow him around wherever he went for the next month. He was also pretty sure he could smell her from here and had little doubt that she would be removed from the premises by Security before too long, but Winslow only needed her to last for a couple more minutes.

The historian positioned himself so that he faced the doorway to his workspace. Then he reached into his briefcase and removed from it a yellowed sheet of weathered, crinkled paper covered in Portuguese longhand.

It was an exactingly created replica of Manuscript 512.

He quickly grabbed the original and slipped it into his briefcase before putting the fake in its place on the table. Once his briefcase was secured shut, he placed the fake in the library tube. He slung his briefcase over his shoulder, picked up the tube and walked out of the examination room.

His plant was still arguing up a storm, going into a full-fledged tantrum now, something about how the government pays the librarian's salary so why couldn't she do what she was asked. Winslow made eye contact with the librarian as he walked over to her desk, making a grimacing expression that said, *I feel your pain.* He spoke loudly in Portuguese over the irate customer as he held up the document tube.

"Heading out for a bite to eat. I'll be back later. Here it is." The librarian shot him a slightly confused look, since he had checked the item out not long ago, and most people, after travelling to a foreign country to view a document, wouldn't leave it after so short a time. But she was preoccupied with the angry woman, and so she didn't think things through as well as she might have. She did not, however, overlook that she needed to open the tube and have a look inside. She uncapped it, and Winslow held his breath while she slipped the fake manuscript out of the tube. His plant was spitting now while she ranted, and as a rain of spittle approached the yellowed paper, the librarian hastily stuffed it back inside its protective cover.

She capped the tube and put it safely behind the desk before smiling at Dr. Winslow. "Very well, senor."

Winslow tensed as she saw him glance at his briefcase. A bag search wouldn't have been out of the question, but now a security guard was entering the room, the librarian looking visibly relieved at his presence. Winslow beat a hasty retreat, avoiding eye contact with his hired help as he trod past the incoming security, who immediately homed in on the out of control woman.

Dr. Winslow, meanwhile, walked briskly out of the Special Collections room carrying his briefcase, which contained a centuries-old manuscript purported to reveal the location of a lost Amazon jungle city. Winslow exited into the hall and turned left, his system brimming with adrenaline. *You've got it! Just keep going...*

Another security guard strode into the hall from up a stairwell on the left, and Winslow's hand clutched his briefcase handle, but the guard merely nodded at him and trotted on past toward Special Collections. *Lady did a bang-up job, would have paid her a hundred bucks for that*, Winslow thought of his decoy as he reached the elevator at the end of the hall and hit the call button.

He fidgeted impatiently as he waited for the elevator. It seemed to take forever but in reality, was only about thirty seconds. He was distraught to see two high-level library staff, wearing suits and ties, accompanied with yet another security guard, step out of the elevator. The men nodded to him in curt greeting but said nothing, and Winslow entered the elevator car. He hurriedly lashed out at the "1" button as the library staffers walked briskly down the hall toward Special Collections.

The doors slid closed and Winslow took a deep breath as he began his descent. He had done it. There was no turning back now. Once the fake was discovered by the staff—and it would be, hopefully later rather than sooner, but it definitely would be—he would be a wanted man. This was expected. But he didn't care. Once he found the treasure of the Lost City of Z, he would have power beyond all reckoning. He would be untouchable. He only needed to act fast enough to find it before he was discovered. He smiled to himself as he felt the small jolt of the elevator car reaching ground level.

Who said retirement had to be boring?

As he stepped out into the main library's grand entrance floor, Winslow scanned the space for signs that he'd been made. He doubted he had been so quickly, but it wasn't impossible. The expansive Information Desk, staffed by four people, showed no signs of anything other than business as usual. One of the staffers talked to a visitor, while the other three were all on the desk phones.

Winslow glanced yet again at his watch as he made his way out through the main exit doors onto the busy street outside. He was five minutes early to meet his cab, but with any luck the driver would be here waiting. He was certain he'd tipped him enough, and no doubt the man would anticipate more if he returned. But the cab was not here. He saw a different cab—a green car, when his was yellow and black—pulling away from the curb, but there were no other taxis here.

He would have to wait out the five minutes. Damn this guy's punctuality, Winslow thought. Complicating matters, a cab from another company—this one was painted white with yellow accents—saw Winslow standing there looking up and down the street and figured correctly that he needed a cab. He pulled over.

"No thank you, waiting for a friend." Winslow called over to the driver as he rolled down the passenger side window. The cabbie shot him an irritated stare before accelerating back out into the street. *Great*, Winslow thought, looking around, *I just made a little scene.* But he saw nothing other than normal foot traffic going in and out of the place. Still, he couldn't stand around here forever. He eyeballed his timepiece again. Two more minutes. He decided it was worth the wait before going with a random new cab or winging it—just setting off on foot and hopping on a city bus or something. The weight of his briefcase in his sweaty palm reminded him that he needed to make a very important phone call, one that couldn't be made until he was somewhere safe from prying ears and eyes.

Suddenly he heard a siren wailing and growing louder. He white-knuckled the briefcase handle hard. What to do? Where to go? He glanced around but saw no obvious opportunities or threats. But the sound of the siren became louder with each passing second. What if it was the police coming for him? He tried to rationalize with himself, telling himself it could be something else—an ambulance or fire truck—not even coming to the library...but no sooner had he completed the thought than his peripheral vision caught the flashing of red lights coming from his left.

Police car. Heading straight for the library. His body flooded with adrenaline, so much so that he tensed enormously, frozen in place. *Not good not good not good!* was all his petrified mind could scream. He felt like an idiot just standing there waiting to be arrested, like the proverbial deer in headlights. But as the vehicle came to a stop a few feet to his right and the doors opened, the two officers walked straight past him with barely a glance and strode—rapidly but not running—toward the main library entrance.

He figured they were either not coming for him at all or they didn't know he was their guy. But surely if he was already wanted, the librarian would have provided a description. His thoughts were interrupted by a car horn as a taxi rolled up to the curb. His driver! Winslow ran to the car, flung open the back door and got in.

"Sorry, I meant to be here earlier," the driver said, "but big traffic jam because of an accident. Where to?"

Winslow gave him the name of a popular coffee shop in downtown Rio. The ride over was made longer by heavy traffic, and Winslow shrunk down in the seat when a procession of three police cars passed them in the other direction toward the library, lights flashing, sirens on. Surely that level of attention wasn't warranted by his decoy, a supposed belligerent visitor? Winslow began to think the theft had been detected. He pulled out his smartphone to search local news, but then gave up; it was too soon for news on something like that.

And then the cabbie was pulling up to the coffee shop, bubbling over with enthusiasm about how happy he was to assist Winslow, exiting to open the door for him, but the historian had already exited on his own. He clutched his precious briefcase which he had held in his lap for the entire ride to eliminate the chance of leaving it behind in the cab. He handed the cabbie three times as much cash as needed for the ride and walked away while the driver was still thanking him profusely.

Winslow was practically shaking as he walked through the outdoor portion of the café, ducking the colorful umbrellas and threading his way past patrons sliding their chairs out and walking to their tables. He entered the inside of the business. He didn't need to be sitting outside, visible to all who walked or drove by.

Winslow found an unoccupied table and took it, not wanting to wait in line at the counter to purchase a beverage. He would wait for them to come to him, and if they didn't he didn't care. He had work to do. He set his briefcase on the table and rested his arms on top of it, holding his smartphone. He looked around to make certain he wasn't being observed: the place had people but wasn't crowded. It was a pleasant sunny day and most customers preferred the outside patio. Satisfied that he was basically anonymous at this point, Winslow placed a call to his contact, one he depended on for his scheme to be successful.

To his annoyance, the phone rang seven times before it was picked up. The male voice on the other end was nearly drowned out by loud calypso music. "Lincoln, turn that crap down, will you? Turn it down!"

During the pause while his associate apparently sought to silence the background noise, a male server approached Winslow's table and asked what he would like to order. Winslow asked for a large black coffee and a plain croissant, and the man disappeared again. Winslow didn't like the fact that this meant he would have to return to the table during his conversation, but he had to order something to appear like a normal customer, and at the same time he needed to move his plan forward. It was critical that he advance it right now, he told himself. Because until the manuscript was analyzed in the lab—

His thoughts were interrupted by his colleague coming back on the line.

"Right then, what's your status, mate?"

Winslow sighed heavily before answering. His associate, an American lab technician by the name of Steven Hoch he had met while on a project to have the papyrus of an ancient Egyptian document age-dated, for some reason called him "mate," because he had gone on a vacation to Australia seven years ago and had adopted the slang ever since. Hoch was a single man with a penchant for partying, and had, like Winslow, lost his university lab job, though in his case for failing to show up for work too many times. Winslow had recognized an opportunity with the lab tech, whose pay grade was several big steps below Winslow's own. With Hoch unable to find a professional job due to his firing, Winslow made him an offer he couldn't refuse: set up and run a temporary lab in Brazil that had but a single purpose: to analyze and reveal the chemical structure and makeup of Manuscript 512.

Winslow reminded himself not to use real names, and hoped Hoch would get the message, too. "The status, *Lincoln*, is that I've got the asset in my possession, and so now it's time to get it to you so you can start the lab work on your end."

Hoch was aware of Winslow's plan to steal 512, he had to be since what he would be doing only made sense if working with the original, physical manuscript itself, not a reproduction.

"Wow, so you've got it, eh? Really went through with it. Wow. How hot are things now?"

"Let's just say that time is of the essence, okay? I'll meet you at the statue in four hours to make the handoff."

The statue was none other than the world-famous landmark of Christ the Redeemer, which had stood atop Corcovado Mountain overlooking Guanabara Bay since its dedication in 1931. A crowded tourist stop, Winslow figured it would be a safe place to make the handoff of 512. From there, it would be Hoch's responsibility to take the document to his lab in the outskirts of Rio. Hoch had rented a nondescript house in a middle-class suburb to set up a basement laboratory to run the tests on 512. Neither a mansion nor a shack, the residence attracted no attention for being either ostentatious or ramshackle.

"See you then, mate. Be careful." Hoch clicked off the call and then Winslow's server walked up to the table with his order. The historian handed him a bill and told him to keep the change. He sipped his coffee and nibbled at his croissant so as not to attract attention by leaving in a hurry. While he drank, he scanned what he could see of the sidewalk and street through the café windows. All still appeared normal, he could detect no sirens in the distance.

It was time to begin making his way to the statue.

CHAPTER THREE

Copacabana Beach, Brazil

The iconic stretch of sand beckoned Dr. Winslow as he took in the sunbathers, soccer and volleyball players, food vendors, exercisers, swimmers and surfers that all cavorted in sea and sun. But Winslow had work to do, and as he rose from his poised sitting position, one that he hoped made him appear relaxed and casual, he was feeling anything but.

Glancing away from the beach, inland, he could see a majestic backdrop of mountains, including Corcovado, on top of which the statue of Jesus lorded over the region. He'd come here to the beach to make his movements more difficult to follow, and because there was a van tour operation that left from the beach to see Christ the Redeemer, where Steve Hoch should be waiting. Winslow had ditched his work clothes for a beach outfit, trading his briefcase for a Ripcurl backpack, which now contained the precious manuscript.

He rose slowly, hoping he looked like a lazy beachgoer rather than a disgraced historian who just stole a priceless manuscript from the National Library. It dawned on him, looking around at the dazzling surroundings, that if his plan worked, a couple of days from now he would be deep in the Amazon jungle for a long time. *Enjoy the sunshine while you can*, he told himself as he began to walk up to the street fronting the famous beach.

But despite the radiance on his shoulders, he couldn't feel warmth. There were still too many unknown variables. After the drop with Steve, he had the field expedition team to deal with. And then there was the library—had they noticed the manuscript was fake yet? Winslow reached the road and saw the sign for the van tours up to the statue. He waited in a short line to purchase tickets for the tour, for which he paid cash in *reals*.

He shuffled onto the van between the gaggles of families and friends, a loner on a mission who appeared to be nothing more than a solo traveler out for a day's mini-adventure. He fought his way to a window seat at the back of the van and slouched against the backrest, facing out the window as an elderly Japanese couple slid into the seat beside him, smiling politely. He tuned out the driver's multi-lingual tour guide chatter as the van got underway, driving onto a narrow, paved road that wound its way up into the mountainous countryside. The ride was slow but mostly pleasant, with the view becoming increasingly fabulous with their elevation.

Excited exclamations erupted in the van as the Christ of the Redeemer statue came into prominent view for the first time, standing seven stories tall, its outstretched arms summoning all of Brazil. The van threaded its way up some more paved switchbacks until it let out in a parking area for the statue. Here there was an outdoor café and gift shop, connected by a paved walkway that straddled the summit of the mountain to the actual statue. Winslow bought a small coffee at the gift shop, telling himself he needed to stay alert, before strolling along the path toward the Redeemer, his backpack slung over one shoulder as with a casual tourist. He rode the escalator the final distance to the statue's base, hoping none of the hundreds of tourists riding in the opposite direction would look too long at his face, which he hid behind large sunglasses and beneath a fisherman's style sun hat. The view was unreal, and he got a glimpse of the beach he had left hours ago, a white crescent miles below, bordered by city buildings. Beyond the city lay an expansive stretch of green, the beginning slope of the mountains, the barest hint of what lay in the country's interior.

He found Hoch sitting on the ground with his back against the statue's pedestal.

Complete idiot, Winslow thought. He threaded his way through tourists posing for pictures in front of the landmark as they imitated its pose. He sauntered up to his associate and greeted him with a fake smile, extending a hand as if to help up an old friend. Hoch gripped Winslow's hand and allowed himself to be pulled up into an embrace that was all for show.

"You dolt, Steve, what are you thinking laying around the base of the statue like a damn sloth!" Winslow admonished under his breath.

"What's the problem?" the lab technician answered, seemingly offended.

"Having your picture taken a million times over, that's what! Not to mention offending more than a few people, I'm sure, by using their sacred religious icon as your personal chaise lounge. Use your damn head! C'mon, let's walk to the café."

Steve said nothing in return but nodded, and the two fell into step as they made their way back to the escalators. They faced each other while standing on the descending stairs, and Hoch nodded at Winslow's backpack. "So you have it?"

Winslow nodded. "We'll grab a table at the café and I'll give it to you. You have room in there, right?" He nodded to Hoch's pack, which was small and full-looking.

"No worries."

"I have a few worries, Steve." Winslow lowered his voice as the escalator neared the bottom of its run. "How's the lab—ready to start?"

The technician nodded. "Good to go. It was easier than I thought to get some of the equipment. I guess because of all the drug labs down here, they need that kind of stuff to—"

"Enough! Stop talking," Winslow hissed, as they stepped from the escalator onto the concrete path that led to the café and gift shop area. "Buy something at the gift shop."

"Like what?" Hoch looked over at the small stand hawking curious.

"I don't know," Winslow snapped, "anything—a mini-statue of the Redeemer, I guess. The point is just to blend in and you'll give it to me and I'll give you what I have. It'll look like a gift exchange."

Hoch cajoled his way up to the cashiers with a lot of muttered *"perdoname's"* while Winslow grabbed a nearby table for two. He shrugged off his backpack and took from it the rolled-up Manuscript 512, original copy. He disliked even having it out here in the humid, salty, tropical air, but considering its intended fate in the next few days, he supposed it didn't much matter.

Hoch emerged from the shop carrying a little plastic bag and joined Winslow at the table. "Here ya go, hope you like it!" he said, handing him the bag with overplayed enthusiasm.

"I'm sure it will give me much-needed spiritual guidance." Winslow took the bag and slid the manuscript over to his associate, who knew better than to give it a close look here. He stashed it in his pack and zipped it shut, while Winslow put his gift in his own backpack.

"Right then, mate, so you coming with me back to the l—"

Winslow glared at Hoch at the mention of the "L" word, laboratory. That was not something they should be mentioning out loud, ever. And for once, he thought it was good Hoch said the word "mate," which might fool people into thinking he was from Australia, rather than serving only to annoy Winslow.

"No, I don't have time to meet you at the *house* today. I'll be in touch, though. Let me know when you're having that party, I'll be there for sure."

The coded language was clear enough to Hoch. Winslow would not be coming with him to the lab. He could have told him this earlier, but Winslow was operating on an abundance of caution. Even his own business partners didn't need to know all his plans. The different phases of his operation were compartmentalized, meaning that each facet of the project was a world unto itself, no one who worked on any one part needed to know anything about the other parts unless it was critical to their own job duties. That made for a more secure setup, Winslow knew. Loose lips sank ships.

"I'll give you a call when I get to the Horse." He could give him that much. Saying the entire name of the camp, Dead Horse, would be too risky, but Hoch would know what he meant.

The lab tech nodded and stood from the table, extending a hand to Winslow. "Good deal, then. I better get back home to the wife."

It was all Winslow could do not to laugh. Hoch, nor he, for that matter, were family men. Nerds of academia was more like it. Living the life, Winslow thought sarcastically. But finding the lost city would make all the sacrifices worthwhile. The late study sessions alone, the publish-or-perish stress, the eschewing of a real social life in order to maintain a competitive edge over colleagues, the extended field expeditions to remote corners of the world…He had given his life for this pursuit and it was about to pay off.

He watched Hoch mix in with the tourists until his backpack disappeared into the crowd. *Good luck, Steve.* He was always a competent lab tech back at their university, but now he would have to be more effective than ever to succeed. And if he didn't succeed, then Winslow wouldn't succeed. The historian shouldered his own backpack and made sure they had left nothing behind at the table before making his way over to the tour van stop. It was time to get back to Rio, and from there to begin making his way to Dead Horse Camp.

CHAPTER FOUR

Copacabana Beach

The sun was setting now and the beach emptying out. Winslow sat on the sand with his backpack strewn casually next to him, an entire arm's length away. Now that it no longer held the rare manuscript, he no longer felt the obsessive-compulsive desire to safeguard it at all costs. He had been relieved of that burden by Steven Hoch, but with that transfer of responsibility came a new set of worries.

Would Hoch be able to decode the document? His work was predicated on Winslow's own highly speculative theory that the unreadable sections of Manuscript 512—those damaged by worms— would be able to be restored, or to otherwise have their information decoded. *The answer is in the paper's chemicals*, Winslow told himself fervently. He just hoped he was right. It seemed like a good theory sitting in his condo back at home in the states, but here, alone on the beach in Brazil, a wanted man or about to be, and with a monumental jungle expedition between him and success, he wasn't so sure.

But he had come too far to back out now, there was no doubt about that. He was all in with no backup plan, and so he had to do his utmost to make it work. He couldn't deny the fear creeping in now, the realization that this was no longer some kind of deskbound fantasy based on theories and conjecture. As a frozen fruit vendor plied his wares (*"no gracie"*), glaring at him ever so slightly with his decline, Winslow activated his mobile phone and placed a call to his field expert.

The phone rang only once but when it picked up all Winslow could hear was very loud live music, with people laughing and carrying on with animated conversation in the near background.

"Where are you, Sal?"

"The Conga Room club, old friend, you should stop in. I'll be playing a set on the congas!"

Winslow felt his temper flare but suppressed the urge to lash out. He would be living with this person in the Amazon for weeks and depended on him not only for his mission's success, but to protect his very life, for one man alone deep in the Amazon wasn't an expedition, it was a suicide mission.

"That's great, Sal, but I'll be there in Araçatuba tomorrow afternoon to finish outfitting the expedition, and so we should plan on leaving just before daybreak the day after that."

"Sounds good, my friend. I will enjoy a last night of music and socializing then, before having only your company deep in the jungle. Have no worry, I am ready to go, and have already completed the preparations we discussed."

"Excellent. I will meet you at the club tomorrow at 4pm. Be ready, friend, for I need to get underway into the jungle."

"Understood, my friend, have no worries. I am ready for this, and most excited to find what you seek."

Winslow ended the call and rose slowly from the sand, deciding he should get into a hotel for the night. He didn't need any trouble, and tomorrow would be a long day with a lot of travelling. While he walked to the hotel—a different one from the one he stayed in last night, to avoid being recognized or drawing too much attention-he mulled over the importance he had placed on his friend, Sal. The entire expedition came down to him, really.

He first met Sal Torres on his first field trip to Brazil nearly a quarter century ago. The young Sal had been a porter on his expedition then, working for his father, a guide who had passed more than a decade ago. Even on that expedition, Winslow recalled, Sal had proven himself both resourceful and willing to break the rules at least a little. When a much younger Winslow—not even Dr. Winslow yet since he was still in graduate school—had lamented the fact that hard liquor was prohibited on grant-funded expeditions, Sal had stopped by his tent that night with a bottle of Cachaça, a kind of moonshine, asking for nothing in return other than to have a couple of shots with him and hear stories of what it's like to live in America.

Over the span of Winslow's career, he had sought out Sal's guide services as both moved up in their respective professions. By the time Winslow was leading occasional expeditions of his own, funded by his own grants, Sal was running his own guide company out of one of the major jungle cities. The two had been working together in this sporadic manner ever since, for decades, spending a few weeks together in the jungle every year or two.

This had made Sal Winslow's first choice, and yet the jungle guide had cautioned the historian against the epic sojourn. You could spend a lot of money and still come back with nothing to show for it, he had warned. You could catch ill and die in the rainforest, the Mato Grosso is so vast, so huge, help will be too far away most of the time should you sustain any kind of serious injury or require a hospital. But none of this deterred Winslow, and his powers of persuasion, combined with the lure of a healthy payday—incentivized by doling it out in chunks—one third on agreeing to do it, one third when the expedition departs, and one third when it returns safely, proved irresistible for the jungle guide.

Winslow found a hotel and checked in for the night, still using his real ID. His entire plan was predicated on the fact that the library wouldn't notice the theft until he was long gone into the jungle. And after that, he thought, bedding down for the night, the Amazon would decide his fate.

#

Next day, Araçatuba

Winslow glanced out the window of the bus and marveled at how much modernity there was in such close quarters to the largest expanse of unbroken wilderness remaining on the planet. A city skyline rose around him as he rode on traffic-clogged streets lined with contemporary businesses boasting free wi-fi as well as street vendors hawking their wares. He found another nondescript hotel and checked in for a single night, paying cash in the local currency. He still had a couple of hours before meeting Sal at the club, so he ventured out for a little shopping spree. The outdoor supplies store was one he had researched ahead of time, so he knew they were reputable and would have what he needed in stock.

Besides, Sal would be bringing the heavy gear, as well as local porters for the trip as far as Dead Horse Camp. Beyond that, Winslow knew, even the lure of money wouldn't entice the locals to venture into the uncharted regions of the Mato Grosso, and he and Sal would be on their own on foot.

Winslow found the outdoor shop and easily picked out the items he was looking for: a large backpack, a hammock, rope, carabiners, cookware, two machetes, a fire-starting kit, water purification tablets and filters. Perusing the aisles of the relatively uncrowded store, he also picked up some simple fishing gear, mosquito netting, bug spray, flashlights, a multi-tool and first aid, including snakebite antivenom kits. He paid about five hundred U.S. dollars for the lot of it, which he wore out of the store in his new pack.

He took a cab back to his hotel and organized his new gear until it was time to meet Sal. A few minutes to 4pm, he left his room and got into a cab, ordering the driver to take him to the Conga Room.

The ride there was uneventful, and soon Winslow was once again laying eyes on the ratty little establishment bordering on a trash-strewn river. "Club" was too grandiose a term, the historian always thought, and seeing it now did nothing to change his mind. The place was as dumpy looking as ever, looking like it would fit right in to the *favelas* clinging to the mountains above Rio. It had electricity though, that was for sure. Even before he opened the door, he could hear the music thumping right through the taxi's closed windows. He paid the driver with a decent but not excessive tip and exited the vehicle. The air outside the establishment was redolent with a cocktail of smoke—cigars, pipe tobacco, cigarettes, hash, firewood—it seemed that if it burned, it was in the air at this place.

Also in the air was the pulsating rhythm of calypso music. Winslow strolled up to the corrugated sheet metal that served as the walls of the place, the conga beats thumping in his chest as he approached. He knew that Sal was behind these rhythms, and so as he entered the club, he turned toward the music, and there he was: Sal Torres, sweating and gyrating away behind a percussion setup, surrounded by horn players and dancing girls. Sweat beaded on his forehead, and his long face was framed by dreadlocks that seemed to flow out of a wide brim straw hat. His eyes were closed as his hands moved back and forth across the skins of his three congas, reaching out occasionally to slap at a bongo or a cymbal.

"You wanna drink?" The words were in Portuguese, but Winslow had enough familiarity, given the context, to know what they meant. He nodded to the female server, who wore a bra and held up a serving tray festooned with neon bracelets. "Maybe a Jell-O shot?" she added, taking Winslow's hesitation as a sign he must not be interested in normal drinks.

He grabbed two bottles of Brahma beer off the tray and handed her some cash. "Thanks." She winked at him and bounded off to a table of loud-talking men playing a game of chance involving both cards and dice. Winslow sauntered over to Sal's end of the band, watching him play for a few seconds before Sal opened his eyes and saw him. When the song ended, Sal stepped down from the stage and greeted Winslow, who handed him one of the beers.

"You didn't put those on my tab, did you, because they might-"

"Relax, buddy, I paid for 'em. It's on me. Is there somewhere we can talk?"

Sal pointed to his watch and turned to the singer in his band, a whitehaired Brazilian wearing a blazer with denim shorts and sneakers with lights in them. The vocalist nodded and then turned to the other members of his band, who launched into a new tune.

Winslow followed Sal into a corner of the dirt floor establishment that was just far enough away and shielded by a thin piece of sheet metal wall to be able to hold an actual conversation. They occupied the makeshift table that had been set up there and watched people dancing for a minute while sipping their beers before Winslow got down to business.

"So are we ready?"

Sal raised his eyebrows. "Are *you* ready, my friend?"

"The lab work is underway, I've got a sat-phone to keep in touch with my tech, and I procured some basic personal gear today that's packed and ready to go. I'd like to head out before dawn in the morning, assuming you're prepared, that is."

Sal nodded, giving a wave to a couple who thanked him for the music as they passed by. "Oh, I'm prepared, Hunter. Air charter is booked for tomorrow morning. My porters and guides are on standby. They'll meet us tomorrow as soon as we get to Cuiabá."

Winslow nodded, but Sal continued before he could say anything. "It's not too late, though, Hunter. To change your mind, I mean."

Winslow reared back in his chair, offended. "I'm in this way too far to back out now, Sal. If you're having second thoughts, let me know and I'll get someone else."

Sal shrugged amiably. "No, no, I'm fine with it. I've got nothing much better to do, as you can see, other than making noise for the locals in places like this...." He waved an arm about the rust-stained walls and smoke-filled air. "Plus, I'd like to help you. You've been good to me over the years, giving me gainful employment when I really needed it. And there's something else, I suppose, too," he added, his eyes taking on a faraway look.

"What's that?"

Sal took a hearty swig from his beer and set the bottle down with a *clack*. "The Lost City of Z. I've always believed in it. I know it's out there somewhere, and I'd like to be with you when you find it."

Winslow nodded slowly as he sipped from his own beverage. "I'm sure you would, Sal. You recall the incentive structure in the contract you signed?"

"Of course, if we find anything, I get a bonus, sure, sure, but that's not what I mean, Hunter. I mean I really want to be there when you find it, for the thrill of it. Ever since I first set foot in the Amazon, I've been hearing about this mythical place. It's the stuff of legend. To be on the expedition that finds it first—"

"—and returns alive, at least, since Fawcett may have found it first," Winslow interjected.

Sal nodded. "To do that would be quite a feat, wouldn't it? The stuff of legend, Winslow."

The same waitress with the tray of goodies stopped at their table and Sal lifted two more beers from her, eyeing Winslow for the cash. The historian fished some bills from his pocket and put them on the server's tray with a smile, and she departed after a little curtsey.

Winslow raised his bottle in a toast. "To the stuff of legend."

They clinked bottles and took a swig. "Tomorrow it begins."

#

Later that night in his hotel room, Winslow placed a satellite-phone call to Steven Hoch. He needed to make sure the lab tech had gotten things underway from his end; his work was too important to leave things to chance, and once in the field, opportunities for communication would be more limited. Winslow used a cheap burner cell-phone he had picked up in town for communicating until he got into the jungle and would rely on his satellite-phone. But that was expensive, and he didn't want to place calls from the hotel which would leave records.

Hoch picked up on the third ring. Winslow reminded himself not to use names or places. "We're set to leave for Green Hell at daybreak. How are things on your end—you get started yet?"

"Haven't burned it up yet, but the preps are well underway. You've got what, a week or so before you get to—"

"No names."

"Right, before you get to your first stop?" Winslow nodded to himself, knowing the tech was referring to Dead Horse Camp.

"Correct. I'll call you when we get there, or if we get delayed. You call me if you have anything before then."

"Copy that. Good luck, amigo. I'll get back to work."

"Do that. And good luck to you as well. Talk to you in a few." Winslow ended the call and stared at the water-stained ceiling, lost in thoughts about his uncertain future.

CHAPTER FIVE

Winslow's hotel room television brayed him awake at 4am by turning on to a local news channel. *Jungle time!* The historian fell out of bed and was making his way to the bathroom when the actual content of the tv broadcast caught his attention. The program was a replay from the previous night's 11pm airing, and Winslow was mortified to see his picture inset in the upper right of the screen, accompanied by the headline AMERICAN HISTORIAN SUSPECTED IN NATIONAL LIBRARY THEFT.

He froze in mid-step with the realization that the jig was up—he'd been found out and the news had broken.

Got to get going, now!

Winslow spurred himself into motion. This hotel hadn't asked him for ID to check in, but the one in Copacabana had. He had been naïve to think it would take longer than this for the theft to be discovered, he realized now, but it was too late for regrets. He had to get out of here right now. Fortunately, he had pre-packed before going to sleep and was supposed to head out at this time anyway, but he hadn't expected to have to hightail out as a wanted man. He glanced at the screen again where the newscaster urged viewers to call the crime hotline number below if they had any information about the theft.

He hurriedly used the bathroom but skipped the shower he had planned to take given that it would be his last one for an unknown period. He took a few precious seconds to make certain he was leaving nothing identifiable behind in the room. He pocketed his wallet, passport, and burner phone. His sat-phone was in the pack, which he double-checked when he opened it to grab a floppy hat that would partially conceal his features. It was meant to keep the sun and then spiderwebs and various jungle creepy-crawlies out of his hair, but he wouldn't even get to those dangers if he didn't escape the ones he faced now. He shouldered the pack and moved to the door. He reached out to open it but instead glimpsed through the peephole. No one there. Then he opened the door, put on the Do Not Disturb / Não Perturbe sign, shut the door, leaving the key in it, and walked quickly out of the hotel, not bothering to check out.

You're a wanted man! It kept running through his head while he ran out to the street, hailing the lone cab waiting there. He got in and instructed the driver to take him to the local airport, thank God not an international one where he'd have to show ID and pass through security, but a small one for charter operations. He drew his hat down tighter on his head, wishing it was light enough out to be able to wear sunglasses. At least the driver didn't try to make small talk with him, so he was able to think about what else there was to go wrong with his best laid plans.

Steve was processing the manuscript in the lab. He wished he had the luxury of time to stay in the lab with him and learn what the results were before trekking into the jungle only to possibly find out that the procedure offered no additional leads, but that was not the case, and besides, he told himself: *Think positive. He'll fill in those missing gaps.*

And Sal should have the charter plane warmed up already by the time he got there, and it would whisk them away to the jungle town of Cuiabá, where he should be able to disappear into the vastness of the Amazon, only to emerge when he had found the riches of the Lost City of Z. With such great wealth, he would be able to live a quiet, easy life of anonymous peace for the rest of his days. That's all he wanted, he didn't want to hurt anyone. Surely there were more important criminals to go after than someone who took a moldy old paper from a library? He chuckled to himself as he recalled articles about people who were fined exorbitant sums for failing to return library books for long periods of time—decades. After he found the riches of Z, he'd hire the finest international legal team money could buy, and that's how they'd spin it—*Our client failed to return a library book! Is that a great crime?*

Yes, it would all work out, somehow.

"Airport coming up, you know which terminal?" the cabbie asked in Portuguese. *Which terminal? Terminal!* That made it sound so huge, like the kind of place that would have security check points and cops, cameras. Could it get any worse? But then he actually looked out the window and saw that, although somewhat spacious, there were hardly any services here. A couple of small hangars, and an even smaller office building, and that was pretty much it. A few small outbuildings here and there, and the obligatory windsock on a high pole and that was it. A couple of pole-mounted halogens lit the place up.

At this early hour there wasn't much activity, so it was easy to spot their plane, as well as Sal carrying gear from his Land Rover over to the aircraft, where he piled it in a heap on the tarmac in front of the plane's open door. He had assistance from two Brazilian porters, one of whom worked feverishly to run the gear from the truck to the plane, while the other stood in the plane and pulled the stuff inside as it was handed up to him by Sal.

Winslow paid the cabbie and dragged his backpack out of the car. He shouldered the pack while the cab drove off and waved to Sal as he jogged over to the plane.

"Morning! We about ready?" the historian called out. It concerned him that the plane's engine was not yet running.

Sal glanced at his watch and then looked up at Winslow, concern of his own evident in his eyes. "I saw the news last night. I did everything we can to step on it, but the pilot said he's going to be a little late, 5:30 takeoff, nothing I can do." Sal held up his hands in a gesture of supplication.

Winslow glanced at his own timepiece: 4:37. He reminded himself to keep his cool. *You got yourself into this mess, now you'll have to get out of it. Less than an hour to takeoff, you'll be all right.* "Well, let's finish the loading. This is all I've got, so let me get it in there and then I'll help with the rest." He shrugged off his pack and dragged it up into the plane, where he set it on the floor in front of one of the two rear passenger seats. Sal would be riding shotgun with the pilot, while Winslow would be in the rear seat. Behind that seat, additional rows of seating had been removed to create an extended cargo hold. It was already at least half full of gear crates. He couldn't suppress a smile as he took in the sight. It was finally happening. The Lost City....

"Grab this, will ya?" Sal's voice shook him from his reverie. Winslow took a crate and hauled it aboard. One of the porters hopped inside and took it from him, moving it to the back of the heap where there was still some empty floor space. Winslow felt a sting on his neck and slapped away a large horsefly. Already the air was warming, like a moist blanket slowly wrapping around him. He couldn't' wait to be underway.

They continued to load the aircraft until the pile of crates on the tarmac was no more, and the cargo bay of the plane was full to the brim. Sal wiped the sweat from his brow and looked at his watch. "Fifteen minutes 'til he gets here."

"You're sure he's going to be here, though, right?" Winslow couldn't disguise the uneasiness in his voice.

Sal's response brimmed with confidence. "Don't worry, he won't turn down the payday. This little job is going to wipe all his bar tabs clean from here to Rio. Then he'll go off on another jag for a few months...he'll be here."

They were the tensest fifteen minutes of Winslow's life. He stayed inside the plane, hunched down in his passenger seat, lap belt on, ready to go, while Sal and the porters parked the Land Rover in the long-term lot and then made their way back to the plane. Every time Winslow heard a vehicle in the distance, he tensed, thinking it was the *policía* coming for him, that they had somehow gotten wind of his whereabouts and plans.

But when Sal and the two porters returned, they had another man with them, the pilot, an American ex-pat who wasted no time climbing into the cockpit and warming up the airplane. Sal made curt introductions, and Winslow was glad that the man seemed to pay no special attention to him. Sal had assured him he knew only that he was flying him and his associate with the gear into the jungle, and that was it. As far as he could tell, it appeared to Winslow that that was the case.

The porters entered the aircraft and squeezed into the seat next to Winslow, not bothering with their seatbelts. Sal climbed in to the co-pilot's seat, shut the door and belted in, while the pilot did the same. Winslow glanced out the window, scanning the tarmac for signs of approaching law enforcement, and then closer to the plane for any equipment that may have been overlooked. But all was in order. He felt the vibrations of the plane's engines as it revved in place. Then the pilot engaged in some radio chatter with the control station, put it into a taxi, and they were rolling out onto the runway.

Jungle bound, at last.

Winslow felt the plane shudder as it picked up speed on the runway, then the unnatural sensation of lifting into the air, followed by the rumble of the wheels retracting into the fuselage. He looked down on the airport, at the roads leading to it, half-expecting to see a procession of police cars, lights flashing, but there was only the early morning quiet of a small, charter airport.

They were looking for him, but they hadn't found him yet. He considered his case from the police's point of view and smiled. They'd think he intended to sell the document on the black market to some wealthy collector. That'd be their first guess. Not to destroy it in order to decode the missing sections. The only person who knew about that was Steve Hoch, and…Winslow turned away from the window and settled back into his seat. *Let's just say that Steve has been more than sufficiently incentivized to keep his trap shut, even when drunk.* By the time the heat figured out that there was no black-market action going on, that this guy stole this document and did not leave the country at all…how long would that be?

CHAPTER SIX

Cuiabá, Brazil

To Winslow, the land below the airplane looked more like the U.S. Midwest than the most untamed wilderness remaining on Earth. "A bit disappointing to come all this way only to see the same thing I could have in Iowa," he said, glimpsing the green and brown patchwork of farmland below.

Sal leaned back from the co-pilot's seat. "A lot has changed since Fawcett's time. Twenty percent less forest overall. But the rainforest is still a vast place. We'll be wandering around in a wilderness larger than the state of Texas. And I've driven through Texas on the 10 freeway. Speed limit is 75 miles per hour in some places and it still takes twenty-four hours—that's drive time, not counting hotel stops."

"I get it. We'll be on foot most of the way, through a jungle the size of Texas."

"Can't wait!" Sal said with an exaggerated thumbs up before turning back around to watch the approach to their landing strip.

The capital of Mattao Grosso, *Cuiabá* was a city of 900,000, known as the gateway to the Pantanal wetlands to the north. A last bastion of civilization amidst an expanse of jungle so wide most people couldn't comprehend it, the settlement was named for the river on whose banks it was situated, the very same river they would follow deep into the uncharted regions of the Mattao Grosso.

Looking ahead past the farmland, Winslow could already see an unbroken expanse of green. Into that he would disappear. The pilot put the plane into a landing pattern and the historian leaned back in his seat.

The wheels bounced a few times on the runway before the smooth rumble of fast wheels on concrete took over.

"Welcome to *Cuiabá,*" their pilot intoned, without emotion. "The best place."

"Best place for what?" Winslow couldn't help but ask.

"For everything, *amigo*." The pilot grinned behind the stick as he put the wing flaps up, decelerating the plane.

Winslow saw only a small building some distance away. Sal already had his phone out, contacting someone about their ground transportation. Winslow tensed in anticipation of the coming journey, he was so excited.

That's when he heard the first police sirens.

The pilot seemed oblivious to the hubbub, going about his duties as he took the plane into a slow taxi toward the still distant airport building. Sal, meanwhile, looked up from his phone, finger poised over the touchscreen as he squinted out the window toward the wailing noise.

"What do you reckon that is?" Winslow asked.

To his surprise, it was the pilot who answered. "Could be a fire truck. There can be small spot fires caused by oil or fuel spills. I didn't hear anything on the radio though," he finished with a frown, reaching out a hand to adjust his VHF airband transceiver.

Sal began speaking softly but urgently into his phone, pausing after a bit to say, "Yes, yes, in sight of it now...good, go then."

"What's happening, Sal?" Winslow wanted to know, a nervous edge creeping into his voice.

"Our two vehicles will be waiting up ahead. Just be ready to start the equipment transfer as soon as we get there."

"But Sal, if that—"

"Not now, okay?" He turned around and nosed subtly toward the pilot, indicating he did not need to be privy to their business.

"Right-O, Sal, getting ready." Winslow stared out his window, sulking while he looked for the oncoming siren vehicle. By the time they had reached the airport building, he could see the red flashing lights.

Sal gave directions to the pilot, directing him toward a cluster of vehicles near one corner of the airport building. The pilot obliged, steering the aircraft toward them. Sal asked him politely if they could go any faster, and the pilot begrudgingly increased their speed by a half-a-knot. *Better than nothing*, Winslow thought, *I'll take it.*

Sal craned his neck to look out the window, since the wailing vehicle was behind them now. "Bad news, mate. It's a *policia*. Not sure what it means, but, they can put the entire airport on lockdown, and we have a schedule to keep, do we not?"

Winslow nodded, too horrified to speak coherently.

"I've already spoken to my head porter. What we're going to do is, we're going to take the lead Jeep—both Jeeps are already there waiting—with only our personal gear, to get things going right away, you understand?"

"Absolutely, yes."

"We'll do that while the porters load the rest of the stuff into the other vehicles. They'll meet up with us later to transfer some of the gear into our Jeep."

"I'm on board with that."

Sal beamed. "Excellent." Then he turned to the pilot. "Any idea what siren's about, mate?"

"Nope, radio still silent. It's police, though, I can see that it's not fire. Almost there, don't open the door until I say, okay? Huge fines for me if they see me letting people out early, and I don't take repeat customers who don't follow the rules."

Uh-oh, Winslow thought. *This guy's paying attention a little bit. He knows we're in a serious hurry to get out of here...*

But Sal, as usual, was a smooth talker. "Your wish is our command, you know that. Just say when."

The pilot nodded as he put the plane through a final series of low speed maneuvers that ended up with the plane a few feet away from a congregation of vehicles—two Jeep Wranglers, along with three pickup trucks and a sedan, parked nearby.

"Okay, thanks for flying with me, you're free to move about the country," the pilot said as he shut down the engine. Sal had his door open immediately with Winslow following suit a couple of seconds later. They dropped to the tarmac with backpacks slung over their shoulders as the police car drove up to the main entrance of the airport building, on the opposite side of the structure.

"Hunter, get into that Jeep there, passenger side, right now. I'll drive. You go, I've got to tell my men what they need to do."

Winslow didn't need to be told twice. He ran to the Jeep as the police officers entered the airport's administrative building, no doubt to ask for a flight log to see who was going in or out. This was a small airport, though, and it bothered Winslow that they knew to look here. He supposed they must have put out a blanket alert to check all airports, but still, it made him extremely nervous.

He dimly registered in the back of his mind that Sal was waving his porters over for a quick huddle, while he flung open the passenger side door of the indicated Jeep—it had a hard top with a rack on top that was not yet loaded with equipment—and got in, dropping his pack into the foot well. He heard snatches of Portuguese as a couple of questions were asked—he could tell the men sounded confused—but then two of them ran toward the plane while Sal ran to the driver's side of the Jeep.

Winslow saw the porters—he counted eight men of either Brazilian or possibly Bolivian descent—swing into action offloading the gear from the plane and forming a human chain to toss it into the other Jeep and two cars. "Where are we going?" he asked Sal, who put the Jeep into reverse to back out of the group of vehicles until he could put it in forward and drive away from the airport building.

"To the jungle, mate, just a little faster than expected."

"Oh crap!" Winslow suddenly slid down in his seat until his head was below the window. "Police are walking over to the porters."

"I see them." Sal sounded calm while he continued to drive at a normal pace for a car merging out onto the access road.

"They're going to talk to the porters. Do they know what to say?"

Sal laughed in response. "The cops will ask them who they're prepping an expedition for, they'll give them my name, and that'll be that. I run a lot of jungle trips, it's nothing out of the ordinary at all. Relax. There's a flask of rum in the glove box if it'll help."

"No thanks. Just get us out of here, please."

"Will do." Sal slowed to a stop as he prepared to turn out onto the main road that led away from the airport and into town.

"What's happening, why are we stopping?" Winslow wanted to know.

"Relax, it's a stop sign."

"What are the cops doing?"

"Still talking to my guys. Sharing cigarettes, now."

"You're positive the porters won't tell them you're supposed to take an American professor or something like that into the jungle?"

"No, they don't know or care who the heck I take. Lots of times my clients are Americans. I told them to say they didn't know who it was, just to be safe, but honestly, it's normal for them not to know who the clients are."

Hunched down in his seat, Dr. Winslow began having second thoughts about his best-laid plans. But he knew all too well it was too late for that. His fate lay with the largest rainforest on the planet, and every turn of the Jeep's wheels took him closer to it.

CHAPTER SEVEN

Diamantino, Brazil

They rolled into the old mining town near the end of the day as the sun began to set. The highways and major roads had long been left behind, and Sal remarked that this would mark the end of their paved road driving.

"I don't see any hotels," Winslow said, looking around at the rows of dilapidated shacks.

"There aren't any. We'll set up a simple camp on the outskirts of town. Probably just as well, given the situation," he added, referencing the historian's wanted status.

Winslow agreed. "Fine with me. Where do we meet up with the rest of the expedition?"

Sal turned off the main drag onto a dirt road that ran down into a watery gully. They splashed through it before bouncing up onto a set of wheel tracks that ran across a grassy field. "I'll get them on the horn once we settle in. They'll meet us tonight, and tomorrow we should get officially underway."

"I'm tempted to say we should try to find a last hot meal in town while we wait," Winslow said, "but…"

"Nah," Sal interjected, "it's not worth the risk. Besides, might as well get used to roughing it. You ready, pal? Next few weeks are going to be epic!"

"Ready as I'll ever be." *Not that I have a choice at this point.*

Sal continued driving the Jeep over the field, the grass of which grew taller than the Jeep on both sides, until they reached the end and it let out into a stand of hardwood trees on the bank of a small stream. He shut off the engine and leaned back in his seat while taking a deep breath and exhaling slowly.

"Ahhh, peace and quiet at last. Back to nature."

Winslow popped open his door and tossed his backpack outside. "Looking forward to it." He stepped out and dragged his pack over to a tree on the bank of the brook. He grabbed a tin mug he had clipped to his pack and filled it from the cool, bubbling stream water and sipped it, savoring the unadulterated taste of pure water.

"We're pretty much as far from the ocean as you can possibly get in all of South America," Sal said as he sat down nearby Winslow with his own pack.

"Deep in the jungle, all right." Winslow unclipped a small tent from his pack and began setting it up while Sal activated his satellite phone and placed a call. He spoke in Portuguese for a few minutes before nodding and smiling at Winslow as he disconnected.

"I sent them our coordinates. They'll be here in about three hours."

"Be dark when they get here," Winslow pointed out, stamping one of the tent stakes into the ground with his boot.

"Yeah, that's okay. We can work a little at night to be able to leave at first light. I take it that's okay with you?"

Winslow grinned at him. "Wouldn't have it any other way. I'll feel a lot better once we depart Dead Horse Camp."

Sal nodded. "We'll get there. It's about a week's travel from here, all told."

"In theory, yeah. We'll see," Winslow said, referencing the fact that in the Amazon rainforest, there was no such thing as normal. Roads washed out or became overgrown, tribes could bar the way, heavy rain could delay travel until it passed. It was all so unpredictable, and yet simply being that deep in the jungle would make him feel safer, that much farther away from the long arm of the law that was right now reaching out for him.

The two men started a small cook fire and prepared a simple meal of beans and some fresh fish Sal netted out of the river. After that, the sun set, leaving them in near darkness, as there was no moon tonight. No artificial lights could be seen anywhere. Sal set up a simple hammock between two tents and said he would sleep in that until the porters arrived. Winslow retired to his tent, where he placed a sat-phone call to Steve Hoch, who answered on the first ring.

"I know it hasn't been that long yet, St—" He cut himself off after almost using his associate's real name. No need for that. He continued. "-Lincoln. But we're in camp for the night and tomorrow it's a long day on the road, so thought I'd check in, see how you're doing."

"Right mate, no worries. No results for you yet, I'm still prepping the equipment, doing some preliminary analyses, but I expect to run something tomorrow morning. Hopefully when I talk to you tomorrow night, the buns will be in the oven."

Winslow nodded to himself, glad for the coded phrase, silly as it was. He had no idea if the Brazilian government or Interpol monitored satellite phone calls, but there was no need to refer to a "manuscript" whatsoever. "Sounds good, glad you're up and running. I'll touch base again tomorrow, probably late afternoon."

"Have a good trip, amigo. Stay safe out there. I know it's hot."

Winslow winced at the double meaning there, also a coded message indicating that he was a wanted man. "It's always hot in South America."

They ended the call and then Winslow spent the rest of his evening poring over his maps and charts, analyzing their potential routes from their current location to Dead Horse Camp.

Before long, his eyes closed, and he was dreaming of the lost city.

#

Sometime later Winslow was stirred awake by the sound of engines rumbling into their tiny camp. He tensed like an animal getting ready to flee from predators, and then immediately felt ashamed of himself. Is this what he had become? Once a respected university professor, and now a hunted animal who startles at every sound? *Pathetic. Focus on your work. Find that lost city. You have no other job to go back to.* The Portuguese chatter reached his ears and he poked his head outside the tent, knowing how silly he was being. *If it was the police, they're not going to knock on your tent like it was the front door of some mansion.* But it was only the porters, the same ones as from earlier that day at the airport. It already seemed like forever ago, Winslow thought, he'd seen so much since then, driving across the country's vastly different terrain, from cities to countrysides to farmland to towns to rainforest and then jungle settlements.

Winslow stepped out of the tent, pleased to see that Sal had already rolled out of his hammock to greet the porters, since he didn't know them at all and his Portuguese, although passable most of the time, was not fluent like Sal's. He was stepping over to greet them when his foot caught on something that pitched him face-first onto the dirt. He heard a noise off to his left after he fell and looked in that direction to see a fat snake slithering off into the leaf litter.

One of the porters ran to it and jumped on it, stabbing his hand down into the leaves. It emerged holding the six-foot long snake by the base of its head.

"Morning, Dr. Winslow," Sal called out. "Fancy python for breakfast, do you?"

"I think it fancies me for breakfast," Winslow said. "How are we doing with the gear?"

Sal nodded. "It's all here. We're divvying it up now. Should be ready to head out in three hours. Get an early bird start, make camp a little early too, late afternoon. Hopefully we have at least two more driving days ahead of us before we have to go it by river."

Winslow nodded, heading for the coffee station the porters had set up by the fire. "Dead Horse Camp here we come."

CHAPTER EIGHT

By the time the sun cast the camp in an orangish glow, the full expeditionary team was underway. Sal and Winslow occupied the lead Jeep, with Sal at the wheel and Winslow riding shotgun. Equipment occupied the rest of the vehicle, including the roof rack up top and four large gas cans on a tailgate rack. The second Jeep carried the four porters who would be accompanying them into the jungle, along with additional gear. The other four porters who had helped with offloading the gear and transporting it to this point would not be needed in the jungle and returned to town by car.

It wasn't long before the caravan encountered their first obstacle. Before the sun was full in the sky, Sal braked the Jeep to a stop in front of a large tree trunk that had fallen across the dirt road. A narrow but deep creek ran parallel to the road on one side, while the other featured a deep depression filled with mud. The net result was to make the road impassable for the vehicles unless something was done about the tree. Fortunately, the porters had a solution in the form of hand axes, but even with two of them chopping away at a time, it took well over an hour to cut the log. During this time Winslow quietly worried, wondering if he had made a huge mistake; if they were encountering obstacles already, what were the odds they'd be able to make real progress once they got past Dead Horse Camp? He checked his sat-phone voicemail but had no messages, not that he expected any. He considered calling Steve to ask how the lab work was going, since he had nothing else productive to do until the tree was cut, but they already had plans to talk end of day, and he didn't want to pester the man upon whom he now so dearly depended. He had made the correct decision not to wait with him in the lab for that work to be done, though, that was for sure.

A chorus of shouts erupted from the porters and Winslow looked up in time to see the stout tree trunk separate in the middle with a last blow of an axe. He and Sal jumped out of the Jeep and helped the porters to drag the tree sections far enough off the road for the vehicles to pass. Then they got back underway, rolling along next to the creek on one side, and uneven terrain on the other. Trees became more closely spaced as they travelled, and after another hour or so they had a canopy over their heads most of the time.

Progress was made in similar fashion throughout the morning, with frequent stops to overcome obstacles such as boulders, trees, piles of branches in the road, or flooded sections of road where timber had to be placed in order to proceed. In one case, a dead cow blocked the way and had to be dragged off. They stopped for lunch in the middle of the road around mid-day, eating a hot rice and bean beef stew cooked up by the porters over a quick fire.

Winslow sweat bullets as he sat in the shade, and not because he was stressed about being discovered by law enforcement out here. It was oppressively hot and humid. Even though they were out of the direct sunlight, the tree layer also blocked any wind, giving the air a stifling, heavy feel made worse by the high moisture content. The droning hum of insects was omnipresent, punctuated by the occasional birdcall or animal cry of unknown type.

They packed back into the vehicles and drove onward, deeper into the Amazon, the road becoming less reliable as the day wore on. Nevertheless, they made progress, and as Sal pointed out, it still beat walking. "Enjoy the ride while you can," he told Winslow after catching an exasperated expression on the treasure-seeker's face when forced to clear the vehicle to clear an obstacle yet again.

"Oh, I am," Winslow said, wiping the sweat from his forehead. "It's not the stopping and starting I mind, it's thinking about whether this was the way Fawcett went. Are we following in his footsteps?"

Sal shrugged. "We'll wind up at his camp. Not sure how he got there, but we'll be at the same spot. And after that, the jungle still looks like it did for him a hundred years ago. Still virgin forest in those parts."

The forest grew ever thicker as they rumbled on along an increasingly narrower dirt road with more and more ruts, potholes and washed-out sections. Winslow wanted to study his maps, to match their progress against them, but he was being jostled around far too much.

About an hour after leaving their lunch stop, the porters' Jeep suddenly stopped behind them, pulled part-way off the road. Sal raised the driver on a walkie-talkie, and he reported that they had suffered a flat tire. Sal stopped the Jeep in the road and he and Winslow got out to stretch their legs while one of the spares was put on. The job was almost done when they heard a rustling of leaves right next to the road halfway between them and the porters.

Not two seconds after that did a primal human—naked but for a girdle of leaves around his crotch, face painted with black, blue and yellow pigment—emerge from the jungle. He carried a longbow and a quiver of long arrows slung over his shoulder, but these weapons were held casually, not at the ready.

Sal spoke to the man in Portuguese, to which he received a reply in broken Portuguese. But then one of the porters trotted over, smiling, and spoke in a tribal dialect that the native could understand. After this brief exchange, three more tribal men emerged from the trees and stood in the road next to their comrade. One of the porters translated for Sal and Winslow while the other talked to the tribal men. They asked where the party was heading, and when the porter described the general location of Dead Horse Camp, the tribal men frowned, and then exchanged glances before quickly changing the subject. They pointed to the truck and explained that they wanted to watch the tire changing process, so they all walked over to that Jeep so that the tribal men could observe the procedure, which was almost completed. A porter showed a tribesman how the lug wrench worked, and then they took turns cranking down the lugs.

When that was done, Sal offered some mainstay goods to the villagers, things that he knew worked well in terms of fostering good will. Bic lighters, cans and bottles of beer and soda, flashlights, batteries, souvenir T-shirts from Rio. Enough to keep them happy so that they allowed them to pass freely through their territory, road or no road, as well as a promise to pass the word on to the neighboring villages that the two-Jeep caravan were good people.

With the tire fixed and gifts given, Sal and Winslow climbed back into the Jeep and drove off as a light rain began to trickle through the canopy. The rain never got worse, but it never let up, either, as they bounced along what was now more of a track than a road. By the time they rolled up to a tiny town with an unpronounceable name, the sun was setting.

"This here is the main drag!" Sal gushed as they slammed into a ditch hard before bouncing out of it. Winslow nodded at the single block of buildings, simple wooden structures. He saw telephone wires but no street lights. The road was still dirt.

"I take it there's no Hilton here," Winslow lamented.

"Not hardly. We'll car camp like we did last night. But I know a place where this Brazilian lady will cook us up a nice dinner for a pittance. This is the last bastion of civilization before we hit the real rainforest, mate. So get your fill." Winslow looked out at the town, saw only a few people walking around. It looked more like a residential neighborhood than a town.

"Can't wait."

CHAPTER NINE

Steve Hoch was ready to start the procedure that would permanently destroy Manuscript 512 in the hopes of elucidating its secrets. He took a deep breath as he double-checked the settings on his machines again—the spectrophotometers, gas chromatographs, computers, chemical glassware, the centrifuges and more—it was all prepped, calibrated, tested and ready to go. Even with the air conditioning on, it was hot down in the basement of the Rio suburb house, so he decided to go upstairs for a quick break before beginning the work that would start by burning part of the precious document.

He ascended the rickety wooden steps to the first floor of the two-story wooden house. It wasn't a shack, but it was also nothing special, particularly in a neighborhood full of equivalent domiciles. On one side lived an elderly couple who had owned it for decades and minded their own business, not social at all, even when happening to see a neighbor while retrieving the mail or taking out the garbage. On the other side was a group of college kids who were social, but only with each other and minded their own business when it came to the neighbors. Which was fine with Steve. He was more than happy to let them do their thing. Let them have their fun. He didn't need anyone snooping around his lab. He told anyone who asked, which wasn't many people, that he was a writer working on a novel who had rented the place to have a place away from his home in the states to work in solitude. So that explained why he was home all the time.

So he was more than a little surprised to hear a knock at the door as he was opening the fridge to see if he had any more Brahmas. Who could that be? He had classic rock playing down in the lab to keep him company, but there's no way it was loud enough to elicit a noise complaint. He could barely hear it up here with the door to the basement open.

He padded barefoot quietly over to the front door. The windows had curtains on them and he didn't want to peek out like an old lady, but there was a peephole on the door. He put his eye up to it and looked out…

…and got the shock of his life when he saw two uniformed *polícia* standing at the door.

What?! Steve took several deep breaths in a row. What was happening? He dug his cell-phone out of his pocket and checked his call log—maybe Dr. Winslow had called or texted to warn him about something—but he had nothing incoming at all.

Another knock at the door, this one louder and more insistent. "Mr. Hoch, *Polícia Civil do Estado do Rio de Janeiro*, we have an urgent matter about which to speak to you, please." The officer spoke perfect English, with an accent, but still. How did they know his name and that he spoke English? He began to feel dizzy and weak in the legs.

Basically, this was the Rio de Janeiro police department. Should he open it? He could pretend he wasn't here, buy some time to figure out what was going on.

"Mr. Hoch, we are going to break down the door and come in if you do not open it."

That settled that. The lab tech wasn't sure what the search and warrant procedures were in Brazil, but he doubted they were the same as in the U.S. Besides, he was only working for Dr. Winslow. If there was something going on, he should have been warned.

Steve backed up a few steps and called out toward the door. "Okay, I just got up, coming—give me a minute!"

He walked up to the door, checked the peephole one more time. Same two cops still there. One car in the driveway, an unmarked sedan. But now there was a neighbor from across the street walking a dog and looking over at his house, obviously curious. *Great.*

Steve opened the door a crack and stuck his face out. "Hello?" Playing dumb.

"Good afternoon, Mr. Hoch, we are with the Rio de Janeiro police, may we come in?"

"Is there a problem, officers?" Steve wasn't sure if that was a good thing to say, but he'd heard it so much on TV he thought he'd go with it. It was just a way of fishing for information that probably wouldn't work, but he figured it was a common reaction and so it would help him to appear normal.

"We just have a few questions to ask you about the whereabouts of your colleague, Dr. Hunter Winslow. May we please come in?"

Uh-oh. Not looking good at all. "Uh, sure." Steve stepped back and pulled the door open. If he said "no," that would be bad, right—make him look guilty? So he may as well invite them in, say he knows nothing, and they'll be on their way. Deep down he knew that was ridiculous, but it was all happening so fast he wasn't thinking straight. *Damn it, Winslow....*

"Been living here long, Mr. Hoch?" one of the officers, the bald one, asked. The other guy had a head of thick curly hair and didn't say much, but his gaze darted constantly around the house.

"Uh, no, just got here, actually." He let his words hang awkwardly in the air while the bald cop stared at him, as if expecting him to elaborate, and the dark-haired guy continued to look all around. Steve mentally kicked himself for leaving the basement door open. It wasn't visible from here, but he could faintly hear the strains of The Doors *Break On Through* wafting up from the lab. *Idiot.*

"And so you are here on vacation? Because you reside in the states, correct, where you work as a laboratory technician with Dr. Winslow at Brown University?"

Suddenly Steve felt trapped into a corner. If they knew he'd been telling people he was a novelist, he was in very deep excrement indeed. Obviously, they knew who he was. He just had to hope they hadn't heard his "cover story." Thank the lord he hadn't told it to many people, he thought.

"That's right. Is Dr. Winslow okay?" Steve played dumb, hoping his facial expression looked like how he pictured it, but not sure. He was no actor, that was for sure.

Baldie shot him a hard stare for a long moment before answering. "Mr. Hoch, Dr. Winslow is currently wanted for questioning in a suspected theft of a rare document from the National Library of Brazil. Can you tell us when the last time was you spoke with him?"

Oh boy. He was really implicating himself the farther and farther this went. *Maybe I should just ask for an attorney...*

A chiming noise emanated from his pants pocket, and he realized it was the ringtone he'd specified for Winslow. *Christ, he's calling me right now for the daily update!*

Baldie glanced at his pants pocket. "Are you going to answer it?"

Steve shrugged. "No, it's quite alright. You're here, they're not, is what my mother always said about answering phones in the presence of other people."

Baldie made an expression of reasonableness. "Your mother sounds like a wise woman. Now about Dr. Winslow, when did you last speak to him?"

Do not implicate yourself. Make them work for it. He'd seen enough cop shows on tv where people basically handed the case to the officers, who then get credit for "solving" a case because the suspect simply admitted to it. That wasn't going to happen to him, *no way, no how.*

"About a month ago, I suppose."

"And what did you discuss?" Baldie pressed.

"He asked me if I would be available to do some lab work on a new project of his…" *Careful, Steve.* "…and I told him I'd be going on vacation for a while—that's why I'm here."

The guy with hair began to walk around the house, looking at items on the walls, at the furniture, the coffee table, everything. Baldie continued the conversation, which to Steve's ears was developing much more along the lines of an interrogation.

"Oh, and how long is your vacation?" Baldie waved an arm at the inside of the house. "Do you always rent a two-bedroom house for yourself in a suburb when you go on vacation, Mr. Hoch?"

Steve thought about the term of his lease—six months, which they had made longer than necessary so as not to draw attention, but now it seemed like the complete opposite.

"Well, it's more of a sabbatical, really. Six months. That's why I was telling Dr. Winslow I wouldn't be available for some time."

"A sabbatical, I see." He paused for a moment while stroking the stubble on his chin. He seemed about to say something further when his partner called out from out of sight, where he had wandered down the hall.

The basement!

He spoke in rapid Portuguese that Steve couldn't pick up, but Baldie gestured that way and said, "Mr. Hoch, do you have any roommates?"

"No, it's just me." He didn't see how he could fake that.

"There is music coming from the basement. Do you mind if we have a look?"

Steve froze there like an idiot with his mouth half open. Part of him was telling him to say no, they needed to talk to his lawyer (*what lawyer?*), and part of him was telling him to let them do it, just make something up, but he had no idea what.

"Sure, be my guest." A million red flags went up inside Steve's head. *It's like they know something. Where's the manuscript?* He tried to remember exactly where he had left it down there in the lab, but he was drawing a blank under pressure. It hadn't been processed yet, he knew that much. It was still in its case down there.

"Come with us, please, lead the way." He walked with Baldie to the basement entrance. Baldie conferred quietly with his partner for a moment, and then turned to Steve. "Do you mind if my partner has a look upstairs while we go down to the basement?"

No problem there. Look upstairs all you want. "Sure, whatever you guys want. I must say, though, this is a little invasive. What's the problem? Dr. Winslow is not here."

"We just need to confirm that for ourselves, Mr. Hoch, since you are a known associate of his. It is a mere formality, a box to tick off showing that we have done our jobs, that is all."

Steve hesitated, then told himself that the longer he paused the more suspicious he would look. He forced words out of his mouth. "All right let me give you the grand tour, then."

"Thank you." Baldie shot his partner a serious look and the partner departed for the second floor. Steve walked down the stairs, Baldie a few steps behind. The music grew louder as they neared the bottom of the steps, and the light was already on, making it clear that this was not some unused space. Steve immediately glanced about for the manuscript. Wanting to find it so that he could draw his attention away from it if possible; this even as he realized how ridiculously out of place all the high-tech lab equipment would look in the basement of what was supposed to be a residential house.

There it is! He spotted it in a protective poster-style tube, lying on a table right out in the open. *Damn it.* Compared to all the other equipment, it was inconspicuous, but not if they were actually looking for it, and given that they knew about Winslow and his working relationship, and that they had gone through the trouble to find him here, that seemed likely.

Baldie stood at the base of the stairs and looked carefully around the room. "What is all of this equipment for, Mr. Hoch?"

"Oh, this? Just trying some experimental methods out during my down time, stuff I couldn't normally do at work. You know, to stay on top of my game."

"Mr. Hoch, do you take me for a fool?" The policeman scowled at him. Clearly his patience was wearing thin.

"Of course not, sir. You asked why—"

"I asked why you have this equipment because I want the truth, not some ridiculous story. Are you manufacturing drugs?"

"No! Talk about ridiculous!"

Baldie spoke rapidly in hushed tones over his two-way radio, and far above on the second floor, they heard footsteps trammeling down the stairs.

"I'm going to have to ask you to turn around and put your hands on your head, Mr. Hoch." Baldie's right hand moved to the pistol holstered on his belt. He undid the catch but left the gun in the holster for now.

"You're arresting me? For what?"

"For running an illegal drug lab."

"But that's not what I'm doing."

"Then what are you doing?"

Before he could answer, Baldie's partner clamored down the stairs into the basement. He, too, was immediately taken aback by the sight of the lab. Baldie spoke to him in Portuguese, and he began walking around slowly, looking at the equipment slowly without touching it.

"What are you doing here, Mr. Hoch, on your *sabbatical*?" Baldie's tone dripped with sarcasm.

And then Baldie's partner saw the tube on the table and went right to it. He picked it up, looked at his partner and then Hoch. "And this would be?"

"Poster tube keeps papers safe for travel."

"Open it," Baldie said, now removing his pistol from the holster. He didn't aim it at Steve but made it clear that he would use it if he needed to.

His partner slipped the document from the tube. He unrolled it, pressing it flat against the table. "Looks like quite on old document to me," Baldie said. "I think we should have the National Library take a look at it to see if it might be Manuscript 512."

Suddenly Hoch had no more fight in him. "It is Manuscript 512. How did you know it would be here?"

"The laboratory equipment you had to declare in order to enter the country with it. We saw it on airline manifests, saw that you were a professional associate of Dr. Winslow's and put two and two together. What we don't understand," he continued, waving an arm at the lab, "is what you are planning to do with that rare manuscript and this equipment."

Steve shrugged. "There are chemical tests that can be performed to try and make the damaged sections of the document readable again."

The two cops smiled at each other. "So you and Dr. Winslow are searching for the treasure that this document supposedly holds the location to—the Lost City of Z?"

"Dr. Winslow is, not me. I'm just his lab tech. He's the one who stands to gain if he finds the treasure, not me. He's just paying me to do lab work like a regular job."

"Like a regular job." Baldie frowned, looking around at the house lab. "And did you obtain a work visa for the country of Brazil in order to do this work?"

"No."

"As I suspected."

"I can see that you suspect something. Am I under arrest or what, officer…?" Winslow realized that neither man had given their names. He looked for a name tag on their uniforms but saw only a generic badge.

Baldie shot him a look that was pure business. "I am Officer Santos." He waved an arm at his associate. "And this is Officer Ruiz. As for your question, that all depends."

"Depends on what?" During this exchange, Ruiz continued to carefully unroll Manuscript 512, slowly shaking his head as he eyed more and more of it.

"On whether or not you will extend to us your full cooperation."

"What exactly does that mean?" Steve asked.

"It means that perhaps you have something we want, and we have something you want."

The cop looking at the manuscript turned around and said something definitive to Santos, who then addressed Hoch. "The fact that you are in possession of a stolen national treasure means that you are guilty of harboring stolen goods. You could go to jail here for a very long time."

Hoch's face grew bright red. "I didn't steal it! Dr. Winslow did it. I didn't know what he was up to, he just said he would be bringing me a rare document that he wanted me to perform chemical analysis on."

"And what is the purpose of this analysis?" Santos asked. Even Ruiz looked up from the manuscript in anticipation of this response.

Steve racked his brain, but nothing was there. He had nothing but the truth. He stared vacantly at the manuscript beneath the cop's hands.

"Mr. Hoch," Santos prompted, "I remind you that you are in possession of a stolen artifact. Your cooperation in this matter will greatly help your current legal situation."

"It's to see if a chemical technique could uncover the illegible words under the damaged sections."

At this, both *policia* turned to look at one another with raised eyebrows. At length, Santos spoke. "And has it worked?" He eyed the unrolled manuscript.

Hoch shook his head. "No. I mean, I don't know yet. I haven't started on the manuscript yet. I just got everything set up and ran some calibration tests to make—"

"How long does the procedure take?" Santos asked.

"We were hoping it could be completed in about a week from the time I start the actual process on the manuscript itself."

"And when had you planned to begin that process?" Santos moved closer to Hoch and made solid eye contact with him.

"I was ready to begin tonight." Hoch saw no reason to hold anything back. This whole idea was beyond crazy, anyhow. What was he thinking, moving down to the South American continent to help a former boss with a pet project that turned out to be completely illegal? He had to end this here and now before it got even worse.

"Mr. Hoch, let us get right to the point," Santos said. "Our prime suspect is actually Dr. Winslow. If you can lead us to him, we are prepared to offer you complete immunity from prosecution in Brazil over this matter."

"Do you know where he is?" This from Ruiz, who had stopped playing around with the manuscript and was focused entirely on the conversation.

"Not exactly," Steve shrugged. "He's in the rainforest, looking for the Lost City of Z. That's what he's doing. As far as where exactly he is, I don't know. He didn't share that information with me because it's not relevant to what I'm doing."

Santos appeared skeptical, eyes narrowed, head tilted while nodding slowly. "Why did he begin his expedition *before* you completed your lab work?" Santos asked.

"That wasn't the original plan. We were supposed to both be doing the lab work together, then he would launch the expedition after seeing the results. But because he was wanted as a result of the theft, he chose to begin the jungle trek early, since he said it would take about a week to get to the base camp he wanted to use, the same one as the famous 1900s explorer, Percy Fawcett."

"So how will he know when the procedure is finished?" Santos asked. "You will meet him at the camp?"

"No, I call him once a day on his satellite-phone and give him an update."

Again the cops exchanged knowing glances, and again Santos fired off another question.

"Have you spoken with him yet today?"

CHAPTER TEN

Mato Grosso, Brazil

The air was still, both in terms of movement and sound carrying through it; a quiet, peaceful night. But Dr. Winslow felt anything but quiet or peaceful as he picked up his satellite-phone yet again. He'd already tried Hoch four times since sundown—why wasn't he answering?

All kinds of dark thoughts swirled through his head as he placed another call to his lab tech: what if he decided to abscond with the manuscript, to sell it on the black market himself? For some people, the manuscript itself would be enough of a treasure, Winslow realized. And then he had to worry if he simply wasn't taking the job seriously enough—he could be lazing about drinking or simply napping all day like a vacationer? He'd thought he'd expressed the importance of the work enough, and had sufficiently incentivized him, but a long, if ultimately not successful, career had taught him that people were hard to predict.

His mind was about to conjure up yet another reason as to why Hoch might not be answering his calls when he heard the technician's voice come on the line.

"Hi Dr. Winslow, sorry I missed your calls, how are you?"

"I'd be a lot better if you got back to me quicker, but things are good on this end. Today was the end of the road for the Jeeps and tomorrow we set off down the river by boat. So we're still on schedule, but again, I'll be in touch with you tomorrow. Try to answer though, because I should be sleeping now—we're up before first light."

"I'm sorry, I had a computer problem I had to fix that was holding up the lab work."

"Did you get it fixed? Are you still on schedule?" Winslow deliberately let the worry show through in his voice.

"I did get it fixed, and yes, we're still on schedule. There's absolutely nothing to worry about."

"Did you start the actual burn yet?" They both knew he referred to the chemical destruction of the manuscript, the point of no return.

"Should be ready to start that in a couple of hours."

A couple of hours....A sensation of...something...coursed down Winslow's spine as he digested this news. In two hours the process would start to show him where the lost city was. *God. I hope I was right about the answer being there but obscured by the damaged sections.* But everything was in place and he would have his answer within the next few days. Anything it could provide to narrow down the search would be invaluable, given the source.

"Excellent. I look forward to your report tomorrow—please answer next time. Is there anything else before we hang up?"

There was a pause on the other end of the line. "Well, anything else?"

Hoch came back on. "No, no that's it. Wish me luck! Talk tomorrow, bye."

They ended the call and Winslow powered his precious sat-phone down. He breathed a heavy sigh of relief. Everything was still going according to plan. No need to worry, for the moment, anyway. But tomorrow was another day. Deciding he better get some sleep, Dr. Winslow shut down his electronics, clicked his battery powered lantern until the yellow night light mode came on, and bedded down for the night.

#

The next morning while the sky was still dark, Winslow awoke to the rumble of two Jeep engines cranking to life. He scooted out of his sleeping bag and crawled out of the tent. If the vehicles were being started that meant he was late for breakfast. He could make it to an early lunch without the food, but coffee was not something he intended to do without. He heard Sal's voice before he was fully outside of his tent.

"You'll have to eat fast, Sleeping Beauty, but I saved some chow and jet fuel for you over here. Grab a cuppa joe and pack up your tent while I heat you a plate of grinds that'll be ready by the time you're done."

"I knew there was a reason I hired you," Winslow said, groggily walking over to the cook fire and accepting a steaming tin mug.

"I knew there was a reason we brought five ten-kilo bags of coffee—makes everyone easier to deal with in the morning. *Carpe diem!*" The sudden onslaught of pouring rain hammering the canopy leaves above nearly drowned out his last phrase. Winslow packed up his tent and gear and returned to the fire. By now, almost all gear had been packed back into the Jeeps, and all four of the porters were gathered around one of them, smoking cigarettes and chatting, waiting to get underway.

The still cheery Sal handed Winslow a plate with a spork and then refilled both his and Winslow's coffee before pouring what remained out on the fire, which, together with the rain, was doused quickly. Winslow chowed down his food quickly; it was surprisingly good, since they had gotten some to go from the previous night's dinner. "Enjoy the last of the home cooked meals," Sal said as he gathered the last of the gear. "From here on out it's nothing but jungle."

They loaded into the Jeeps and drove into thick rainforest only a few minutes from camp. The road became little more than a pair of ruts in the earth, while overhead, the canopy closed in much tighter. Before long they came to a large river, a tributary of the Xingu that flowed downhill for thousands of miles as it wound its way to the South Atlantic Ocean.

An abutment of green tangled growth obscured the tracks any further into the rainforest along the river. They parked the Jeeps and got out, one of the porters meeting with Sal to gauge the river. Its brown water flowed slowly, but with immense power. Winslow knew there was no way a person could swim against it. If one fell in, one had to keep themselves afloat until the river's course carried them into contact with either one of the banks, or a tree that hung out over the water; something before they were sucked down into a whirlpool and drowned or were knocked out by being carried down a fast-moving eddy, mini-falls or even whirlpool, dragged under to bang into a rock.

"This heavy rain might swell the banks some, but the level's already low so we should be okay for today," Sal said, looking upriver.

Two aluminum jon boats, each with an outboard motor and complete with a canvas Bimini top, were hauled down from the Jeep roof racks and dragged into the river. Sal started up the outboards while the porters and Winslow loaded the boats with their supplies. Winslow, Sal and one of the porters would ride in one boat, while three porters would ride in the other, with the gear split between each. With everything loaded, the boats were very full, but comfortable enough while holding the entire expedition.

Sal and one of the porters parked the Jeeps in a spot of firm ground well away from the river bank, with his business card on the windshield, in case anyone wondered whose vehicles they were and wanted to call his satellite-phone to find out. With everyone on board the boats, Sal at the helm of the one he was in, they pushed off the bank out into deep water.

The river was about a quarter-mile wide, and tiny islets consisting of little more than a single tree or two dotted the brown water here and there. A flock of birds glided low over the river to their left, downstream, as they motored out into the middle of the river, where the current was fastest. When they got there, they cut the motors to conserve fuel, since they were drifting at a good clip toward their downstream destination. The resulting quiet settled like a blanket over each boat crew, and for a time they floated silently down the river in the pre-dawn stillness.

By the time the sun was up in the sky, a pot of instant coffee had been made and passed around, and spirits were high. Even Winslow had the makings of a smile on his face. *This is it*, he thought, *I'm doing it, for better or worse. Whatever's going to happen is going to happen, there's no turning back now...*

"Okay, need you to sit all the way inside the boat now, please, going to start her up to maneuver around this islet." Sal's voice wrenched Winslow from his escapist thoughts. He slid down from where he was sitting with his back to the water on the boat's rail so that he occupied one of the bench seats. Sal fired up the motor and accelerated while maneuvering them around a clump of trees growing not far in front of them. When they reached the other side, he used his walkie-talkie to radio the lead boat to ask if more obstacles were forthcoming. Upon receiving the "coast is clear" signal, he killed the outboard again and relaxed. They all knew that their destination, a tribal village of an Amazonian people known to be friendly enough to outsiders, was still a two-day boat journey away, assuming there were no hitches.

There was nothing to do for now but to literally go with the flow, however, so they enjoyed the ride as best they could, snapping off a few photos of their surroundings, with Sal knowing better than to make Dr. Winslow nervous by taking his picture.

"Figure they're out looking for you in all the wrong places right about now, eh?" Sal offered, testing Winslow's mood. Personally, even though he had worked with Winslow over the years, it made him a little nervous to be this deep in the bush with someone who was under so much stress. He could see that he tried to play it off like it was no big deal, but the signs were there. The constant rubbernecking, the sweaty forehead, the darting eyes and continual questioning about who knows what.

"I reckon so," he said, turning away from the porter who was scouting conditions up on the bow platform.

"You're a crazy bastard, Hunter, I'll give you that."

"That's a real compliment, coming from you."

"Touché." Sal's radio crackled, and he picked it up. "Say again," he said into the microphone. A pause while Winslow couldn't hear what was being said, and then, "Got it, out." He moved back into position to operate the outboard while saying to Winslow, "They're saying that the river narrows up around this bend and we might want the motor on to help make the turn."

Again, they got situated in the boat and Sal started the outboard. They motored slowly to the bend in the river and then saw that the lead boat had already disappeared around the next bend after that. Sal negotiated the river, and after a series of "S" curves, the river straightened out again although remained narrower, about half the width as before.

The porters in the other boat began tossing out chicken scraps to use as bait and netted up a few lunchable fish before piranhas made fishing impossible. Winslow watched as the water seethed and boiled with them, shuddering as he imagined what would happen to a person should they fall into the water at that moment. He felt the tropical noonday sun beating down on his neck and retreated below the shelter of the canopy to lean against a bushel of bananas on the bench seat. With the motor off and the lapping of water against the side of the ship, he soon grew drowsy.

The last thought he had before drifting off to a nap was how Hoch was doing in the lab.

CHAPTER ELEVEN

Rio de Jainero Suburb

"Another Café do Ponto, Senor Hoch?" Officer Santos extended his arm holding the coffee cup out to a bleary-eyed Steven Hoch, who accepted the beverage. He'd slept less than three hours after being told he would basically be on supervised house arrest until they were able to bring Dr. Winslow in for questioning. Santos's partner was still here, too, although he had stopped snooping about hours ago and now mostly sat around staring at Hoch, making him nervous.

Funny thing was, although he had thought he was ready to begin the process of destroying Manuscript 512 in order to chemically treat it and hopefully reveal its missing words, he really did encounter computer problems, but they happened after reporting to Winslow that was the reason for the holdup. Call it karma, he thought, but he had worked through the night and most of the morning to get everything on the computing side of things correctly configured, pushed by the *policia*. To his surprise, they had ordered him to go ahead with destroying the document.

"Well, are you ready to begin?" Santos sat down near Hoch on a lab stool. He awaited Steve's reply eagerly, with a sly grin on his face. The whole thing seemed surreal to the lab tech, and a little bit off. The cops were asking him to destroy the rare document that they had just tracked down?

"Are you sure you want me to run the full experiment—I mean actually run it on Manuscript 512 itself—or you mean walk you through the steps in a dry run. Because, again, doing this will de—"

"—destroy the document, we know, Mr. Hoch, we know. But as you yourself pointed out, if Dr. Winslow doesn't get information that seems genuine, he'll know...*something is up*, as you say in your country."

"And if that happens," Ruiz, who rarely said anything at all, chimed in, "our concern is that he will flee the country, perhaps by entering Bolivia or Peru through the Mato Grosso region of the rainforest."

"So you want me to literally destroy the stolen document and then work with him—while you watch—to translate or otherwise decode the missing words?"

"Precisely." It was Santos who spoke, but Hoch's question drew nods from both *polícia*. "It's the only way for us to know where he's going before he gets there."

Steve hung his head in his hands for a moment. "He's going to know I turned him in. Our professional relationship will be ruined…"

Santos gave him a stern look accompanied with a lecturing tone. "You want to preserve your relationship, senor, fine, but I guarantee you it will cost you a lengthy stay in a Brazilian prison."

Steve returned a look that said, *What choice do I have?* "From the time I place the manuscript into the first machine, we'll have a few hours to wait for the results."

Santos nodded. "That would be a good time for you to get some sleep. You have been up for a long time now, and this work no doubt requires a clear mind."

Hoch had no rational arguments against this, so he merely nodded and turned to the manuscript, which had been returned to its tube for safekeeping following the officers' initial look at it. "So you're asking me to take it out of the case and run it through my machines to destroy it and see what we can learn about possible additional content in the process."

Both *polícia* nodded at him. There was no need to clarify the situation any further. They both waited with arms crossed for him to indicate his decision with actions. They tensed when he got up from the stool, but then relaxed as he walked over to the scroll, picked up the tube, uncapped it and removed it from the protective case.

It was time for Steve Hoch to get to work.

#

Matto Grosso

This morning Winslow had an easier time of rising before the sun. He participated in making breakfast with the rest of the group, making an extra pot of coffee to keep his spirits lively, hoping to transform the excitement into positive energy in spite of everything that could go wrong. Facing another long day on the river, they broke down camp in between bites of rice, fish and boiled plantains, with an extra treat of cinnamon buns, and then loaded it all into the jon boats. Absolutely no sounds of civilization could be heard outside of their own camp, only the cacophony of nature in full swing, a lush chorus of insects humming and birds chirping punctuated by the occasional random animal call.

They hoped to make it as far as the tiny village of a known friendly tribe, and then to camp there for the night. Beyond that point, the river's course took it the wrong way from their starting point of Dead Horse Camp, and they would have to go the rest of the way on foot.

"Last day to enjoy a ride for some time," Sal said, expressing this fact.

Winslow nodded. "Another day of sitting on my fat ass, I'll take it."

"Just be ready to work those legs tomorrow, boy. But remember, we take it one day at a time. We still have a full day's river journey ahead of us. It's not exactly like taking a train from point A to B. But we'll make it."

A chorus of shouts erupted from the porters at that moment. Sal and Winslow ran over to a spot a short distance from the cook fire, on the edge of the camp clearing, to see what the fuss was. They found the porters gathered around a hairy spider with a central body the size of a basketball, one of them prodding at it with a tree branch.

"Holy—what kind of spider is that?" Winslow asked, horrified. He could not stand spiders ever since his mother had sent him to get something from the attic as a child and he found it infested with daddy long legs.

"The poisonous kind, Hunter. That's all you need to know. You see one—don't touch it and do what they're doing and don't make it feel welcome." Then he raised his voice. "Come on, everyone, let's get underway, shall we. This little guy can have the camp now."

The team straggled over to the boats and boarded for the day's trip, again with Sal and Winslow in one boat, with a different porter this time, and three porters in the other boat. No precipitation currently fell but it had rained on and off throughout the night, leaving the river swollen and flowing swiftly, with a hint of whitewater.

Narrow and twisty, both boats proceeded with the aid of the outboards to negotiate the curves and sudden obstacles including fallen trees and boulders. Winslow applied liberal amounts of bug spray over his long sleeves and long pants, since they were biting right through the fabric. After the river widened and became straighter, it also became steeper, and they picked up speed as they floated down a thickly forested grade.

A sack of onions tumbled over the side of the boat and the porter snagged it, almost falling overboard himself in the process, but Winslow steadied him with a hand until he was fully back inside.

"Nice catch, there's no more porters to hire out here!" Sal quipped from his captain's position at the outboard tiller.

"Trust me, I know we need these guys," Winslow replied. Then he thought about what they would do when they reached Dead Horse Camp, the point at which the porters would return home, under no obligation to proceed further. All four insisted they would not go that deep into the Matto Grosso. Winslow still held out hope that once they actually got there, if things had gone smoothly until then, that they would agree to go on at least a little further, perhaps if they could grease the wheels with a little bonus payment.

After a time the slope flattened out and the river's water calmed without becoming any wider. They passed a settlement of another known tribe, the women and children bathing and washing clothes at river's edge, waving to them as they drifted past. The porter in Winslow's boat tossed them a bushel of plantains as a gesture of goodwill, and soon the tribe was left behind as the jon boats ventured ever deeper into the rainforest.

To combat boredom, Winslow used a pair of high-powered binoculars to peer high up into the canopy trees, randomly picking a spot. He was often surprised to see an animal there, a howler monkey, a sloth, some kind of parrot...the forest was packed with an amazing diversity of life, even with the habitat destruction of recent decades, and although Winslow was an historian by trade, the wonders of life in this riotously profuse region did not escape him. What other biological wonders did the deepest regions of the rainforest hold? What animals did the citizens of the Lost City of Z know? He told himself that he was genuinely curious about the lives of the actual people of Z, whoever they were, that he was investigating the lost civilization as a researcher who could shed light on humanity and contribute to the body of scientific knowledge, rather than his interest being solely as a greed-driven treasure hunter out to further his own aims at any cost.

But deep down, as he accepted a flask passed to him from Sal at the helm, he knew which one he was.

CHAPTER TWELVE

Rio de Jainero Suburb

Steve Hoch frowned to himself as he removed the manuscript from a chemical bath and transferred it to a machine that would cast it with ultraviolet light. The handwriting on the document, some 250 years old, was now all but ruined, chemically degraded to the point of near-illegibility. And that was only the first pass. The process would have to be repeated more times, and by then the original writing would be virtually erased.

With the exception of the already damaged parts.

He fed the portion of the manuscript with a damaged blotch of worm-eaten words—an irregular splotch approximately one-by-two inches, removing words and part of words from parts of three lines—into the machine and put his eyes up to the attached scope. He heard Santos's shoes shuffling across the concrete floor of the basement as he moved closer to see exactly what he was doing, while Ruiz remained farther away, lounging on a lab stool. Steve slid the parchment into position and then fine-focused the scope as he targeted the compromised area.

Oh yeah, there we go… He backed away from the 'scope just to make sure that he was focused in on the right area of the manuscript—the destroyed part. Because he was seeing words, not opaque blotches. Satisfied that he was indeed focused in on a worm-eaten spot, he then put his eyes back to the 'scope while the *policía* watched him carefully.

The writing was faint, not even what most people would call legible yet, but it was there; that much was unmistakable. He had wiped away part of the damaged portion and revealed the original writing beneath. He backed off the 'scope again and his gut did a little tumble when he saw the rest of the manuscript on that page that had been subjected to the treatment—it was correspondingly degraded by about the same amount the worm-eaten section had been improved. Even though he knew that going into this, to actually see it in action was both heart-wrenching and spirit-lifting at the same time. Sure, he was uncovering the secrets of Manuscript 512, and by extension hopefully the Lost City of Z, but at the same time he was destroying a document that was a quarter of a millennium old.

"Well, what are the results?" Santos wanted to know, interrupting his thoughts.

Slowly, Steve turned to him. "It's working. See for yourself..." He removed the parchment from the machine and laid it out flat on the lab bench. He pointed to the revealed writing with the capped tip of a pen. "Look there—remember how it was damaged?"

Santos leaned in for a close look, shooting a quick look to his partner that no doubt said, *Watch my back while I'm hunched over,* while he did. The cop examined the document closely for a few seconds and then stood up, grinning. "I see! There is writing under the damaged part that is now almost readable, where before it was not visible at all. Still," he added, part of the grin fading, "it is not yet a decipherable word."

Steve nodded. "I know that. This was only the first pass. I will have to make at least one, maybe two more passes to fully bring out the letters without degrading it too much."

"With each pass taking about as much time as this last one?" Santos inquired.

Steve thought about this a second and then said, "Actually, each pass should take a little more time than the one before it."

"Then you better get started."

#

Winslow's butt hurt from sitting on the boat's metal bench seat, even with a life jacket as a cushion. At this point he would have preferred to get out and hack his way through the jungle, machete swing by machete swing, but he knew after a couple of days of that, he would wish he could float down a river again. The jungle was not an easy place however you decided to make a go of it, he decided.

The river itself, having reached relatively level ground, calmed down and widened. They shut off the motors and drifted, relishing the peace and quiet as well as not having to use too much fuel, which would be increasingly difficult to replace the deeper into the jungle they went. As he stared out at what looked to be an impenetrable wall of green on either side of the river, Winslow was tempted to use his sat-phone to check the latest news on the library theft story, but he knew that using the device for anything other than essential contact was a mistake. He didn't think it was traceable to him, but battery life was critical, as was simply dropping it overboard. Plus, the paranoid side of his brain implored, who knew—maybe the authorities were in fact monitoring sat-phone communication originating from Brazil that looked like it might have anything to do with the theft. Wouldn't be all that difficult probably, not that he was a technical expert in the matter.

Even the usually talkative Sal grew silent the deeper into the forest the river took them, while the porter sat on the prow of the boat with a walkie-talkie, watching for obstacles to navigation while chatting occasionally with his peers in the other boat, which was about a hundred feet ahead of them. Winslow brought out a map of the Matto Grosso and once again studied the region, tracing his projected routes and alternate routes, letting his mind wander with possibilities. What would they do if they couldn't get through this way...or that way? But deep down even he knew that the jungle was anything but predictable, that there were simply too many variables involved—both known and unknown—for this kind of planning to have much chance of turning out to be helpful.

A group of crocodiles basking on a mud bank drew the attention of both boats as they passed by, especially when two of the large ones—Sal guessed they were twelve-footers-slipped beneath the water while heading for the jon boats. To err on the side of caution, they fired up the motors and sped away from the crocs until they were sufficiently far away to drift silently once again.

Winslow was lost in his thoughts once again, staring at his maps without even really seeing them anymore, when Sal's voice cut into his stupor. "So what are you going to do if we find it?"

"Huh?"

"If we find it, what are you going to do?"

"Find what?"

"The lost city, and the treasure that supposedly goes with it." Sal eyed him with an unwavering stare while they glided past a tree filled with blue and yellow macaws.

"I don't know. Never really thought about it," Winslow lied, while peering over the bow of the boat from beneath his wide-brimmed hat. "Probably start documenting it so that I can publish some papers, get some academic recognition."

"Academic recognition? Is that all you want?"

Winslow shrugged. "That's what started this all for me. I can't say for certain how it would change me if we come across a large treasure, I guess."

Sal shot him a knowing grin. "Sure you can. Besides, after you go through what we're going to have to to find it, you won't have any reservations about partaking in the spoils, believe me, not that I truly believe you do, anyway."

Winslow decided to shift the conversation away from his motivations, which no doubt were transparent enough at this point, to something else that concerned him. He turned around to check on the porter in their boat, but he was facing forward toward the other boat, chatting softly on the walkie-talkie.

"Do you think there's any truth to the rumors? That the city, or the treasure or both, is cursed? All those expeditions that never returned…"

Sal looked away from the tree canopy, where he'd been watching a large python coiled on a tree branch that overhung the river bank, and levelled his gaze at Winslow. "I'm not sure they're rumors at all, if that's what you mean. Something is up with that region, I can say that without hesitation. All those expeditions that were lost without a trace…and the stories I've heard…"

"What stories?" Winslow didn't know why he wanted to torture himself with tales of expeditions gone wrong to the very region they were about to enter, but there was a lot of time to pass as they drifted down the river and it kept his mind off of his legal predicament.

"Stuff I hear in the bars, whispered late at night after too many drinks." Apparently, Sal felt no need to elaborate, so, after waiting for the call of a tall white bird that looked to him like a crane or an egret to finish its *whooping*, he took the bait.

"Such as?"

Sal chewed on a piece of dried fish while he talked. "There was this one guy—an American college dropout, late twenties, decent guy, smart guy. Came down here alone to lead eco-tours into the rainforest. Started out with established companies, working for them on routes they'd done for years. For about six months he did that, but on the weekends he was known to go out on his own, deeper into the jungle, finding his own way with a handheld GPS, basically blazing his own trail."

"Why do I get the feeling this doesn't end well?"

"Because it doesn't. After about a year he quit his job at the tour company, said that the little nature walks just weren't doing it for him anymore, and that he was going to start offering custom 'extreme adventure eco-tours' or some such nonsense deep into the bush. And he did that for a few months with decent results. Attracted a few clients he'd meet by hanging out in the clubs—including the Conga Room. He'd take people out and they'd rave about the 'adventure of a lifetime' and this and that…"

Sal squinted down river.

"And so, what happened?"

"So one day, the kid says he's going into the bush alone for a week to scout out new routes for his business. Said he wanted something to attract upper echelon clientele from all over the world, something that he could market as a 'premiere adventure experience' or some load of crap like that."

"Let me guess, his new route was in the Matto Grosso?"

Sal snorted. "Oh yeah—almost all of his work was. He'd routinely take people to Dead Horse Camp."

'Wow."

"Yeah, and it was on one of these scouting missions where he tried to venture beyond Dead Horse where things went wrong for him."

"What happened?"

"Kid didn't come back for damn near six months. Strangest shit ever. No messages sent out from him, sat-phone calls, nothing. One day, he just shows up at the port town of Corumbá, stark fucking naked and raving mad. He could speak, but only nonsense over and over again. He'd say something like, "They were talking to me," when people asked where he came from, and then later in the police station, he'd say, "They've been there forever," for a few days, and some other weird stuff. But any attempts to clarify were only met with similar statements that were meaningless without context. He was diagnosed as clinically insane and deported to the States. No one ever heard anything about him again."

After a moment of silence to digest this, Winslow said, "Nice story." Then he went back to staring at his research materials, this time a printout of Manuscript 512. His gazed bored into the eaten-away sections as if he could implore them to reveal what they had read. Meanwhile, glancing at his watch, he hoped Steve Hoch was doing exactly that.

CHAPTER THIRTEEN

Rio de Jainero Suburb

Steve Hoch had just completed a second pass on the damaged section of Manuscript 512 when his satellite phone warbled on the lab bench. He and the two *policia* stared at it like it was a ghost. Santos moved to the phone, picked it up and handed it to Steve. The lab tech left the 'scope he was looking into and answered the call, putting it on speaker. He put a finger to his lips to remind them to stay quiet. Both of them nodded, and then Dr. Hunter Winslow's voice carried through the tinny speaker.

"You hear me?" Steve noted silently that Winslow was still carrying on with his habit of not using names, not that it mattered anymore. He spoke into the phone while glancing at Santos and Ruiz.

"Loud and clear, buddy. How goes it out there, everything okay?"

"We just got off the boats to make camp. It's all on foot from here on out. Reckon about three days to the camp."

Steve looked at Santos and mouthed the words *Dead Horse Camp.* Santos's partner made a scribble in a notepad with a pen.

"So pretty much on schedule, then, that's good news."

"Yeah, you make it sound so easy," Winslow came back. "And how about you, are you on schedule?"

Hoch eyed Santos and Ruiz in turn before saying into the phone, "Yes, the first round of treatment has been successful!"

"Really, that's excellent! Did it work—can you read new sections?" The excitement in Dr. Winslow's voice could only be described as unbridled. Hoch's tone was more cool and soothing.

"Nothing new is actually readable yet, but in the one section I've treated so far, it's definitely revealed writing. I can see words there, but I need to do another chemical pass to make it more legible."

"How long, how long for that?"

Hoch glanced at his watch, at the lab equipment, at his *policia* monitors, then back to the sat-phone in his hand. "Tell you what. I know you're excited about this, so I'll work through the night."

"Excellent. Don't forget the bonus schedule. You know I'll make it worth your while."

"Thank you. If the procedure goes well, by the time you're up at first light, I'll be able to call you with new words. I'll have to email you a picture, which is going to be expensive and take a few minutes, but you knew that."

"Yes, of course, I can't very well have you read the words to me, can I, they're in 18th century Portuguese for crying out loud!" Winslow's laughter was cut short by the sound of a gas generator starting up and a couple of men shouting instructions in the background. "Okay, I should get going and let you get back to work. Excellent progress, and I look forward to hearing from you before we leave camp in the morning."

Hoch looked at the *policia* as he said his next line. "You're still on track for your first destination, right?"

"Yeah, yeah, Sal—I mean my guide–says it shouldn't be too washed out and that it looks like the next day at least, should be fairly normal, for the Amazon, that is."

"Sounds good. Get some sleep. Talk to you in the morning." Hoch disconnected the call and made eye contact with Santos and Ruiz, both of whom appeared energized.

"Good work," Santos said to Steve, while looking at the lab equipment. "Once you are able to feed Dr. Winslow the missing pieces, we will know where he intends to search."

"We also know something else," Santos's partner said, snapping his notebook shut after jotting something down. "The name of his guide— did you hear?" he said to Santos, who nodded.

"Sal."

"You think that's Sal Torres?" Santos looked to Hoch. "Have you worked with Sal before?"

Steve quickly shook his head. "No, I only know that Dr. Winslow has worked with him as a jungle guide going back a number of years, and that the guy has been living down in Brazil for a while."

"Does he play the congas?" Santos asked Steve.

"I couldn't say. Dr. Winslow's guides are his business. I'm just the lab technician."

Santos nodded. "I see."

"I can say, though," Steve continued, "that in addition to the guide, who must know the jungle well and be a little crazy himself to agree to lead anyone that deep into the Matto Grosso, Winslow also hired a group of local porters."

Both cops nodded. "Yes," Santos said, "the police talked to them at the airport."

Santos's partner stood and gathered his keys. "Dinner time, gentlemen. I will go get us some takeout."

Steve nodded. "I'll get back to work on the manuscript."

Ruiz left the basement up the stairs while Steve sat down at his lab bench under Santos's watchful eye.

#

Matto Grosso

"We're not going to have to listen to that thing all night, are we?" Winslow complained to Sal, as the gas-powered electrical generator hummed and rattled from its position on the edge of camp. It powered an array of utility lights on stands that the porters were using to organize gear for the transition from the jon boats to foot. Since they had arrived at dusk, they now needed to prepare for the next day in almost full darkness. The canopy was thick over their heads, completely filtering out what little light remained.

"Until it's time for sleep we do," Sal said matter-of-factly, sipping from a cold Brahma brew. "It's a lot of work to move everything off the boats and organize it into packs. Gonna take some time."

"Can we even take it all?"

"We'll leave the two boats pulled up on land here, filled with extra provisions that the porters will pick up on their way back for their return trip after we leave Dead Horse."

Winslow's expression became thoughtful, concerned. "You don't think there's any chance at least one of them will decide to stay on— even for increased pay?"

Sal gave him a look that was a mixture of pity and disrespect, like one reserved for someone who didn't comprehend the gravity of their own situation. "No, Hunter, like I said, these guys will not go in there no matter what. I will ask them, just to make you happy, when the time comes, but I already know the answer, and so should you. It's going to be just you and me, pal."

"I know that. I'm okay with that."

"Well I hope so, amigo, because if you're not, you've got a couple more days to change your mind. After that, it's Welcome to the Great Unknown, with only my sorry ass for company."

"I'm fine with it, Sal, really. I was just asking, that's all. Anything to make things easier for us and improve our chances."

"Right now, grabbing us a couple more brews would improve our chances," Sal smiled.

Winslow walked over to a cooler and pulled a couple of cold bottles from the packed ice. Even over the sound of the generator, he could hear the cacophony of jungle noises—screeching monkeys, chittering birds, rustling leaves. This place is absolutely untamable, he thought, but then he conjured up all that farmland they'd flown over and knew that it wasn't so. It was tamable, and even vulnerable. But he thought, as he walked back to Sal with the beers, that probably made the parts of the forest that remained that much more resilient, didn't it?

#

Rio de Jainero Suburb

Steve Hoch didn't even want to know the time because he felt like he was running out of it, so he avoided looking at any screen that displayed the hour—his sat-phone, his computer, and did his best to concentrate on the instrument displaying the portion of Manuscript 512 now being subject to his chemical treatment. His only worry regarding time was that he might forget to call Dr. Winslow, but with his *policía* lab security detail, as he jokingly thought of them, he realized there was little to no chance of that. It seemed like the *policía* wanted him to stay in touch with his boss even more than he did. No surprise there, Hoch supposed. The man had stolen a national treasure from their museum and they wanted him to face justice for it.

Steve still thought it odd that they were allowing him to destroy the manuscript little by little in order to string Winslow along that everything was business as usual, but he wasn't entirely sure what to make of that. Brazilian law was different from that of the U.S., that was one thing. For another, they may be testing whether this person claiming to be Steven Hoch was really a lab technician, and not some imposter aiming to throw things off track. After all, they had probably figured out by now that the irate library patron in Special Collections just before Manuscript 512 went missing was actually a paid distractor hired by Dr. Winslow himself. What if the "lab tech" was too?

Hoch supposed that, like any cops, they had to be thorough and so he couldn't blame them for thinking that way, if in fact that's how they were thinking. He was a little giddy himself from the developments, and all he knew at this point was, *I'm cooperating so they should go easy on me, and the work itself is interesting to boot.* He would just have to run with it.

However, as he removed the document from the 'scope to check the effects of his latest round of chemical treatment, he shook his head as he examined the page that he had restored—not the now-readable damaged section, but the rest of that page. It was now seriously degraded, damn near unreadable, Steve thought. He eyed the rest of the document, the damaged sections occurring regularly all the way through to the end. By the time he was done with this process…he shuddered at the thought but had to face the reality: the entire document would be a ruined, bleached out mess, with only a few legible words here and there that weren't present before.

"Is there a problem, Senor Hoch?" Santos asked, leaning forward from his nearby lab stool. Steve showed him the washed-out page. Santos shrugged in response.

"We knew this was the likely outcome going into this, right?"

"Yes, but to actually see it…you still wish me to continue with destroying the document?"

He and his partner nodded enthusiastically. "There is no other way," Santos stated. "Serving justice to international criminals is more important than preserving some old piece of paper."

Ruiz nodded in agreement, and Steve wondered if perhaps these men were simply after professional advancement, that they would make themselves look good before going out of their way to help the library preserve a single document out of thousands. He wondered what he would do in the same situation and supposed he couldn't really blame them.

And the benefit of the work, he thought, turning his attention to the worm-damaged section he had just treated, was that a group of words was now readable where before they were not. He could not read Portuguese, much less 250-year old handwritten Portuguese, so he held the paper up to Santos's eyes so that he could have a look. The detective squinted at the document for several seconds before responding.

"It's hard for me to read, like if you had to read Old English from Shakespeare times, but I think it says something about directions, north of this, east of that…"

The three men looked at each other with the realization that they appeared to be uncovering the specific location of the Lost City of Z. Hoch was the first to recover enough to voice next steps.

"Dr. Winslow can actually read this, so, in keeping with our plan, I'll take a picture of the new words and send them to his sat-phone, so he can take a look. Then when I call him, he'll hopefully be able to tell us what it means."

Santos nodded his approval. "And after that you will continue to process the rest of the document. There is a long way to go," he concluded, "but it appears that your process is working. You should be most proud of yourself."

Hoch wasn't sure how to take a compliment from a member of the non-scientific community who had an ulterior motive, so he went with a simple, "Thanks," and then proceeded with the plan. He took two pictures with his phone—one of the entire document's first page, to show Winslow the overall results of what he had done, and then another that was a closeup with sufficient detail to make the revealed words readable. Then he emailed both of these images to Winslow's sat-phone, noting aloud to the *policia* that it was past end of day and so Winslow should have made camp by now if everything had gone all right.

CHAPTER FOURTEEN

Matto Grosso

Winslow had just taken his first sip of beer when his satellite phone vibrated in the pockets of his moisture-wicking cargo pants. He nearly dropped his beer in the hurry to pull the device out and answer it. He spoke loud enough to overcome the sound of the generator running nearby.

"Talk to me, buddy, how's it going?"

"Good, man, how's it with you—you made camp?"

"Affirmative, we're setup for the night, got about as far as we'd planned by boat. Tomorrow we strike out on foot for a projected two-day trek to you know where."

"Excellent, how's everyone holding up?"

"So far so good, we're all still alive and kicking. So how's it going on your end?"

The chit-chat ended, Winslow held the phone a little closer to his ear. This was the reason for this call.

"Did you get the two images I emailed?"

"What? No, wait hold on…" Winslow pressed some buttons on his phone and then let out an exasperated sigh as he spotted the two new messages. "Sorry, didn't see those earlier, I must have notifications off for emails to save the sat-phone batteries. Anyway, stay on the line, let me take a quick look…"

The historian opened the pictures, first the shot of the overall document, where he could plainly see the chemical damage Hoch's procedure had dealt to the rare document. Then he opened the closeup of the revealed portion, and zoomed in a little…

"Oh wow…wow!"

"So you're looking at it?"

"Hell yes, I'm looking at it! Unbelievable—it worked!"

"Yeah!"

"Congratulations! Nicely done, old friend!"

"Thanks. So what the heck does it say?"

"Has to do with directions! Let's see, the preceding sentence says..." Then Winslow interrupted himself. "Aw heck, let me get back to you tomorrow after I unpack this a little. No need to rack up a big sat-phone bill while you sit there and wait for me to figure it out. I'll work on it tonight in my tent and I'll talk to you tomorrow. But Steve?"

"Yeah?"

"Keep going on the document. Don't wait for me, just keep it going."

"You bet. Talk to you tomorrow."

They ended the call and Winslow dropped the sat-phone into his pocket while Sal nodded to it. "Your lab guy came through?"

Winslow nodded. "It appears so." Winslow raised his beer bottle in a toast. "I'm going to retire to my tent early tonight, so I can work on decoding this thing, Sal. But it looks like we might be getting some more specific information over the next few days straight from the source— I'm talking about the 1700s source who drafted Manuscript 512 upon which Fawcett based his expeditions. With any luck, this new info will inform our expedition after we get to Dead Horse."

"Well, you know we have some kind of luck," Sal said, "or we wouldn't have even made it this far. Let's just hope it continues."

Winslow nodded and retreated to his tent with his beer and his sat-phone images.

#

The next morning before dawn, Winslow was up before Sal. Knowing that the 512 process was effective had energized him. He'd had a difficult time falling asleep the previous night, poring over the image and deciphering its meaning, but he was reasonably confident that he had done it. He would think about it some more while he trekked through the rainforest today, but he thought it made sense to him. He needed the next piece of the puzzle from Hoch to continue, but in the meantime, he was making his way toward Dead Horse Camp and the beginning of his true search, and he couldn't be any happier.

By the time he had lit the cook fire and brewed the first pot of coffee and poured himself a mug, Sal was out of his tent. He ambled over to the fire and gratefully accepted a mug of steaming brew. "Well aren't you up bright-eyed and bushy-tailed. I'd have thought you'd be up half the night deciphering those lab results."

"Don't think I wasn't," Winslow grinned after another swallow of caffeinated beverage.

"So do we know where to head yet from Dead Horse?"

"Not yet, because what I have is still incomplete and depends on what comes after it, which my lab tech is working on now. But the technique works, that's the important thing, it's just a matter of time."

"Glad to hear it," Sal said, wandering off to check in with the porters, who were huddled in a conference or prayer of some sort over by where the jon boats had been pulled up onto dry ground.

Winslow finished his coffee and then broke down his tent and packed everything up for the trek. He donned his backpack, testing its weight, carefully adjusting the straps, for he would be walking with it for the foreseeable future. He was glad now that he'd purchased the best one that was in stock at the shop—lightweight and durable, breathable, moisture-repellent and with a good combination of organization and roominess inside. Satisfied the pack would work, he shrugged it off and turned his attention to his footwear. Wool socks under leather hiking boots that laced up the ankles, with nylon covers over them to keep them from getting soaked. A piece of moleskin carefully placed at the chafe points inside the boots. This he'd learned from experience, painfully so, and now he could not afford not to be at the peak of his abilities— physically and mentally.

Winslow carefully attached a small fixed blade knife in a sheath to his belt and strapped his machete scabbard across his back. He practiced pulling it out, rapidly, warrior style, before sheathing it and then applying bug spray liberally to his boots, pant legs and long shirt sleeves, even the top of his wide-brimmed hat.

Kitted out up and packed up, Winslow poured one last mug of coffee, put out the fire and walked over to Sal and the porters, who were now done stocking the boats with the provisions to be left behind. Sal turned to him as he walked up.

"Be light out in about fifteen. You ready?"

"Ready as I'll ever be."

"Good." Sal nodded to the porters. "Then let's get underway, shall we? The jungle awaits."

The four porters hefted their heavy packs and made their way to the edge of camp opposite the river, which curved away from their upcoming route. At the edge of camp, a faintly discernable game trail offered a break into the formidable foliage. It was only wide enough to permit single-file passage, so two porters led the way, then Sal, then Dr. Winslow, with the other two porters bringing up the rear.

The procession parted a swarm of gnat-like insects that hovered over the gap in the jungle like a cloud, the gap closing as the humans passed. Winslow was glad for his bug spray, and he wondered how the porters got by without it. He knew Sal used it, albeit more sparingly than he. Whatever, he thought, tramping into the rainforest, *whatever it takes to get it done.*

Winslow knew they were deep into the wilderness when he heard the cry of a big cat somewhere nearby. The porters stopped, Sal stopped, Winslow stopped.

"Jaguar," Sal hissed, pronouncing the word so that it had three syllables, which Winslow found extremely irritating. The snap of a thick tree limb breaking reached their ears along with the rustle of leaves, and then the cat was heard no more. The party moved on again, a little warier of what might lie in wait around them, only a few feet past the greenery through which they could see. The jungle was like an ocean that only allowed the visitor to see a few feet into it at a time.

In no time at all, Winslow found himself sweating profusely, his moisture-wicking pants soaked all the way through with sweat. He had to continually adjust his hat by tightening the drawstring beneath his chin after low-hanging branches threatened to knock it off. In the brief few seconds the top of his head was exposed, he had to sweep it clear of thick, ropey cobwebs. It was a great fear of his to have some egg-bearing creepie-crawly scurry into one of his ears and bore into his brain where it would lay eggs. Winslow imagined he would feel a strange itching sensation when it first happened, then pass it off as nothing important after the bug fell dead deep in his brain. But then, when the eggs hatched, a massive brood of tiny arthropods would scamper around his brain, causing him to lose complete control of even the most basic motor functions...

"Hey Doc Winslow, you listening to an iPod or something back there?" Winslow realized that Sal had been talking to him and he hadn't even heard him, so lost was he in his macabre fantasy of jungle-borne obliteration.

"Sorry, Sal, was just thinking about stuff, you know, there's a lot to plan for."

"I get it, pal. Just asking if you're hungry. I still have some of that fish jerky if you want some."

"No thanks, Sal, I'm good."

They marched on in silence for a time, the jungle air growing more still the deeper they penetrated. It became darker as well, with Winslow taking off his sunglasses to see even though it was late morning and very sunny above the trees. He liked the sunglasses for eye protection, though, and wished he would have thought to wear clear safety goggles like the ones Sal wore, though he knew he complained about them fogging from time to time. There was simply no easy way through this jungle, Winslow mused. He imagined how it must have been for Fawcett, during his time nearly a century ago, when the technology was not nearly as good and the rainforest even larger and more unadulterated. *But Fawcett had already vanished into history, and now it's my turn*, Winslow thought as he stepped over a thick tangle of vines that snaked their way across the footpath.

It was at that moment that Winslow felt a stinging prick on the left side of his neck. Not a minor irritation, but a sharp, drop-everything-what-the-heck-is-that kind of sting. He couldn't stand it anymore and screamed out while simultaneously swatting his neck with his left hand, producing a sharp slap that rang out in the still, damp air. Sal whirled around and eyed him carefully.

"What is it?"

"I don't know, something stung me." Soon the porters and Sal were gathered around him, asking him to move his hand away so they could get a look. Sal dug out a first aid kit while two of the porters whispered to one another while gawking at Winslow's injured neck.

"Is it bad?" he asked them in Portuguese.

"They're saying spider," Sal said, tone sullied.

"What kind of spider?" Winslow asked. "Is it poisonous?"

An awkward silence permeated the team.

"I said, *is it poisonous*!" Winslow said, louder now.

"No," Sal said at length.

"It hurts like a mother!"

No one said anything, and the porters all still stared at...not Winslow's neck, but Winslow himself.

"Well, is there anything I should do for this, or what?" Winslow asked, looking at Sal and his thus far unopened first aid kit.

Sal appeared to startle out of some thought, for he suddenly shook his head and looked down toward his kit, hands moving to open it. "Of course, I'll get some bite salve on that right away. We'll disinfect it first..."

Sal pulled out a moist towelette of disinfectant and applied it to Winslow's bite, which was a small red puncture wound about one millimeter in diameter, but sunken fairly deep and very pronounced and red. Then he delved back into his kit and came back with a couple of extra-strength Tylenol, which he handed to Winslow along with a flask of unknown liquid.

"Take two of these."

Winslow started to open his mouth to question how it would help, when he reminded himself that he was not at the doctor's office at home, this was the Amazon rainforest, and he would have to deal with what was on hand. He popped both of the pills into his mouth at the same time and then chugged the flask without asking what it was until he swallowed the pills. He finished by taking an extra swig of the liquor--he was pretty sure it was rum now--before handing it back to Sal.

"Feel better already," he said, dusting himself off. "Why were they acting like it was such a big deal?" Winslow glanced at the porters, who still talked amongst themselves in hushed tones while occasionally casting nervous, darting glances at Winslow.

Sal eyed Winslow but said nothing.

"Out with it, Sal, seriously, what gives?"

Sal let out a long sigh and straightened as he turned to face Winslow. "The spider that bit you is a rare one." He held out a hand to stave off the obvious question. "No, it's not poisonous., But it's rare enough to even see one, let alone get bitten by one, that they consider it an omen of sorts."

"I suppose not a good one."

Sal slowly shook his head.

Winslow shrugged. "Whatever, as long as it's not poisonous and I'm not allergic."

Sal nodded. "Let me get that bite ointment on there. That should pretty much do it." Sal then applied an insect bite cream and asked again how Winslow felt.

"Well the coffee was wearing off, and now I'm wide awake again, so I guess there's a silver lining."

Even one of the porters laughed at this, and soon the expedition was once again underway. They picked a course along the constrictive pathway, now little more than a game trail, the barest promise of a passage through the unending green cloak. Winslow trooped along behind Sal, surprised that his own spirits were as high as they were given the painful bite or sting or whatever it was, but he wasn't complaining. This was the jungle and shit happened. He'd signed up for it, and in a no-backup-plan kind of way, at that, and so he would have to find a way to cope with it, even have a little fun if at all possible.

After a while, Winslow zoned out into a kind of semi-functional trance, automatically scanning for obstacles and potential dangers with his eyes while putting one foot in front of the other and swiping errant vines away from his face. As the team progressed, the lead porters had to use their machetes more and more often. The jungle became thicker the more they penetrated.

They broke for lunch next to a mini-waterfall, a small creek that dropped perhaps ten feet into a larger, slower-moving river below. The porters remarked that the going was good so far, and that if it continued, they would easily make Dead Horse Camp by end of tomorrow. What went unspoken was that there was of course no guarantee of that. This was the Amazon, and the only constant was change. Sal and Winslow dined with the porters as one large group, sitting cross-legged on the ground, then lounging for a bit once the meal was done to rest up for Round 2 of the day's trek.

Winslow thought about calling Steve early, but then decided against it. They had a working communications protocol, so he might as well keep it going. If it ain't broke, don't fix it, right? He opted instead to lay on his back and stare up at the dark green underside of the canopy while listening to the porters' small talk in Portuguese. Sal also lay on the ground but sharpened his machete while doing so. One of the porters whistled and Winslow looked to see him pointing up into a nearby tall tree. A three-toed sloth bear-hugged its trunk about thirty feet up. One of the porters mimicked a bow and arrow, aiming at the beast, but no one made any move to hunt. Although sloth meat was edible, they had enough provisions to reach Dead Horse, and that was the focus for the moment.

Before long they were back on the trail, parting the sea of green in search of the lost city while Winslow thought about the new directions uncovered in Manuscript 512.

CHAPTER FIFTEEN

Rio de Jainero Suburb

Steve Hoch grinned like a Cheshire Cat as he pulled the manuscript from his machine. The document itself was now even more ruined overall due to his chemical ministrations, and yet the next couple of previously unreadable damaged sections were now just about legible. One more pass and they should be readable! He made a computer instruction to dial down the amount of chemicals used so that he wouldn't overdo it. He wouldn't want to have to explain to Dr. Winslow—not to mention the *policia*-that he had screwed up and destroyed the document entirely.

But for now, all was good. He held up the historical document while Santos and Ruiz walked over for a closer look. Again, Santos leaned in very close to eyeball the results of the lab work while his associate maintained some distance, as though Hoch were a dangerous animal that couldn't be trusted. After all, he was only useful to them so far as he could lead them to Winslow; if it became clear he couldn't do that, he would then be facing jail time and therefore may become desperate and be inclined to run for it or even worse, fight back.

"It is almost, but not quite, readable," Santos noted. Hoch nodded.

"One more pass. Fire up some coffee, guys, I'm going back in." No sooner had he completed the sentence than his cell-phone warbled on the lab bench a couple of feet away.

Hoch moved to it and eyed the caller ID, then snatched it up. "It's Winslow," he said to the cops, who motioned for him to answer it. Steve snatched up the phone, mentally telling himself, *act normal,* before answering the call.

"We made camp. I'm exhausted, but it looks like we could make it to our destination by end of day tomorrow, next day latest. How goes it on your end?"

"Sounds good. I've made more progress on two more sections, but neither are readable yet. I've just put them back into the machine for a second pass, which ought to make them legible. So I'd say on tomorrow's call, I'll have—"

"Do you think you'll have those results before sunup tomorrow?" At this, both *policía* also eyed Hoch expectantly. He nodded before speaking.

"Yeah, probably."

"Okay, go ahead and email images like you did before, as soon as it's done, that way I can look at them and be thinking about what it means while I'm trekking all day tomorrow."

Hoch looked to the cops, who both nodded their approval. Then he said into the phone, "You got it, boss. Then we'll talk end of day like usual, right?"

"Yes. I'll let you get back to work. Time to eat and go to bed, here. Good luck."

They ended the call and Steve set the phone down. Santos nodded to the manuscript on the table. "Complete the second pass on this section, then do as you said and send Dr. Winslow the images."

"You got it." Steve once again buried himself in his work under the watchful eye of the *policía*.

#

Dawn next morning, Matto Grosso

Winslow was not quite as quick to awaken as the previous day, but he was still up at the same time as Sal, which he took as a good sign. *You can get through this*, he told himself as a mantra for the coming day. *Stick to the plan.* They made coffee amidst the chatter of birds in the pre-dawn stillness while the porters cooked a pot of rice and gathered leaves to make a herbal tea.

Winslow was halfway through his first cup, chatting with Sal about what the route for the day would be like (more of the same from yesterday was the consensus), when he remembered that he was supposed to check his sat-phone for messages from Steve. *The next part of the document!* He got up from the cook fire and retrieved his sat-phone from his tent. The blinking LED told him he had messages awaiting, and sure enough, there were three images from Steve. One again showed the entire document so that he could see what he was looking at and the extent of overall damage the process was causing, while the other two were closeups of the newly revealed sections.

Dr. Winslow opened the first of these, aptly named Section 2, which came after the first section Steve had elucidated. He smiled to himself as he stood in his tent reading the words. He nodded to himself and then opened Section 3, which was also perfectly legible, though shorter in length than the first two sections. He would have a lot to think about today, that was for sure.

He quickly broke down his tent and readied his pack before trotting over to Sal, who was dousing the cookfire, a hissing tower of steam cascading up into the canopy. Apparently, Sal could read the excitement in Winslow's eyes, because he asked him, "How's the document processing going?"

Winslow nodded along with a big grin. "It's working. I've got some directions that are still incomplete, but by the time we make Dead Horse, we should be able to do better than wander blindly."

"I'll drink to that!" Sal hoisted his metal coffee mug and clinked it into Winslow's, spilling a little on the ground where it immediately attracted a small colony of ants. "Let's saddle up. Dead Horse here we come. If we're lucky, we can sleep tonight in Fawcett's old camp."

They broke down their campsite and, a half-hour later, were pushing out onto the faintest of game trails. Winslow had blisters now, a particularly pesky one on the side of his right foot, even using moleskin, but he did his best to block out the discomfort. He would try to dress it up tonight in camp, with the shadow of Fawcett standing over him.

The porters up front had to use the machetes a lot to clear foliage off the path, and the going was slow. The insects were so numerous they darkened the air with their droning swarms, and Winslow wondered if the DEET spray he used actually attracted the creatures. But it was the spiders that caught their attention.

Strange, hairy arachnids with bodies the size of tennis balls and pencil-thick legs, like tarantulas but the hair was greener, allowing them to blend in with their surroundings. They dropped from the trees onto the hats of the expeditioners, and soon quiet curses in multiple languages became the norm as they were swiped off heads and bodies and trampled underfoot.

Winslow, having had enough of spiders, was particularly disturbed and asked the group to move faster to get away from them. He asked Sal if they were poisonous, but no one knew, and no one seemed that interested. The spiders were simply another mystery in a jungle full of mysteries. They did pick up the pace some, though, and the spiders became less numerous over the next couple of hours, but never disappeared completely.

Winslow stared out into the rainforest away from the path, wondering what secrets it concealed. It seemed amazing to him that anyone could find anything in such a vast place, but here he was, not only giving it his best shot, but having his life, or at least his freedom, depend on his best shot. He brushed another spider off his shoulder and tried to keep his mind off the negatives by focusing on the directions that came from the new manuscript sections.

They were not quite as clear as he had hoped, but there were more sections yet to be uncovered. He was pretty sure that so far, they indicated that Z lay to the northeast from Dead Horse, a different direction from what Fawcett was rumored to go in. But Fawcett was known for deception.

"*Problema!*" His thoughts were interrupted by the Portuguese word spoken by one of the porters ahead. He soon caught up with Sal and the porters, who were gathered around a huge tree fall—actually, several trees which had fallen together and now blocked their tiny path.

"Got to be six, seven trees," Sal said. "Makes me wonder if someone deliberately knocked them over to block the path."

"Who would do that?" Winslow asked.

One of the porters answered. "It's a warning." His explanation was that simple.

"From who?" Winslow asked.

"From the universe."

"The universe? So you're saying these trees fell naturally?"

"Yes. A warning."

Sal intervened by jumping part way up onto one of the trees and then stepping down again. "This isn't passable. We're going to have to cut our way through around the outside until we can get back on the path again."

The porters didn't look too enthusiastic about it, but they went to work all the same, swinging their long blades into the still living foliage on the left side of the treefall.

"Glad they're not giving up," Winslow said in a low voice to Sal.

"They won't give up before Dead Horse. But this definitely won't make them want to go beyond Dead Horse, either. The closer we get, the more spooked they become." Sal eyed Winslow and saw the worry lines on his face. "You're going to have to come to grips with the fact that it's just you and I after Dead Horse. They won't go past it, I'm telling you."

A chorus of shouts came back from some ways into the bush, where the machete progress had been interrupted by something. Sal waved an arm at Winslow and trotted off toward the commotion. When they got there, three of the porters were coming the way they had come. They stopped when they got to Sal and he held a hand up, asking them what was wrong. After a minute of rapid-fire Portuguese, Sal turned to Winslow and said, "Human skeletons, two of them, I think."

Winslow stared blank into the woods. "Recent. Or…?"

"I'll take a look." Sal moved ahead into the thick foliage, Winslow taking slow and tentative steps behind him, noting the grim faces on the porters as he went around them. Sal was out of sight all of ten seconds before turning back around, shaking his head as he walked up to Winslow. "Christ, you can still see some of the clothing. These remains are not that old. Clothing doesn't last long out here." He waved an arm at the jungle that now thoroughly enveloped their team.

Winslow swatted away a horsefly the size of a strawberry. "Do we need to report the bodies?"

Sal stared at him like he was crazy. He took a step closer to him and lowered his voice. "Only if you want to wait around for authorities to get here, then derail our expedition by filing out reports back in Rio. There's no one we can help by reporting it, and I would think you, of all people, would want legal intervention the least of all."

"Absolutely agree," Winslow said. "Glad we're both on the same page."

Sal held his gaze for a moment later before nodding and turning to one of the porters. They huddled in conference for a moment, pointing first this way, and then that, before coming to an agreement. Two of the porters started hacking a new trail into the jungle.

Sal turned to Winslow. "We'll be heading this way."

Winslow nodded while adjusting his pack. When he looked up again, Sal and the porters had already moved into the bush, hacking furiously with their long blades. He took a deep breath and followed, cringing at the idea of the dead bodies so near to him. Another bad omen, he thought. *Weird spiders, now dead bodies…what's next?* As he pushed his way through the plant life, he almost longed to be a professor again, when teaching classes was more important than research, when he was happy to simply have a job and not be so competitive. Because look where that had got him. But those days were long gone now and there was nothing he could do about it, so he picked his way through the Amazon after Sal and the porters, wishing for Dead Horse Camp.

#

Later that day

After the first hour they found their way back onto the game trail further into the jungle, and that allowed them to travel a bit faster. To Winslow it felt as though they trekked into a never-ending tunnel of greenery, but eventually, almost as if through a fog, he heard Sal's voice: "We're here."

The sun was beginning to set as they walked into Dead Horse Camp. There was nothing special to mark the place; in fact, if it weren't for the GPS coordinates, they'd have no way to know for sure they were even here. But both the porters, Sal and Winslow's own GPS all said that they were at Percy Fawcett's infamous camp, the place where he'd shot his horse nearly a century ago.

The team dropped their packs and sat down on the ground, even the porters too exhausted to begin making camp right away. "Hard to believe, isn't it?" Sal said, looking over at Winslow.

"That we made it?"

"No, that this jungle is pretty much exactly the way Fawcett saw it. This part of the Matto Grosso," he emphasized, waving an arm at their leafy surroundings, "is still unchanged by development. It's all but inaccessible, as you've seen." He grinned at the lounging Winslow, who nodded in response.

"Hopefully what Fawcett was looking for is unchanged as well."

"If it was ever there, you mean." Sal chuckled at his own words.

Dr. Winslow glared at him, then tried unsuccessfully to shift the glare into a mysterious smile. "It's there, Sal. It's there."

Sal shrugged it off. "Let's set up camp, then. Tomorrow we set out into the great unknown."

CHAPTER SIXTEEN

Rio de Jainero Suburb

Steve Hoch smiled as he peered through the stereoscope at Manuscript 512. The work was running smoothly now. And whoever that explorer guy was who wrote this thing, Steve thought with a smile, he sure was a crafty son of a gun. He had to know that putting ink to paper with regards to X-marks-the-spot treasure directions was a bad idea, yet at the same time necessary to pass the information on. The same conundrum faced by pirates and treasure hunters throughout the centuries. And yet the author of 512 had found a way to not only encode the information, but to make it look as though the encoded sections were due to accidental critter damage. *Genius*.

For as Hoch continued to work, it became clear that there was no way that worms had randomly destroyed specific parts of the document corresponding to keywords that, when taken as a whole, gave a different set of directions to none other than the Lost City of Z. No possible way. He should have had them destroy other parts of the document as well, Hoch thought. That would make it harder to decode the hidden meaning, though.

He carefully eased the document from the lab machine and took a look, aware he was under the watchful eyes of the two *policía*. They reminded him it was almost time for his call to Winslow in the field. Hoch nodded. This latest round wasn't completely uncovered enough to be read, but there was one new set that was already done.

But as he progressed on the work, as he neared its inevitable completion, he began to contemplate his own fate with increasing distress. The three parties involved—himself, Winslow, and the *policía*, had very different stakes indeed. Winslow, of course, wanted the lost city for himself, both financially and academically. He saw it as a way to restore his former glory, this time with a lot more money. The *policía* sought to bring those responsible for the library theft to justice—and that meant both Winslow and himself. And Steve himself? He sought simply to make a buck, without even having to get his hands dirty by entering the jungle.

So who was the real fall guy, here? If Winslow managed to disappear into the jungle and never come back, who would take the blame? At this point, Steve would. Hoch was under no illusions about that. And the *polícia's* promise of leniency in return for the extensive cooperation he was giving them? Well, that could evaporate into thin air, couldn't it? What could he do about it if they decided to renege on their promise? They weren't judges, after all, they were only cops. They would say and do what they had to in order to cover their own asses. Not to mention that he was a foreigner here, in a country where he knew next to nothing about due process and legal procedures.

He wasn't sure if it was the cheap Brazilian energy drinks they'd begun feeding him so that he could stay up and work more hours, but he began to feel edgy and paranoid, like he had to do something drastic if he was to make it out of this situation with his freedom intact. Not to mention his life. What was to stop these cops, once he finished decoding the manuscript, from simply offing him? Taking him out of the equation altogether. Because there was something else at play here, wasn't there? They were very interested in Winslow's precise location and movements, as well as future movements dictated by what the manuscript revealed, but as he started to open his mind and think more outside the box, to think bigger, more strategically, something darker occurred to him.

What if these cops were after the Lost City of Z treasure *for themselves?* A police salary didn't go all that far in the States, and he couldn't imagine that Brazil was very different. They probably have a lower base pay but treat the bribes they receive like tips, Hoch thought. Still…finding a lost horde of precious metals would certainly be alluring to them, there was no doubt about that.

"Senor Hoch, are you okay?" The sentence broke him from his thoughts and came to him as if in a dream.

"Yes, fine, thanks."

"Would you like another energy drink? We need you to be at your best for this work. It is very important for all concerned."

"Sure."

Santos nodded to Ruiz, who fetched a tall, slim multicolored can from a cooler of ice and tossed it to Hoch, who made a show of cracking it open and pouring some down his throat. Santos, meanwhile, made a production of checking his watch.

"It is time to make the daily call to Dr. Winslow."

Hoch nodded and glanced at his sat-phone while guzzling the beverage. "Yeah, we've got new material for him." He picked up the phone and dialed Winslow's sat-phone.

#

Dead Horse Camp

The sounds of snoring permeated the campsite. Even the two porters who were still awake reclined in restful poses. No one had even bothered to pitch a tent, all of them were so exhausted. When the sat-phone on Dr. Winslow's person began chiming, no one noticed except for the single porter who was still awake, and he did nothing about it. The expedition had made Dead Horse on schedule, but it had taken a physical toll on all of them. In order to be up early tomorrow, they would need more sleep than usual.

Ten minutes or so passed and then the sat-phone sounded again. Winslow rolled over on his bedroll, hiding his ears from the intrusive noise. He dreamt of lost treasure, endless freedom and great power, oblivious to his ringing phone, or to the ring of spiders that crawled around the perimeter of the camp like programmed automatons.

#

Rio de Jainero Suburb

"He's not answering." Steve Hoch held the sat-phone out so that Santos and his associate could hear the unanswered rings.

"Try again?" Santos's partner suggested.

Santos shook his head. "This was the second try ten minutes apart. Something is wrong." He stared at Steve as he said it.

Hoch held up his hands in a gesture of helplessness. "Maybe they're still on the trail?"

Santos glanced at his watch. "It's dark out. No one, not even the tribal people, distance trek at night."

"Then maybe they ran into some trouble. I have no way to know." Steve locked eyes with the cop. "I could send him the latest images of my results."

"No. We want to give him every reason to want to be in contact. If he hasn't received them from you, it is certain that he will want to be in contact."

Steve threw his hands up. "Then I suppose I should get back to work on the manuscript?"

Santos made brief eye contact with Ruiz before responding. "Yes, do that. Make sure your phone is on and receiving calls, in case he calls you. If not, you will try him again at dawn, when they should be breaking camp."

Hoch nodded. "They were close to Dead Horse." Hoch was jittery now, starting to have strange thoughts. *Maybe I should head out to Dead Horse on my own and see if I can find the city myself. Hook up with Winslow out there.* He knew deep down that it was a notion that was beyond ridiculous. He wouldn't know where to begin to get all the way out there. Besides, he mused, he needed to complete the lab work to know where to find the city of Z.

"I suggest you get started on the lab work, Mr. Hoch." Santos held out a hand toward the machine Steve had been working with, as if inviting him to a grand party.

Hoch felt something different well up inside him, an undercurrent of resistance, that he was reaching his limit of being pushed around. But he controlled it by sipping more energy drink, and without letting on the can was now empty, he set it quietly on the lab bench. Then he took his place back at the bench and carefully re-inserted Manuscript 512 into his machine.

CHAPTER SEVENTEEN

Dead Horse Camp

Darkness still gripped the camp when Dr. Winslow awoke from his slumber. He felt padding beneath him but was staring at the canopy leaves above, so he was not in his tent…And then the grueling trek of the previous day came rushing back to him, the arduous trek to…Dead Horse Camp! They were here, at the starting point of the real search for the Lost City of Z! Funny, he thought, he had always imagined the night in Dead Horse would be a celebration of sorts, of knowing they'd reached the kick-off point and were about to embark into the unknown. But the reality was much different; they were so tired they'd passed out without so much as making a cook fire.

What's this? He felt something long and heavy and *moving* on him and sat up in time to see a fat snake slither off his legs and into a pile of leaves on the forest floor. Winslow let out a shout of surprise, but it wasn't sustained enough to wake any of the others. He felt his pockets for the mini-flashlight he kept there and checked himself for puncture wounds, but apparently the snake did not bite him. The spider bite was enough, he did not need any more animal wounds.

But what really got him up wasn't the snake, but the realization that he missed the sat-phone call from Steve Hoch. The new data! Hurriedly, he found the phone and lit the thing up, hoping to see the New Message icon when it booted, but to no avail. He was hoping maybe Hoch had emailed him the new data, but maybe he didn't have any new readable sections yet. Definitely time for a chat, though. The results thus far were promising, but he needed to know what the rest of the damaged sections said. Checking his watch, he saw that it was 4:59am. Time to call Steve. He dialed and expected to wait a few rings, but the call was answered after the first. Winslow recognized Hoch's voice.

"Hey, I tried calling last night, everything okay on your end?"

"Yeah, we made camp late after a hell of a hike. We all passed out as soon as we got here. But we did it. Starting today, we're in prime hunting grounds. How are things going with you?"

"I have a new set of images to send, and you know what that means."

"You decoded another section?"

"Two more."

"Outstanding. Great work! What are we about, halfway through the document now?"

"Almost, yea. I should have a new one later tonight. Did the ones I sent so far mean anything to you?"

A pause while Winslow considered the ramifications of the question. It was best to say as little as possible about operation specifics over the phone, any kind of phone. "By themselves, they're inconclusive. All I can do so far is speculate on a direction until more text comes in, but I think what I have so far combined with my guide's knowledge of the area will give us enough to go on for the first day. After that, *amigo*, I'm counting on you."

"Okay, well that makes sense. Like I said, I should have—"

Winslow didn't listen to the rest of what his technician said, because in the background he heard someone cough. It couldn't have been Hoch himself, because the cough came over a perfectly formed word. *So then who was it?* He couldn't hear a television or radio in the background. Winslow decided to brush it off. He was barely awake. He needed to get ready for today's exploring, and he needed to let Hoch get back to work so that he would have the best possible chance at locating Z.

"Okay, Steve, listen—I should get going and you should get back to it, okay? Send me the images first and keep up the good work."

"Will do." With that, the call ended, and Winslow was once again left alone with the sounds of the forest. He looked around the legendary Dead Horse camp, trying but failing to see what was so wild and deadly about the general area, compared to the rest of the Amazon, that was. Until his phone beeped with Steve's incoming image set. He snatched up the device and downloaded the files.

He was still studying them, putting them into context with what had come before them as well as the original main part of the document, when Sal rose from his position on the ground beneath a sprawling fern. He ambled over to Winslow, still yawning. "Christ, what a way to spend our last civilized night."

"I didn't realize we were still in civilization." Winslow looked around at the dense, seemingly impenetrable jungle that now surrounded them on all sides.

"By comparison. So here's the game plan: we'll have a last team breakfast together before the porters head back. Then you and I will set out on foot." Sal paused to glance at Winslow's sat-phone. "Have you got new information specific enough to base our search with or should we just head northeast?" That direction would take them into the heart of the largely unexplored Matto Grosso territory. Before Winslow could answer, it started to rain, a thick, drenching downpour that made a racket as it pounded against the tree canopy over their heads. A distant crack of thunder was heard, and then the porters began to stir. Dawn was officially at hand in Dead Horse Camp.

As Sal had said, they made a large production of the morning meal with a big cook fire and lots of food, coffee and tea. They ate well beneath a tarp tied overhead between four trees, and during the meal Winslow kept nudging Sal to ask the porters to continue on with them until he finally relented. He asked the lead porter, who shook his head quickly and firmly before pointing in the direction from which they had arrived. The other three porters all nodded.

"Offer them more money," Winslow urged Sal. He wanted as much support as possible going into the unknown. He would still do it without the porters, but he was firm on doing everything he possibly could before ruling out something that could help their expedition.

Sal relayed this offer in Portuguese to the lead porter, who at first appeared surprised, then a little angry, and then stone-faced as he once again shook his head firmly. Sal shrugged while facing Winslow.

"Sorry old chap, it's just you and me. You still up for it?"

"Of course." Winslow sounded offended.

"All right, then drop it, okay? It's a done deal. The four of them will be leaving us with what supplies we can carry on our own before heading back to collect the Jeeps and take them back to Diamantino."

"Let's go over the gear one more time," Winslow said after clearing his large plate. "Besides the basics, we'll need some climbing gear—ropes, carabiners. We have that?"

Sal waved an arm for Winslow to follow. "Our friends have already laid everything out nice and neat for us to choose from. Whatever we don't take, they'll take back with them." He pointed to an array of climbing gear laid out on the ground. "I'll take these ropes and 'biners here, how about you take those?"

"Fair enough." The two explorers began divvying up different types of equipment in similar fashion, knowing that to carry too much was to slow their pace through the jungle, limiting the amount of territory they would cover. Carry too little, on the other hand, and they would be ill-equipped in the face of some disaster. They came to a duffel bag with some vinyl material inside of it.

"What's this?" Winslow asked.

"Ah, this is our boat, should we choose to take it. It's a two-person inflatable raft with a pump. Pretty-heavy-duty but still lightweight. You never know when we might want—or need—to float down river or cross a pond. But it does add bulk and weight. It's an option, that's all."

"I like the option."

"Do you like it enough to carry it, is the question." Sal grinned.

"I think so."

"Done." Sal nodded to one of the porters and dragged the raft bag to the pile of gear they'd be keeping with them. "Let's move on. Now first aid is not something we can afford to skimp on." Winslow agreed, and Sal continued. "In addition to what we've already been carrying on our persons, I suggest we take on additional snake bite kits each, as well as insect sting ointments, more bug spray, more Quick Clots, more general first aid supplies including splints, ice-packs and wraps."

"Sounds good." Winslow's voice sounded far away, like he was somewhere else in his mind, which he was, thinking about the Lost City of Z. Would he find it after going through all of this trouble? And was the law still actively searching for him in Brazil or would they assume he left the country by now?

"Stay with me, Dr. Winslow. Over here we have small stuff, but very useful. Extra hammocks, batteries, walkie-talkies, flashlights, water filters, and a multi-tool. There's also another Personal Locator Beacon, which I suppose you don't want, although I have one on me, as a backup to our satellite phones."

Winslow shot an uncomfortable glance at the PLB. "I don't have room for that."

Sal moved on to the rest of the gear, and by the time daylight filtered down to them through the trees, they had decided on their final equipment list.

"Time to pack this stuff up now," Sal said, dragging his frame backpack over to the mound of gear. The porters gathered around them, offering help moving things around, waiting for them to finish packing so that they knew for sure they could leave. It took some doing, but an hour later, Sal and Winslow had carefully organized and packed their gear into their two backpacks. Satisfied they weren't forgetting anything, they said their goodbyes to the porters, who then blessed the two explorers before retreating back into the Matto Grosso the way they had come.

Sal and Winslow were alone in Dead Horse Camp.

CHAPTER EIGHTEEN

Dead Horse Camp

Winslow walked slowly around the camp, peering into thick brambles of foliage here and there, until Sal asked him what he was doing.

"Checking to see if I can find the bones from Fawcett's horse," he said with a smile.

Sal gave a bellyaching laugh. "Bah! I doubt even bones last a hundred years in the Amazon! It's time we go over our game plan, Hunter. Now, we know Fawcett publicly announced he was going one direction, but in actuality took his expedition—only one person larger than our current configuration, I might add—in another direction."

At this, Winslow walked back toward Sal and the center of camp where their packed gear lay waiting on the ground. "Right, Fawcett said he was going northwest, but really went northeast. And what new info I have so far from my lab tech and Manuscript 512, which Fawcett obviously did not have access to, seems to corroborate the northeast direction. So we should probably start out that way."

"Figures," Sal said with a heavy sigh. "That's the most difficult direction to go in from here."

"What's so difficult about it compared to what we've been doing?"

"Don't get me wrong—the easiest way to go from this point is back the way we came. So there is no easy way. But if I had to pick one way that really sucks, it'd be to the northeast. I've been maybe five miles in that direction, max, one time. And I've heard stories. It's super-dense forest, very primeval, unbroken by any development other than some of the most savage tribes, one or two of them reputed to have no contact with civilization."

Winslow remained positive. "Well, that does sound like a good place for a lost city, doesn't it?"

Sal tipped his head. "You got me there. Not that you couldn't hide or bury a city in pretty much any part of the Matto Grosso. But if you're telling me that's the best place to start, then okay."

"I think it's the way to go."

"Let's head out then. Say goodbye to Dead Horse Camp."

Winslow waved a hand at the site while picking up his pack and slipping into the straps. He cinched his pack's cummerbund tight and bounced up and down in place to test it out, wincing a bit with the heaviness of it. They were carrying about twenty-five percent more weight than they had been up to this point, when they had the porters. But it was doable, Winslow decided.

"Remember, our pace can slow down now, since we're not trying to reach a specific place, but to look for something. So just relax and take it easy, we don't have to go fast, we just have to go."

Winslow nodded in agreement while Sal shouldered his own pack. Then the two explorers, machetes in hand, walked out of Dead Horse to the northeast.

#

A mile or so out of Dead Horse, Winslow's neck started to throb. At first, he passed it off as strain from all the gear lifting to leave camp, but then he remembered the spider bite. The afflicted area throbbed in time with his pulse, not hugely, but enough to be noticeable where before it was not. He continued walking with one hand on his neck, a few steps behind Sal, who still hacked here and there with his machete. They were not even on so much as a game trail but trekking through the open spaces between canopy tree trunks.

Lianas and hanging vines of all sorts connected the tree trunks like a massive botanical spider web, and they had to constantly duck and weave to make progress in any single direction. Both of them used an old-fashioned compass to follow a specific heading. They saved the GPS unit batteries for when they really needed them. The forest floor had a thick layer of leaf litter here, as though it had been undisturbed for a long time.

Never in his life had Dr. Winslow been in such a forbidding and remote location, and it dawned on him now as his neck throbbed, that he could easily die out here. It wouldn't take much. Help was too far out of reach; there was nowhere to land a helicopter here. When they came to a shallow ravine where the forest floor dipped before rising back to level again, Winslow caught up with Sal at the bottom of the depression.

"Neck bothering you?" Sal indicated Winslow's hand on his spider wound. Winslow took his hand away and showed Sal the injury. The rainforest guide's brows furrowed in concentration and he sucked in his breath.

"How's it look?" Winslow asked. "It's pulsating."

94

"Looks weird. Kind of a greenish color. Not real good, mate, I'm afraid. You don't want gangrene on your neck. Rot your brain right out of your skull, I tell—"

"All right! What can I do about it is all I need to hear, thank you very much!"

Sal took off his pack and broke out the first aid kit again. "Let me try applying some different stuff. And here, take one of these—antibiotics." He handed Winslow a white pill, which he downed along with some water from his canteen. Then he squeezed some white cream out of a tube and smeared it on Winslow's neck.

"Stings," the historian commented.

"That means it's working. All right let's see what that does." He packed away his first aid kit and looked around the forest before powering up his GPS for a position check. "We're actually making fairly decent progress," he said after the device booted up and acquired satellites. "Better than I thought. You up to keep going or want to take an early lunch break?"

It was mid-morning. Winslow said he wanted to keep going, so Sal took a heading with his GPS, powered it off again and the pair of explorers set off once more into the deepest jungle.

The dim light beneath the canopy made it feel like evening as they picked their way through the tapestry of greenery. Animal life was plentiful here—sloths, a tapir, even a jaguar was sighted while moving deeper into the Matto Grosso. After a while the forest opened up enough to allow them to walk side by side, both men slashing occasionally with their machetes, but able to walk normally for long stretches at a time.

"See, you'd never know it was like this in here if you didn't hack your way in like we did," Sal commented.

"Right, it's a regular walk in the park in here." Winslow rolled his eyes as he grabbed hold of a hanging vine and swung Tarzan-style across a soft, muddy spot in the forest floor, landing on semi-solid ground on the other side, splashing mud up the side of his pants.

"Well, I don't see that lost city yet, so it can't be all that easy."

"We'll find it. I know we will. I just hope no one's found it before us." Winslow rubbed at his neck.

"Slim chance of that, my friend, unless maybe they're dead..." They walked on for some time with that kind of banter, attempting to take their minds off the daunting task ahead, finding Z.

CHAPTER NINETEEN

Rio de Jainero Suburb

The work became a kind of productive blur where Steve Hoch lost all track of time, losing himself in the details of what had to come next, nothing less and nothing more. The cops would bring him energy drinks, snacks and coffee at regular intervals, and he would keep feeding the manuscript into the machine and adjusting its parameters to cleanse the damaged sections to the point they were readable. Winslow was in the prime area now, and so he really had to step on it to get it done.

When he took the document out to examine the results of his latest round of treatment, he saw that he was about half way through the manuscript. And the latest round had been successful with no refinements required—he had uncovered the text behind the damaged section with a single pass. He took notes on what exactly he had done to be able to repeat that process going forward; it would significantly reduce the time it took to complete the manuscript.

Santos came over for a look at the work. He took a photograph of the completed sections of document, then urged Hoch to keep working. "Power through it. The quicker it is solved, the quicker this will all be over."

Steve glanced at the time on the screen of a laptop that was running one of the lab machines. "A few more hours until I call Dr. Winslow."

"How much more do you think you can realistically have ready by then?"

Steve eyed the manuscript. "Maybe three-quarters."

"Excellent. Do not go past that point without telling me, however."

Hoch locked eyes with the cop. *He doesn't want me to give Winslow all of the information. Does he plan to send a team in to the location?* He didn't know, but with Ruiz eyeing him with one hand on his gun, he knew he didn't have much alternative but to get back to work. Regardless, one thing was certain: his work on the manuscript was almost done. He was now confident the process would reveal 512's full content.

The question was, what then?

#

Matto Grosso

The forest was thick again. Any forward progress came by forcing their way through intertwined vines and thick ground cover. Winslow's neck still throbbed despite the medications.

"Next suitable location for camp, and I say we call it a day," Sal said, hacking a clump of plant shoots out of his way.

"No arguments here," Winslow agreed. "I want to hear from Steve, anyway. We don't need to head an inch in the wrong direction out here, I can see that now."

Sal belly-laughed from a few yards ahead. "Yeah, starting to see that about this place, eh? If there is a lost city here, I can see why it got lost, and stayed that way."

Not long after this conversation, a stream bubbled out of the ground and ran ahead of them into the thick trees. They followed it, the understory so thick that at times they had to stoop to be able to walk beneath it. For a hard mile they scrabbled through the underbrush, stamping out strange insects, spiders and other segmented creatures as they went. The forest was literally crawling with strange critters that seemed to feed off of the stream.

But when they came to a mound of rock and elevated ground where the stream disappeared into, they faced a choice: get wet or turn back. Sal took off his pack.

"Tell me we're not going to camp here?" Winslow asked, looking around at the trees threatening to consume them, to simply integrate them into themselves and make them a part of the forest forever.

"Give me some credit. I've got an idea that could save us a lot of time. I didn't lug this thing out here for nothing." Sal tossed the rubber inflatable raft onto the ground. Winslow eyed it with consternation before watching the stream disappear into the rock mound.

"You think we can float through it?"

"Sure, why not? I can see daylight on the other side from here, so I know it goes all the way through. Still, have a flashlight handy, because you never know."

They inflated the raft, which was all of eight feet long and four wide. It barely fit the two men and their gear, but it did fit. Sal launched the raft into the stream, making sure to hold it by the single rope attached to a grab line. They tossed their packs inside first, then waded out into the stream until they could flop into their rubber craft without fear of pressing it into the bottom and causing a tear.

They had one collapsible paddle between them and Sal used it as a pole to push them off the bottom out into deeper, faster flowing water, where they began to drift downstream toward the opening in the rocky mound. Both explorers had to duck as they passed beneath the stony lip and into the watery tunnel. Winslow clicked on a headlamp in order to have light in the tunnel but keep his hands free, while giving Sal enough light to steer the craft with the paddle. Only the occasional dip into the water of the blade as a rudder was needed, as the current moved the light raft along at a decent clip.

Hanging mosses brushed against them as they floated through the passage, a narrow oval of light visible some ways ahead. Winslow peered into the dark waters, catching silvery reflections from his light off of moving things, mystery creatures. He shuddered at the thought of what they might be and made it a point to keep his gaze fixed ahead at where they were going rather than into the water.

"Something tells me Percy Fawcett didn't go this way!" Sal joked from the back of the raft where he held the paddle.

"Unless maybe he built a raft out of tree branches."

Their voices echoed in the aqua-tunnel as they drifted through the passage toward the light. As they neared the opening, Sal let out a groan.

"What is it?" Winslow asked.

"I thought something didn't look right about the light." He pointed at the entrance, which had a semi-opaque look about it. Sal took a closer look as they flowed toward it. He was surprised to see a massive spiderweb covering the entrance. Comprised of thick, rope-like strands, it was not the kind of web that could be simply swatted away. They couldn't maneuver around it, either, since it was positioned over the entire entrance. And there was nowhere to go but through it if they wanted out of the tunnel. Even if they opted to paddle all the way back the way they came, the current was too strong to go against for any length of time.

Sal's voice rang out in the darkness. "Here, take this to fend it off." He handed Winslow the paddle. He smashed the blade of it into the spider web, but it bounced right off and he almost lost it overboard. He tried again, this time swiping the edge of the blade sideways through the web as he was about to pass through it. This action tore through the silky trap creating an opening to pass through, but it also rained a multitude of trapped insects down into the boat, where they scurried out of sight into the various vinyl folds.

Sal got down low to avoid the web and then cursed as the small army of bugs sought shelter beneath his body. He tossed some of them overboard, winged bugs, smaller spiders, centipedes and strange critters he had no idea about. He knew only that there was a good chance at least one of them was poisonous and could sting or bite him with nasty results, so he tossed them out or crushed a virtual avalanche of bugs.

Through it all the little raft kept floating downstream in the dark tunnel, the stream becoming wider and more powerful as it neared the end. Up front, Winslow checked to make sure they were not approaching a waterfall, but although the slope of the stream increased, it remained mostly   level.

"Into the light!" Sal yelled in mock triumph as they passed outside of the tunnel into the jungle once again. The canopy was still very thick here, and although compared to the tunnel it was light, for mid-day it wasn't that bright.

Winslow looked around, noting that either bank was shallow enough to easily get out on. "How long should we ride the river?"

"As long as it's going our direction anyway, we might as well take the ride, right?" Sal brought out his compass and took a heading. "We're still on track, but it looks like we veer west up ahead."

The small river did shift course, but before long it meandered back onto their desired heading, so they stayed with it in the raft. For another hour or so they drifted through a seemingly endless forest, until the stream jogged west and stayed that way.

Sal steered the boat to the right-hand bank and steadied it there while Winslow tossed out their gear before jumping out himself onto dry land. Then Sal exited, and they pulled out the raft. "Amazing this thing's still intact," he said, letting the air out of it and rolling it up until it fit back into its carry bag.

After a brief break to drink water, during which Sal noticed Winslow's neck seemed to be getting greener in color, they set out on foot again through the understory. Sal mentioned the possibility that if they couldn't find a suitable ground site to camp at, they would have to sling hammocks from the trees and sleep suspended in the canopy.

"I have a feeling that before long, I won't care where we camp as long as I can get some rest," Winslow panted, stepping over an exposed clump of tree roots.

"I'm beat myself, not going to lie." Sal hacked his way farther away from the stream. Then he paused and looked around. "I've got an idea."

"Uh-oh."

"Don't worry, sometimes they work. How about this: I think we can clear a large enough space up ahead there, where it opens up a little, by cutting down a few of those smaller trees. Sound good?"

Without even answering, Winslow moved ahead to the area Sal pointed out. Sal joined him and the two of them cut down small trees and shrubs until they had cleared an area that was barely large enough to set up a camp within.

"It's a good site because we're close to a water source, the stream, and it's on our projected course. Speaking of which," he said, glancing at Winslow.

"Right, hopefully my lab guy has some more clues for me."

CHAPTER TWENTY

Rio de Jainero Suburb

Steve Hoch couldn't help but let out a whooping holler as the machine he monitored completed its pass on clearing up another damaged section of Manuscript 512. He reflected to himself how the damage must have been intentionally inflicted, whether by worms or otherwise, to precisely cover certain keywords in this way. He carefully removed the document from the machine and inspected it with a magnifier.

Not only had he completed most of the entire document now, but what had been revealed, even to his and the *policía's* limited knowledge of ancient Portuguese, appeared to contain very specific positional information regarding the lost city. He couldn't wait to phone Dr. Winslow with the news.

#

Matto Grosso

The camp had a claustrophobic air as darkness settled in for the night. The ring of trees and foliage surrounding their camp was so tight that outside their little cleared circle, the light of the cook fire was not enough to see by. In order to relieve themselves even a small distance from camp, they had to bring a flashlight. Winslow returned from just such a sojourn, the smells of their modest dinner tantalizing his taste buds, when his satellite phone screen lit up a split second before he heard the ringtone. He picked it up, nearly salivating over the prospect of any more specific info from Steve. Sure, they'd had some rough guidance up to this point, but actually being out here in the wilderness like this…it was sobering.

"You hear me?" came Hoch's voice.

"Loud and mostly clear, old chap. We are camped for the night in some very dense, hard to-penetrate-jungle. I hope you have something for us, I really do."

"It just so happens you're in luck!" Hoch's voice was unmistakably enthusiastic, Winslow noted. "I had a bit of a breakthrough with figuring out how to do less passes—and—"

"Just give me the gist of it, please."

"Right. So there are only two more damaged sections remaining."

"Only two? That's great!"

"That's right, I'll be sending over the image sets right after this call."

"Excellent work!"

"I'll get back to it. Good luck, buddy, and be safe out there!"

They clicked off the call and Winslow and Sal stared at one another for a moment before Winslow set the phone down.

"Chow's on," Sal said. "Hopefully by the time we're done eating you'll have those new images."

#

As they finished eating by the fire, a sizable cat, by the sound of it, growled somewhere nearby. Sal stood and walked to the perimeter of the camp, drew his machete and shouted into the dark. Winslow took the opportunity to check his sat-phone for the new material from Steve. Sure enough, he had new files waiting. He opened the images and lay back in a hammock to think while he examined them. He brought up the earlier images so that he would be taking these in context and used a notepad and pencil to take notes. Sal came over after scaring off the feline and asked how it was going. Winslow told him he needed a few minutes to decipher what he was looking at.

But it was all starting to make sense wasn't it? What had before seemed too general now became crystal clear. Landmarks were given in general terms in terms of rivers, and days' travel by land or river. Winslow figured those travel times hadn't changed much in this part of the forest, if at all. He called Sal back over and reviewed what the new text meant.

"Is there a confluence of four rivers that you know about, within about two days from here over land?"

Sal thought about it for a moment before saying, "I think there might be three rivers that come together, northeast of here, in our continued direction. Let me check a map..." He visited his pack and returned a couple of minutes later with a well-worn paper map. He opened it up and smoothed it out on the ground.

"Here's our current position, here." He drew an X with a pencil on the map. Winslow nodded as he looked on while Sal continued, tracing an imaginary route with the eraser end of the pencil. "Now, here's where I would call the outer limit of two days' travel through the jungle, and you can see...." He brought the pencil point down on a spot on the map where three blue lines intersected. "...the confluence of not four, but three rivers, here. But there aren't four anywhere else, as you can see, for hundreds of miles around. Unless they are very small streams, not big enough to put on a map. Or maybe there used to be four a couple centuries ago, but one dried up. It's possible," Sal finished, thinking aloud.

"Or," Winslow said, leaning over the map now, "what if one of them is underground, like the one we rafted down?"

Sal's eyes widened as he considered this during a beat of silence, except for the din of insects. "I say, that would be possible. You mean if the fourth river is passing beneath the point where the other three meet, but underground?"

"Yes. And there's something else you couldn't know unless you read the new text from Manuscript 512." Sal made eye contact with Winslow while waiting for him to continue.

"It refers to something underground. The wording isn't specific enough for me to get any more than that out of it. There is still a small amount of the document left to uncover."

Sal thought about this for a moment. "I think it's safe to say it's worth heading to the confluence of the three rivers. Once there, we can see what it looks like, check for an underground river. Two hundred-plus years...things could have changed."

"How difficult will it be to get from here to there?" Winslow asked, staring down at the map while the cat began to growl again somewhere in the forest. Sal glared in that direction before answering.

"We can get there end of day tomorrow if we're lucky."

CHAPTER TWENTY-ONE

Matto Grosso

"At this rate we're not going to get there today." Winslow's voice was as shaky as the wet terrain on which they trudged: moist, spongy earth made even less stable by the heavy downpour that fell since before sunrise. All around them the unchanging tapestry of tree trunks and green leaves closed them in, making it feel like nothing existed or ever existed outside of this natural but deadly realm. Machete blades were kept in near constant motion to make any progress, but slash and walk they did, through the rain that dripped from the trees like water from a house gutter, concentrated into small streams in certain areas, near dry in others where the roof of leaves was too dense for water to trickle through.

"We'll get there. Just keep moving." Sal was resolute, and he practiced what he preached, steadfastly moving through the forest, slowly but without many pauses, forcing Winslow to keep up. His neck throbbed even worse, and from the way Sal gawked at it now and then, he knew it must be severely discolored as well. Adding to the creepy factor, he seemed to be followed by a trail of small spiders now. He couldn't recall them not being here since they set out from Dead Horse. They followed him like he was the pied piper or something, circling around him when he stopped but not climbing onto his body. Sal said it was normal, but something in his voice told Winslow he wasn't being totally earnest in that assessment.

Winslow focused on the bright spots—he was homing in on the lost city at last, and he was far from the long arm of the law. He didn't see how anyone could get to him here, but at the same time he knew he couldn't last here indefinitely, either.

They broke for lunch in a random spot between a cluster of trees that offered barely enough space to sit down. As they finished their meal, they heard a rustling in the trees and Winslow looked up to see a medium-sized monkey drop to the ground in front of them. He tossed it part of a plantain and the primate snatched it up, sniffed it and ate it. Then the two explorers checked their position via GPS and then set a course to follow toward the confluence of the three streams.

They set off again, with the monkey following them in the trees above. Before long Winslow realized there were two of the primates, one on either side of them. He wondered if they had ever even seen a human before. They worked their way through the oppressive forest, and after a couple more hours they had a procession of spiders and monkeys trailing after them. Winslow's muscles were sore, his neck throbbed, sweat poured from everywhere, bug bites covered his body, blisters stung his feet, and yet he managed a smile as he thought about how every step took him closer to Z.

The day wore on and they navigated through the rainforest, the going slow and tortuous, yet steady. Winslow was about to suggest a break when Sal held up a finger and stopped walking. "Shh, hear that?"

Winslow craned his neck and held his breath. He was about to say he couldn't hear anything when the sound of faint rushing water reached his ears. "Stream!"

"Sounds like it's that way." Sal pointed off to their left, and they made a course correction with the aid of a compass and moved out. The monkey jumped ahead of them from limb to limb, as if it knew where they were going. The stream grew louder until they could see it; not a large waterway, but deep and fast-flowing.

"I only see one stream, though," Winslow said.

Sal pointed downstream. "Yeah, I think we go this way for a while to get to where it crosses with the others."

"You think? I'd hate to have to come back up the other way if you're wrong."

"Yeah, me too, so let's just hope I'm right." Sal paused to check his GPS and cross-referenced it with the map. "As best I can figure it, that's how it is, so let's move out."

They trekked downstream, the monkeys ahead of them in the trees, the spiders trailing them on the ground. The terrain gradually descended as they followed the stream. After a while Sal set up the raft and said that since they weren't coming across the other streams yet, it would be faster to float downstream, so they set it up and launched into the river. Winslow was glad for the opportunity to sit back and relax while making their way through the jungle by water, leaving both the spiders and the monkeys behind.

Both of them studied the map and the GPS while they rode the river, with Sal becoming more convinced that they were in fact heading in the right direction. The forest grew even thicker around them as they drifted along the stream, until a loud bubbling, over and above the stream they rode, came to the fore of the auditory landscape.

"Another stream joining this one up ahead," Sal announced. Both men knelt in the raft to give them as high a vantage point as possible.

"We need four streams joining, though," Winslow said.

Sal said nothing for a minute while they floated closer to the new waterway. The two streams joined into what could be called a single small river, wider and flowing faster. The two of them gripped the safety line on the perimeter of the raft as they bounced and jostled their way into the single large river. The bottom was shallower here, making it more turbulent, as well as occasional boulders that cropped up as obstacles they had to steer around to avoid puncturing their fragile craft. They had just become comfortable with the new waterway when a furry form dropped into their boat from a tree branch above.

"Monkey on board!" Sal shouted. He made a move toward the animal, but it deftly scurried along the outside of the tube to the middle of the raft where it perched while making clucking noises. When Sal and Winslow closed in on it from either end, it jumped across the middle of the boat and landed on the opposite tube, where it assumed the same position.

"Just let it ride with us," Winslow said. "It's not hurting anything."

"Maybe it smells our food," Sal suggested.

"Maybe, but it's not trying to get at anything, so just let it be for now."

They drifted with the monkey down the river until a group of downed trees that had fallen across the river blocked the way, making the river impassable for the boat. Sal steered the raft to the edge while Winslow kept an eye on the monkey, and they clambered out onto land. They considered putting the raft back in on the other side of the blockage but saw that there were other downed trees after this one, that had toppled when the banks became unstable due to heavy rains. They hiked instead, and Winslow was quick to complain about the exertion level after sitting in the raft.

The monkey stayed with them, too, though keeping its distance now up in the lower tree branches. The spiders were back, too, a living stream of them, small arachnids that flowed along the ground like a living conveyor belt. Sal checked their position again via GPS and told Winslow they were heading in the right direction. The forest was slightly easier to walk through here, though the machetes still lashed out frequently. Darkness was beginning to fall on the forest floor when Sal let out a shout and called back to Winslow.

"I see it! Three streams converging."

"We need four converging."

"I know, Hunter, but maybe one's underground, remember? Or maybe two hundred years ago there was a fourth. All I'm saying is, this is the place I thought of when you read me that description. Do you want to check it out or should we go some other way now that we're all the way here?"

Winslow stopped walking. It was the first sign of irritation he'd seen from Sal since they set out from the airport in Araçatuba. He would have to be careful, as he could not afford to alienate Sal. Without him he would be unable to continue out here.

"I'm not suggesting that, Sal. You're right, let's check it out."

He said nothing, and they cut their way through the brush toward the converging streams. When they got there, they stood on the lip of a natural bowl, at the top of which the river they had been riding tumbled off in a short waterfall into a churning bowl where two streams emptied into. From there, a single river washed straight out into the rainforest and continued its downward journey toward the distant Atlantic coast.

"So we've definitely got three rivers converging here," Sal stated, staring down into the stormy bowl. "What do you say we drop our stuff here and have a little look around to see if we can find a fourth?"

Winslow was more than happy to ditch his heavy pack for the chance to walk around unencumbered. He and Sal split up on either side of the washbowl, with Winslow taking the right side down and Sal the left. Winslow stood on the bank of the circular confluence, picturing the uncovered words of Manuscript 512 while staring into the turbulent water. He started to walk along the bank, poking his head into an outcropping of rock here, and peering down into the water there, looking for signs that a fourth waterway joined the others.

But it was Sal who found something first. "Over here!" Winslow looked downstream and spotted the jungle guide at one end of a very large toppled tree. The trunk seemed to still be rooted into the ground about a hundred feet from the river itself, with the other end of the trunk hanging over the river some distance from the churning washbowl.

Winslow ran back up to where their packs were and back down around the other side to where Sal stood by the tree. He didn't see what was so special about a downed tree, but he wasn't finding anything, so he was eager to check it out and at least hear Sal's thoughts. He wasn't expecting what he found when he got to the tree that stuck out over the river.

"Check it out." Sal pointed authoritatively at the end of the tree, which was only a few inches above the water level. "See those ripples?"

Staring intently at the spot on the already moving water, Winslow could barely make out the spreading of wavelets from a central point. "Water's pouring out of that tree?"

"It would seem so! Let's check out the other end of it." Sal and Winslow jogged away from the river to the root end of the tree while the monkey chattered unseen in branches over their heads. Winslow stamped out multiple spiders on the way to the other end of the tree, but they got there without too much trouble.

And it was worth the trek.

"Well, lookey there!" Sal exclaimed.

"I'll be damned," the historian said under his breath.

The tree was completely dead, hollowed out, with only the outside of the trunk remaining intact. Into this hollow tube flowed a steady stream of water that emerged out of the ground, through the tree trunk and into the river.

"A fourth river joining the other three!" Sal said, voice heavy with import.

"I'd call it a stream, but okay, so we found it. But found what?" Winslow stood straight again and looked around, seeing only the river, the roiling cauldron where the first three rivers joined, the fallen tree stream emptying into the river, and the trees all around them...

And the spiders at their feet. A thick rope of them scurried along the ground past their boots, apparently not interested in them, but going somewhere. None of them carried prey items such as small insects; they simply transited along the ground. Winslow scanned ahead the line of them to see where they were going. They moved deeper into the forest, away from the river. Winslow began to slowly follow them, walking in their direction, a few feet away from them so as not to interfere with whatever it was they were doing.

He walked slowly for a minute or so until he could see that the procession of arachnids went to a cluster of intertwined trees that reached far up into the canopy.

"Where are you going?" Sal called from back at the stream tree.

"Looking at this grouping of trees over here. All the spiders are going to it." Sal had no reply to this, but Winslow could hear his boots crunching over the twigs and dried leaves on the forest floor as he walked in his direction.

"Look at them," Winslow said, stopping a few feet shy of the thick tree cluster, "they're all going up there."

"Okay, is there some reason that matters?"

"It's just weird. These spiders have been following us ever since Dead Horse, and now they're all marching up into this odd-looking tangle of trees. How many trees do you think there are there?"

Sal walked up to Winslow and craned his neck up to examine the botanical formation. "Probably nine or ten. It is unusual. I don't think I've seen that many stuck together like that before."

"Looks like we could practically make camp up there, there's so much space." Winslow moved over to the base of the tree, careful to avoid stepping on the spider. The trunk closest to him had thick roots spiraling up it, and he placed his right foot on one of them and started to climb.

"Whoa, cowboy, whatcha doing?" Sal sounded concerned.

"It's like a ladder. I'm going to check it out up here. Be right back."

Winslow ascended the root ladder, climbing about ten feet until the intersection of trunks themselves offered a convenient platform on which to rest. He eyeballed the path upward, noting that due to the spacing between trunks, he could easily keep climbing.

"Gonna go up a little higher," he called down to Sal, and then began to ascend toward the canopy. This part of the climb required a little more attention to detail, but he was able to do it and, in a few minutes, called down to Sal a good thirty feet from the ground, in a nest of sorts where the tree trunks intertwined.

"Thought maybe I'd get a decent view of our surroundings."

"See anything?" Sal responded, his tone giving away that he was unimpressed with the idea. In the tree, Winslow slowly turned 360 degrees before answering.

"Not really, I'm not high enough to see over the neighboring trees, so—" He cut himself off mid-sentence as he took in a curious sight. "Hold on, this is weird..." Winslow stared straight down into the space between the intertwined tree trunks. It looked like it went a long way down, but the dim light wasn't sufficient to penetrate far enough for him to see clearly.

"Hey Sal, do me a favor and toss me up a flashlight, will you?"

"A flash—what for?"

"Just do it, I'll explain when I get back down," Winslow shouted down from his perch in the trees. He heard Sal muttering something but saw him go back to his pack. In the meantime, Winslow observed the spiders walk up the tree in their thick line, on one of the opposite trunks from where he stood. The strange thing, Winslow thought, was that they kept coming up the tree, but none were going down.

Until he realized that they *were* coming down, but down the inside of the tree. He hadn't noticed that little tidbit before he requested the light. He was probably going through a fair amount of trouble just to illuminate a giant spider nest. But then Sal was running back with the flashlight in his hand, and tossing it up to Winslow, who missed it on the first toss and had to endure a round of cursing about how he lacked coordination. He caught it on the second try, clicked it on and then trained the beam down the space between the trees.

He had a hard time processing exactly what he was seeing. Yes, there were spiders crawling down the inside of the hollowed-out trees; yes, it extended down to the ground…but wait a minute, Winslow thought. It went farther than the ground, didn't it? It seemed to extend even below that.

"So what is it?" Sal asked from below.

"It's weird. It looks like it goes even deeper than the ground."

"Deeper than the ground?" Sal screwed up his features in disbelief, or like he might not have heard correctly.

"Yeah, like it goes underground. I think. But here's the really strange thing: I see something glittering down there."

"Glittering? Are you sure it's not just the reflection of your light off some water trapped at the bottom of the trunks?"

It was not a bad guess, Winslow knew. He took his time examining it again, angling the light in different ways, to be certain it wasn't that. "No, I don't think so, because the glittering things are all fixed in place. If it was water, they—"

"Okay, fine. Go down and have a look, then. I'll be taking a breather." Sal sat down on the ground, leaning against the trunk of another tree while staring up at Winslow.

In the intertwined trees, Winslow let the flashlight hang from its strap around his wrist while he climbed down into the hollow space between the trees. He was not within a single tree, but inside the gap left where all of the trees joined. He was able to use irregularities in the bark as hand and footholds in order to make his way down in a controlled fashion. At ground level, he began to see the glittery, sparkling things he noticed from above.

They were not water.

CHAPTER TWENTY-TWO

Matto Grosso

Winslow placed his feet on a solid surface and removed his hands from the tree trunks as he gaped in wonder. Jewels. Perhaps quartz, perhaps something more valuable, he wasn't a geologist, but they were large, the size of fists to soccer balls and completely lined the inside of the tube-shaped space from here down.

And looking down, he could see a most amazing space indeed.

Below the ground level, the trees opened up into what could be called a small chamber. Winslow climbed down into it, using the large crystals as hand and footholds until he stepped onto a smooth floor made of sanded stone. He could faintly hear Sal's voice from outside, asking if he was all right. He craned his neck upward and yelled that he was okay, needed a few minutes to look around. He doubted all of that would be audible, so he resumed his exploration before Sal grew too impatient.

He held his flashlight and aimed the beam around the chamber, which was small, with the open ceiling leading up into the tree grouping, and walls made of the same smooth stone as the floor, except they were also studded with the large crystals. He could see now that this was an antechamber of sorts, as it was featureless except for a corridor to his right that led to another space.

Winslow had to stoop to pass into the next area. It, too, was a smallish chamber studded with sizable crystals, though this one had a solid ceiling of smooth stone barely higher than Winslow's head. Overall, the room was only a little larger than the antechamber. He could no longer hear anything from outside now and knew he would need to hurry up and get back before Sal really became worried when he called for him and received no response.

But, oh lord, what is this?

Set into the floor of this room was a most peculiar contraption. Winslow knelt next to it in order to get a closer look and allow his adrenaline-fueled breathing to slow.

Three circular wheels of sorts set into the smooth stone floor, themselves also comprised of the same smooth stone, but with a hairline groove delineating the circular shapes. Each circular section had its perimeter lined with a complex set of interlocking crystals. Winslow looked around the room and saw no other openings or significant features of any kind, only an enclosed space housing these devices.

He grabbed one of the crystals on the wheel closest to him and pulled it. He drew in a breath as the wheel started to turn, producing clicking noises as the crystals from the adjacent wheels ground against each other. When he stopped pulling, the wheels ceased moving and they appeared as before.

His flashlight beam winked out for a second and he was plunged into complete darkness. He smacked it against a palm and it flickered back to life. Deciding he better get Sal down here to look at this right now, Winslow exited the mysterious chamber back into the antechamber, where a narrow cone of natural light made a circle on the floor. He climbed up the crystal rock ladder into the space between the tree trunks themselves, above ground, and then continued to climb the trunks until he was once again in open air, encircled by the tree trunks.

"Was starting to worry, Hunter, you find anything interesting in there?" Sal stood on the ground below, a sign that perhaps he was preparing to come after his expeditionary partner.

"You've got to see this, it's incredible! Grab a flashlight and come on up here."

Sal's expression darkened. "Are you kidding me? I'm taking a break, Hunter."

"Sal, relax, we'll make camp here for the night. You have got to see this right now."

"Fine, give me a few minutes to go bring my pack over here." With a sigh of exasperation, Sal pushed himself up from the ground and walked over to their packs by the confluence of rivers. He put his pack on and carried Winslow's in his hands back over to the crystal trees. Then he took a flashlight from his pack and began to climb the same way Winslow had.

"Coming up now, Hunter."

"Excellent! Watch out for the spiders!"

"I see them." The sheer number of parading arachnids was somewhat frightening, as they formed a heavy train nearly a foot wide and three inches high, but at the same time, their course was very well-defined and therefore easy to avoid. Sal easily ascended the tree to where Winslow waited at the entrance to the hollow gap. The historian reached out a hand and pulled his jungle guide up to the crux of intertwined branches. Then he pointed straight down into the space between the trunks where he had dropped down minutes earlier.

"It's down there. Good idea to bring the headlamp."

Sal adjusted the elastic band of the light he wore on his forehead and tapped the switch to turn it on. "Let's do it."

"I'm excited to look at this in more detail," Dr. Winslow explained as they descended slowly and precisely inside the trunks. "I barely had time to check it out and my light was giving out on me."

They made it down to the antechamber after Sal paused to examine the crystals lining the inside of the trees. His face took on a confused expression. "This is really strange. Very weird. This is obviously fashioned stone, sanded to a clean finish…" He trailed off with a tinge of wonder in his voice as he visually appraised the space. "Like some kind of new age tree house."

Winslow snorted. "Wait 'til you see the next room." He led him into the main chamber with the crystal wheels, where Sal stood there, mouth agape.

"I am flabbergasted," he said.

"Have you ever seen any kind of arrangement with these types of crystals in the Amazon before?"

"Hell no. Maybe in Sedona, Arizona…" He trailed off with a quiet laugh. Winslow pointed out the thin grooves surrounding each of the three wheels, finishing by saying, "You see how the crystals of each wheel interlock with those of the next?"

Sal nodded as he walked slowly around the three crystal wheels set into the floor. "What could their purpose be? Three smooth stone wheels with elaborate crystal structures, below ground inside of a bunch of trees?"

"We were led to this place, Sal, we didn't find it by accident."

Sal looked up from the crystals to meet Winslow's gaze. "You think these have to do with the lost city?"

Winslow shrugged. "If they don't, that would almost be even stranger at this point, wouldn't it?"

Sal nodded. "Stone wheels with interlocking crystals at the confluence of the four rivers. Let's suppose for a moment that they are part of Z. What is their function?"

Winslow paced the confines of the small chamber. He directed his gaze up, where the ceiling was featureless, smooth stone, to the walls of the same, then back to the floor. "Let's look at the crystals. How many on each wheel?"

Sal counted for a time and then said, "Sixteen on each."

"Okay. With the red ones being shorter but fatter, the white ones tall and skinny, and the pink ones in between."

"Right, they all interlock depending on how the wheels are positioned."

"Let's try turning it—I'll spin the wheels and you watch closely what the crystals are doing."

Sal stood close to the middle wheel, on the opposite side from Winslow.

"I feel like what's-her-name on Wheel of Fortune," Winslow said as he put a hand on one of the tall white crystals and began to spin the wheel. It moved slowly at first, with dull clicking sounds as the crystals from the opposing wheels knocked against each other. But then as the spin picked up momentum, they began to turn more smoothly and the clicking sounded like a smooth, continuous ratcheting as opposed to a clunky knocking. Winslow gave a final push with his arm and let go of the wheel, standing back to watch it spin. The other two wheels remained stationary while the middle one turned. The wheel gradually slowed, the individual clicking of the crystals coming into contact with one another becoming more distinguishable.

The wheel came to rest, and all was quiet. Sal looked around the enclosed space. "Walls don't seem about to come down or anything like that."

Winslow pointed to the crystals. "See how different crystals are now coming into contact with one another?"

Sal stared down at the middle wheel for a second. "Uh-huh."

"The more I think about it, the more it seems like these wheels and crystals here are a puzzle, a puzzle to be solved that will unlock something."

"Unlock what?" Sal appeared unimpressed, strange crystals or not.

"Something that leads us to Z. Take a look, here..." Winslow pointed to the middle wheel. "See how we have a pink crystal between two white ones on that wheel, and between a pink and a red one on the other wheel?"

"Yes."

"I think that means something. Like, if we spin the wheels until certain crystals are touching, that something will happen."

Sal shrugged. "Which crystals, and what will happen?"

"I don't know. But I'd like to find out, wouldn't you?"

#

They set up a simple camp including a small cook fire. Sal prepared a meal while Winslow set out a pair of walkie-talkies, two flashlights in

114

good working order, and his camera. He felt like that should prepare them sufficiently for their next trip into the crystal room. He sat on a log next to Sal by the fire and discussed the odd crystal wheels and what they might mean. He had barely finished eating when he heard his satellite phone ring over by his bag.

Steve! He had forgotten all about the lab work. A jolt of adrenaline shot through him. Were the strange crystal wheels hidden in the trees connected somehow to the Lost City of Z? They had, after all, followed the directions provided by the uncovered information in Manuscript 512. Eagerly, he snatched up the sat-phone and accepted the call.

"Good news, buddy," came Hoch's eager but strained voice. "I've done it! All sections have been revealed. I'll be emailing you the last image set after this call."

"What does the last section say? Can you give me the gist of it verbally?"

He heard Hoch take a deep breath before saying," Listen, you're going to think I'm smoking crack or something, okay? But I'm not."

"Just tell me what it says, and I'll be the judge of your character, all right?"

"The second to last damaged section was the most extensive one— the longest—in the entire document. It reads—are you ready?"

"Go ahead." Winslow turned away from the racket Sal was making as he sharpened his machete on a stone nearby.

"It reads, and I quote: 'The blood of the spider will reveal the final key'."

Winslow waited for more, or for some kind of explanation, but the line carried only silence, during which he shivered as he pictured the conga-line of spiders that had followed him—basically led him—up into the intertwined trees and then down to the room of the crystal wheels. And then there was the word, *key.* In the context of a puzzle...*could it be?* At length, he said, "That's it? You're positive you didn't leave that section incomplete, or that there are no more hidden sections of text anywhere in the document?"

Hoch snorted. "Yeah, I am. What do you think I've been doing here, playing with myself? I've been staring at this thing and working with it damn near 24/7 for days."

"Okay, relax, I'm only trying to be thorough. You've done an outstanding job and I won't forget that."

A pregnant pause occupied the line. "I appreciate that. So getting back to the manuscript, that's it for that second-to-last section, yes. However, there is one final unreadable section, but it's a lot shorter than that one. But get this: I already ran it through the same process as all the others, and it didn't work."

"Not at all?"

"No, not at all, as in—it had no effect on the document, or the text that it may or may not hide."

"Does that part of the document seem different—does it look or feel different than the other damaged parts?"

"No, it doesn't. It's indistinguishable from the other damaged sections. Maybe I can run some more tests while you keep moving. How are things on your end, by the way?"

Winslow clutched the handset tighter as he spoke, again picturing the spiders. "Listen, this is very important, and it's going to sound weird as hell. But I assure you I'm of sound mind. I can have Sal verify if you like."

He heard a laugh emanate from the other end of the line. "Well, he's never been of sound mind himself, so I'm not sure I'd put much faith in that."

"Okay, listen: we're in camp now, next to a most interesting feature that the new information you've been sending appears to have led us right to."

"That's great! So—"

"There's something here. Something not natural. We'll be checking it out in more detail first thing tomorrow, but it's manmade, and underground."

He heard a gasp emanate from the phone. "You mean like an old settlement or something—old camp buildings?"

"No. Much different than that. And there are spiders here. Lots of them."

"Spiders? Did they bite you, are you okay?"

"I'm okay." Winslow felt his neck throb. "But a huge line of spiders followed us into the tree and down underground where I found this…this construction…I think it's a puzzle." And then the implication hit him so hard he had to sit down before his legs gave out from under him.

"You still there?" Hoch's voice inquired.

"Yeah. Listen, this is going to sound weird, but I know what has to happen."

"What?"

"I need you to bring the document here, to me, so that we can put the spider blood on that last section. It holds the key, that's what it says, right?"

A beat passed while a stunned Steve Hoch processed what he was hearing. "You want me to take the manuscript to you? How would I even get there? Why don't you bring some of the spiders back to the lab here?"

"Because then we've to get all the way back out here again, and we're already here." He looked over to see Sal nodding vigorously in agreement with him. "If you bring me the manuscript, we treat it with the spider blood, and it should reveal the key to this physical puzzle we found."

"That sounds pretty iffy. What if we put the spider blood on it and nothing happens?"

"Everything else revealed in the manuscript turned out to be accurate so far, right? It led us here."

A pause, and then, "Where is *here*? What exactly have you found?"

Winslow couldn't exactly blame the man for wanting to hear the reasoning that was about to send him into one of the most unbroken and inhospitable jungles on the planet for days, so he recapped the discovery of the converging rivers and then the crystal wheels underground beneath the trees.

#

Rio de Jainero Suburb

Steve looked over at Santos and Ruiz while Winslow described the crystal wheels. Santos scrambled for a piece of paper and motioned to his associate for a pen. He scribbled his note fast, to get it done before Winslow stopped talking and Hoch would have to reply. Santos dropped his pen and handed Hoch the paper with his message. Hoch read it while Winslow was describing how the crystals on the wheels interlocked:

Tell him OK, you will meet him at his location (get GPS) in a couple of days. Say you know a local guide who can make the arrangements to get you there. Ask him if it is in the budget for helicopter travel, or else it will take much longer.

Hoch read the note and looked up in alarm at Santos. He didn't know any guides, but he figured they did and they wanted him to go. Santos gave him a slow nod, meaning *yes, that's what I want you to say.* On the other end of the line, Winslow wrapped up his strange yet compelling description of what they had found.

Hoch made eye contact with Santos while responding to Winslow, trying to muster up the appropriate level of enthusiasm. "That's amazing! We have to see what it does. All right, tell you what: since I've had no luck here in the lab with the last key section, I'll do as you suggest and bring the manuscript to your location with the spiders."

"Perfect! Let me know if you have any trouble with the guide, because I can have Sal hook you up with someone he knows."

Santos cast Hoch a warning glance. Hoch said into the phone, "If I can arrange helicopter travel, can I be reimbursed? That'd make it a lot faster since we know exactly where we're going at this point."

"Good idea. Sal and I will be sitting around on our asses until you get here with that code, so do whatever you have to do to get here as fast as possible. You know I'm good for it."

Santos smiled at Steve before he replied. "Perfect. I'll call you tomorrow when I'm underway." He made eye contact with Santos to make sure the promise of communication didn't somehow go against his plans, but he gave no indication that it did.

"Sounds good. So, I will need the GPS coordinates of your current campsite to give to the guide."

At this came a hesitation. Then, "I will send them to you. But listen, make sure you guard those coordinates. Don't give them out unless you're sure the guide can take you to this general region, first. Like I said, Sal knows people—"

"I understand, don't worry. The info will be guarded."

Steve told Winslow he would be in touch when he was underway and ended the call. He looked to Santos and Ruiz. "Looks like we're going to the jungle."

CHAPTER TWENTY-THREE

Matto Grosso

Two days later

Steve Hoch tensed in the back seat of the modified Robinson R44 Raven II helicopter as it hovered over the verdant canopy, its rotor wash buffeting the tops of the trees. He saw the pilot look over to Santos, in the co-pilot's seat, and then Ruiz in the back seat with Steve and the load of expeditionary gear and supplies.

"We're about five miles from your coordinates. I'd like to get you a little closer but I'm having range anxiety." He tapped his fuel gauge.

"We can hike in," Santos stated. The helo pilot turned to look at him. "You're going to have to. Probably take a full day," he said, gazing down at the impenetrable layer of green below, before looking back to his fuel gauge and adding, "Let's drop the gear."

In the back, Santos's associate opened the cargo door, and they were immediately blasted with rotor wash. He and Sal shoved the gear, which had been bundled with a helo drop in mind, each crate covered in layers of tarps to cushion the blow when it crashed through the trees and landed on the ground. The pilot held the chopper's position while they dropped all the gear crates. Steve could not hear them crashing through the trees above the sound of the chopper's engine.

"Now it's your turn," the pilot shouted, turning around, a big grin on his face. "I recommend you use the basket instead of going out like the gear, but it's up to you. I've done my job either way."

Hoch and Ruiz pushed a small basket, large enough to carry one man at a time, out the open door. The pilot flipped a switch for the winch and tested it, briefly lowering down, then back up again. "It works. It won't get through the trees though, so, like we went over in the briefing, you're going to need your climbing gear on and then get out of the basket onto the top of the canopy to climb down from there. Be careful. Who's first? Be quick about it." He tapped his fuel gauge again.

Ruiz raised a hand. "I'm next to the door already, so I'll go first." The *policia* deftly climbed into the basket and gripped the sides with both hands a second before the pilot flipped the switch, and it began to descend toward the canopy.

Steve watched the process carefully, knowing that he was up next, like it or not. He couldn't believe he was being forced to do this, that his only alternative, would he not agree to this expedition, was to rot in a Brazilian jail until matters were resolved by the courts, and then possibly facing more jail or even prison time. What a mess he had gotten himself into. But this was the way out of it for him, it had to be. He looked out over the canopy, knowing that Dr. Winslow was down there somewhere, and that he was about to come face to face with him. He wasn't looking forward to that. He certainly didn't want to confront him after he was arrested for the theft, knowing that his employee had been responsible for leading the *policía* straight to him.

"Let's go, Mr. Hoch!" Santos yelled from the front seat, where he was positioned to move to the back as soon as Steve left the chopper.

Steve gripped the metal bar of the basket and climbed into it, watching the carpet of tree canopy through the mesh wire of the basket, the thunderous roar of the helo's engine blocking out all other sounds. He felt a jolt and then he was dropping toward the jungle. He looked up and saw Santos's head sticking out of the 'copter door, the sun glinting off his mirrored glasses. Below, he watched as Ruiz slipped deeper into the trees, pulling his red climbing rope down after him until no trace of him was visible.

The basket moved fast enough that he had no time to ruminate on everything that could go wrong; he had to make sure his climbing harness, the use of which he'd been hastily instructed on only hours earlier, was rigged properly and ready to go. By the time he did that, there were leaves poking up through the bottom of the basket. It was time to jump into the jungle.

The lab technician saw that the basket wasn't moving any lower, so he did as instructed and clipped a line off onto the bottom of the basket and fast-roped down through the soft leaves. Once he was beneath the canopy, he continued descending until he found a branch sturdy enough to support his weight. He stood on that, got his footing and handholds, and then tied himself a safety line to the branch he was on. That done, he unclipped the rope from the basket and tossed it high enough to show that he'd disconnected. The basket was retrieved for its last round trip, to bring Santos.

Hoch made the mistake of looking down when he heard Ruiz call up to him. The *policía* was trying to do him a favor by pointing out a favorable route down, but oh, how far down there was to go. They had to be over a hundred feet above the ground! Steve didn't have a fear of heights, but not many people were used to being so high above the ground in a tree, and he found the experience unnerving. Still, he told himself, it beat jail time, and so he concentrated on what he had to do in order to get to the ground safely. He cautiously put one foot down, then the other, followed by one hand and then the other.

By the time Santos's feet poked through the canopy, Steve was already a good twenty-five feet lower. He shouted up to him, to give him an idea of where to go, then resumed his path downward. Once he slipped on a branch and fell but grabbed it before he fell off. His safety rope would have stopped him, but it would have meant a long fall during which he could hit branches.

He heard Ruiz yell up that he was on the ground, although he couldn't see him through the leaves. He spotted a small monkey below him at one point, but the primate skittered off when Steve made eye contact with it. After a lot of careful placing of his hands and feet, Steve finally dropped down to the ground by hanging from a branch by his hands and letting go.

He flexed his knees and went into a roll, landing in a heap on the ground, but an intact heap with no serious injuries. He was irked to see Santos drop onto the ground not long after he regained his own feet, but he took pride in the fact that he had done it at all, and that he had at least made it to the ground before Santos.

The three of them looked at one another in the dim light of the jungle floor. They had made it.

"Let's set up the gear." Santos pointed to one of the bundled crates lying on the ground nearby. A couple of them had lodged in the crooks of tree branches and had to be retrieved by climbing. When they had gathered them all on the ground at their drop site, they opened them and distributed the loads in the three backpacks that were included in the crates.

Santos activated his GPS unit, which had been pre-programmed with Winslow's coordinates. He pointed into the dense jungle. "It's that way."

Hoch gave his machete a couple of test swings, and the three of them set out.

CHAPTER TWENTY-FOUR

Matto Grosso

Winslow glanced at his watch. "They should be here soon."

Over by the cook fire, Sal checked on a pot of rice. "I hope they brought some extra food."

"I just hope they brought the damn manuscript, because we're not getting anywhere without it, that's for sure."

The extra days of waiting for Steve to get here had given the two of them plenty of time to further investigate the crystal wheels, and indeed, the entire surrounding area. But the upshot of it was that they were no closer to understanding the puzzle than before. The only thing left to try was the suggestion of the manuscript. The spiders continued to patrol the area, a long line of them flowing up and into the tree, then out again and to the confluence of rivers where they disappeared into a hole in the ground, only to return along the ground on the opposite side of the tree.

They heard voices before they saw the men. Sal hushed Winslow, who was about to call out to them. "Let's make sure they're not tribal first." But they were able to pick out Portuguese words, and so Sal relaxed as the voices drew near along with the hacking of machetes felling plant life in the arriving party's way.

Winslow cupped his hands to his mouth and shouted in the direction from which the newcomers moved. "Steve, is that you?"

"Yes!" The reply was immediate.

"Over here! You found us!"

Some more hacking and then three men appeared in the clearing of the small camp. "A minor miracle, that," Steve said. Winslow was taken aback by his lab tech's physical appearance. He was used to seeing him in a starched white lab coat, with protective eyewear on, pens in his pocket, pressed slacks and loafers. Even in Brazil, he wore linen resort-wear and maintained a clean-shaven look. But the same person was now a bedraggled, dirty creature with an overgrown beard, dark circles under his eyes, small cuts and scrapes over much of his visible skin. But he had decoded the manuscript and had brought it to him all this way.

"Looking good, Steve! Glad to see you made it in one piece. Who are your friends, here?"

Sal also appeared eager for the answer to that question. A long-time jungle guide services provider in the Amazon, he did not recognize either of the two men who had brought Winslow's lab tech into such a remote corner of the Matto Grosso on such short notice.

"These are my faithful guides, Gabriel and Filipe." The two *policia*, Santos and Ruiz, respectively, extended hands and shook Winslow's and Sal's in turn. "A pleasure to meet you, Dr. Winslow," Santos said, when it was his turn to shake his hand. "I have heard marvelous things about your work."

Winslow thanked him, and it was Sal's turn to greet him. "I'm impressed at how quickly you were able to get here, even with a chopper. I could never convince a pilot to come anywhere near this far out into the bush," Sal said, obviously seeking an explanation.

Santos, now going by the name of Gabriel, smiled amiably. "A little trade secret of ours. I confess I do not usually have to resort to such extreme measures, but our client—your associate, here—assured us that the situation was urgent, and that he was willing to pay in order to have an appropriate response time."

"And we appreciate that," Winslow said, not wanting Sal to put the guides off by attempting to ply them for trade secrets. "Planes, trains, or automobiles, I'm just glad you got here as quick as you did. Welcome to our humble camp!"

Steve and the two *policia* looked around at the partially cleared patch of jungle and the lowly cook fire with its meager implements. Winslow could sense they weren't impressed and decided to get right down to business. "Look, there's something I need to get out in the open before we begin," he said, eyeing the two undercover *policia*. "What we've found here is of a sensitive nature—"

"Steve told us as much," Santos said, nodding. "I can assure you that our guide services are one hundred percent confidential."

"We are no strangers to taking people into the jungle who wish their motives to remain private," Ruiz, now going by the name Filipe, said.

Winslow nodded. "Excellent, then it sounds like we understand each other. With that said, since we have limited supplies out here, let us get right down to work, shall we? I think the first step should be to give you a tour of what we've discovered. I've laid out some basic gear over here that we might need down in the rooms we found." He showed them the flashlights, walkie-talkies, and climbing gear he had laid out earlier, and then the *policia* and Steve produced their own equivalent gear from their packs. That done, Sal and Winslow led the entire party to the intertwined trees and explained the layout of the space inside and the underground chambers. Sal and Winslow climbed first, to demonstrate, and then the others followed, with Steve going after Santos but before Ruiz.

They descended into the space between the tree trunks in that order, one at a time. Winslow explained that the first room was an antechamber with nothing of importance that he could discern other than as an architectural passage to the main chamber that housed the crystal wheels. The five of them passed through the antechamber and crowded together into the crystal room, where Sal and Winslow proceeded to demonstrate how the wheels spun while the crystals interlocked.

"I've had a good deal of time to think about this mechanism while waiting for you to get here," Winslow said, adopting his old professorial tone, "and I think the different crystals—there are three types according to size and color—operate as a sort of combination lock."

He paused to let this sink in, and at length, Steve broke the silence. "So you think the last unreadable section of Manuscript 512 holds the combination—to this?" All of them eyeballed the wheels doubtfully. It suddenly seemed like an awful lot hinged on this strange contraption. But Winslow was resolute.

"I do, yes. And unless anyone has further questions, I think we should break for lunch and then proceed to the next phase of our operation—making that last fudged section of the manuscript, which you just referred to, readable."

"And that phase will involve the spiders?" Santos asked, pointing to a thick rope of arachnids tumbling over one another as they moved into the chamber on one wall, then up to the ceiling and back out again, like a living conveyor belt.

"Precisely," Winslow said. He removed a plastic Tupperware-style container from his pack. "I will collect some of the arachnids in this, and then, in camp, extract their blood. Then we can apply it to the document and see what happens."

Again, this seemed not to inspire the utmost of confidence in anyone, but at the same time, no one had any better ideas, and they had all come a very long way to be here. They agreed, and Winslow handed the container to Sal. "You're taller, would you do the honor of collecting the specimens?" Sal shot him a withering stare but took the plasticware and moved to the nearest wall where the procession of spiders moved along it up high by the ceiling. He tentatively placed the container near the moving stream, but the spiders deftly moved away from it as a single unit, as if someone had waved a rope.

He tried again, more decisively this time, and a good number of the spiders fell into the container before they began to fall out of it while the rest of them moved around it. "That'll do, that's good!" Winslow exclaimed, backing away even farther from the falling spiders while clutching his neck.

Sal slammed the lid onto the container, crushing a few spiders in the process, sending streams of viscous green fluid sluicing down the sides of the plastic. "That's the stuff, there," he said, backing away from the wall with the sample container.

"Let's get outside," Santos said, and no one had any arguments. They filed out the way they had come in, climbing up out of the antechamber, noting that the spiders had reassumed their normal marching formation. Sal placed the sample container in the small pack he wore, and the party exited the hidden tree lair without incident. Back on the ground at the camp, Sal wiped the outside of the container down with a towel and handed it off to Winslow.

"Here you go. I hope it works." He leveled a stare at the historian, who nodded and turned to Steve.

"I'll need your help preparing the, ah…the elucidation solution."

Steve stole a quick glance over to Santos, who remained poker-faced, before replying, "That's what I'm here for. I brought some implements to help with that. Let's get our field lab set up over there." He pointed to a small cleared area in a corner of camp, away from the cook fire but still within sight. He and Winslow retreated to that area, where they set up a basic four person camping tent to serve as a lab, while the others set up the regular campsite for the night. "This will shield us from rain and wind, and help to avoid contamination problems," Winslow said as they snapped the tent poles into place. Then they brought the spider container, the manuscript and Steve's field lab supplies into the lab tent.

Inside the tent, Steve opened a plastic Pelican box and took from it a glassware version of a mortar and pestle—basically a bowl and a grinding utensil, but clean with no imperfections and not used for any other purpose but lab work. He set up a folding footstool and placed the spider container on the top step, and the glass mortar bowl on the bottom step. He explained how the procedure would work to Dr. Winslow.

"I'll grind up the specimens—some will run out and escape during that process, but that's okay, and we can always get more if we need to…" He nodded out the tent door toward the intertwined trees. "Then we should have a bunch of that greenish blood substance in the container, which I'll transfer to the bowl below. At that point, I'll stir it up, purify it as best I can by removing any foreign particles I can see, and then we should have a 'spider blood' solution that can be applied to 512 by using a brush."

"All right. I'll get the tent flap." Winslow closed up the tent while Steve moved to the sample container.

"Actually, I'm going to need you to open the lid so that I'm ready to get right in there with the grinder." He held up the glass pestle implement. "But first, we both need to put these on." He tossed Winslow a pair of white latex gloves and donned a pair of his own. "Sterile technique is not exactly possible out here, but let's keep everything as clean as we reasonably can."

Winslow snapped the gloves into place and moved to the sample container. "Ready?"

"Ready." Steve stepped up to him with the pestle. Winslow removed the lid from the container and backed away before dropping it along with a couple of spiders that had stuck to it into their makeshift trash can.

Hoch went to work right away with the pestle, grinding the bulk of spiders into a thick paste even as a lot of them crawled out of the container and spilled out onto the stepstool and onto the tent floor. He continued to grind away at all corners of the container, and soon there was a soupy gruel sloshing around in the bottom of the plasticware. He set the pestle down and turned to Winslow. "Lid, please."

Winslow handed him the lid and Hoch snapped it in place. He took a paper towel and cleaned the outside of spiders and blood, then he shook the container vigorously for about a minute. "This will help to homogenize the liquid inside and evenly distribute the contents."

Both of them eyed the clear container of greenish, sludgy fluid as Hoch held it up to the light and slowly turned it this way and that. "All right, I'm going to take a closer look at it now." He set it down on the step stool again and removed the lid. With a pair of tweezers, he extracted a few spiders and parts of spiders that had managed not to be ground up, as well as a few pieces of dirt, leaves and tree bark. Satisfied the container now contained pure spider blood, he replaced the lid on the container. Then he turned to Winslow.

"We're ready for the document."

The historian nodded and pulled the poster tube from his pack, uncapped it and took out the rare document. He unrolled it, unable to keep from shaking his head at the ruination Hoch's lab work had wreaked on the paper, until the very bottom of the manuscript was laid bare. He set flat stones on the corners and sides of the paper to act as paperweights and then pointed to the last remaining damaged section.

"So this is the part here that we're hoping the spider's blood will reveal?"

"Correct." Hoch eyeballed the section for another few seconds and then turned back to his lab implements. "Let me select an appropriate brush to apply the solution with." He went to his supply box, picked up a couple of brushes and then took one over to the document. He placed it next to the damaged section and nodded. "I think this'll do."

He took the container of spider blood and set it down next to the manuscript. "I think we should start with one layer, let it dry, and see what happens. We can always apply more later."

"Sounds good," Winslow agreed. He removed the lid from the spider blood container and Steve dipped his brush into it. He was about to dip it into the blood when he said, "Hey, I just noticed your neck. What happened?"

Winslow made uneasy eye contact with him. "Spider bite a few days ago. Different kind of spider than these. Guides said it was a rare one. I'm okay, though. Let's get on with it, shall we?"

"You got it." Steve dipped the brush into the spider blood and let it drain off the brush so there wouldn't be any excess. Then he brought the blood-laden brush over Manuscript 512 and deftly stroked it across only the last remaining damaged section. Both treasure-seekers held their breaths as they waited to see if the blood would have an immediate effect.

But nothing happened.

They stared at the blood on the parchment, but the damaged text remained unreadable. Dr. Winslow stroked the now thick beard on his chin as he stared at the document as if willing something to happen.

"Some chemical reactions take time." Steve said, putting the lid back on the blood container and setting his brush down. "I suggest we break for supper and then we'll take a look at it. If nothing's happened, we could try another application."

#

Dinner was a tense experience for Steve Hoch, because he was constantly wondering whether Sal or Winslow was on to the fact that his two jungle "guides" were in fact undercover Brazilian *policia*. And then he had his own misgivings about the *policia*—were they in fact *working* undercover, or were they moonlighting for their own benefit? It seemed like they'd had remarkably little input from any kind of headquarters or station or whatever it was they had down here, but then again, Steve knew little about how Brazilian law enforcement operated. Still, he grew increasingly worried that they would not keep their word to him once they had what they needed to bust Dr. Winslow for the library theft. And there was a darker thought as well. *Were they even really interested in bringing Winslow to justice, or did they want the Lost City of Z, along with the supposed priceless treasures it holds, for themselves?* It was certainly possible, wasn't? Corruption wasn't uncommon down here.

But as the conversation turned to the document processing, the spiders' blood and the likelihood of it working, what they would do if it didn't work, and so on, he forgot about it. Finding he was ravenously hungry after all of the travel to get here, he devoured a meal of *feijoada,* a bean stew with pork and beef, washed down with a couple of cold Antarctica beers from an ice chest. He told himself that things weren't so bad, he'd get through this ordeal okay, and then as soon as he could, he'd be on the first plane back to the States, never to return to Brazil or the Amazon again.

Best laid plans.

CHAPTER TWENTY-FIVE

Matto Grosso

After dinner, all five of the party gathered in the lab tent. The tension was palpable as Winslow picked up Manuscript 512 and pointed to the end of the document where they had treated the section with spider blood. To his, and everyone's great surprise, where before there had been only a dark green smear, there were now legible characters.

"Well I'll be," Steve said. "Looks like it worked!"

"Let's take it outside so we can look at it comfortably," Santos suggested.

"Let's take a picture of it first," Steve said, "in case the effect is temporary, or it continues to degrade the manuscript. Just to be on the safe side."

All agreed that was a good idea and so Winslow snapped a photo of the new section with his camera. Then he took the manuscript outside and laid it out on top of a crate where they could all gather around and look at it.

The revealed code was a simple one, consisting only of three numbers and three letters:

8 B 2 R 3 V

"I'll be damned if it doesn't look like a high school locker combination," Sal said.

"Sort of," Winslow said, "but there are letters, too."

"The combo locks had letters, too: 'R' for right and 'L' for left."

"But there are three letters here, 'B', 'R' and 'V'."

"Besides," Santos interjected, "if the letters indicated direction, as in turn Left or Right, in Portuguese, those letters would be 'C' for "*Certo,*" which is right, and 'E' for "*Esquerda,*" which is left."

"Okay, so let's think about what it all might mean," Winslow said. "Remember, Manuscript 512 was written by a Portuguese explorer 250 years ago who reported sighting a lost city."

"Z," Sal added.

Winslow responded, "But it wasn't known as Z until Percy Fawcett dubbed it that in the early 1900s. It was just reported to be an ancient city filled with treasures, deep in the Amazon jungle."

"So getting back to the crystal wheels, then," Santos prompted. "What could this code mean in that context?" He stared down at the document. "8 B 2 R 3 V?"

Winslow looked at Sal while he spoke. "You said it reminded you of a locker combination."

Sal nodded. "High school, yeah. You know, 24 Right, 16 Left, 22 right, that kind of thing."

"But in this case, we've got three separate wheels," Santos pointed out.

"Three wheels, three numbers, and three letters," Winslow added. "So it seems to fit."

"So let's think about the numbers for a minute," Sal said. "What can they mean?"

"It's got to have to do with the crystals on the side. Hold on..." Winslow took out his digital camera and brought up one of the images he'd taken of the wheels. He pecked his finger on the screen, while counting softly, then showed the screen to the others. "There are twenty-four crystals on each wheel."

"None of the numbers in the code are higher than twenty-four, so that's good," Sal confirmed.

Winslow pointed to the image. "So the crystals could be numbered, one through twenty-four, though we don't know where the 'one' is. Let's think about the letters again."

"Think about them as the first letters of Portuguese words," Santos said, "since the manuscript itself was written in Portuguese." They all agreed, and Winslow continued.

"You already established that it's not 'right' or 'left' in terms of which way to turn the wheels. Could it be 'clockwise' or 'counter-clockwise'?" He looked to the native Portuguese speakers, the *policia*. Both of them shook their heads. "Those both begin with 'S'," Santos stated.

Winslow went on. "Okay, so it's not that. What does that leave?" He stared down at the image of the crystal wheels again while holding the display out for the others to see.

"The crystals themselves," Sal said.

Winslow nodded. "Let's consider them. Twenty-four on each wheel, eight each of three different colors and sizes. The white ones are tallest and skinniest, the red ones are widest and shortest, while the green ones are in between in size."

"Ah!" Santos's exclamation was so loud, sudden and without preamble that it startled the rest of the group. "I think I know: 'B' for *branco,* the Portuguese word for *white."*

Ruiz picked up the narrative. "'V' for *verde,* or *green* in English."

Sal then appeared confused. "I happen to know that 'red' in Portuguese is *vermelho,* though, which doesn't fit. Unless the 'V' isn't for *verde,* but for *vermelho?"*

Santos stared at the picture on Winslow's camera some more. "We've been calling them red, but maybe they are pink. Because, in Portuguese, the word for 'pink' is *rosa."*

"There's our 'R'!" Sal rejoiced.

Winslow recapped the thinking. "So we have 'R' for the pink crystals, 'V' for the green ones, and 'B' for the white ones. Agreement?"

They all said yes, and Dr. Winslow continued. "Now let's put it all together, numbers and English words. The code as we are interpreting it says: 8 White, 2 Pink, 3 Green. Do we agree?"

No one said they didn't agree, so Winslow carried on. "All right, so then what does that mean?" He held up the image display for everyone to see.

Sal shrugged. "It must be indicating certain stones of the right color."

"Yes," Santos said, "like the combination to a lock. Each wheel needs to be turned to a certain stone, and then it unlocks…whatever it is that it unlocks," he finished with a shrug before swatting away a buzzing insect from his face.

Winslow nodded. "So if we assume each color of crystal has a number, 1-8, with there being a total of twenty-four crystals on each wheel, three of each type, how do we know which crystal corresponds to which number? Where is number one?" He pointed to the photo on his camera screen.

A long pause ensued, after which Sal ventured, "I would hope we can assume that the wheels have been left in the default position. We could also look at the mechanism of the wheel, see if there are any markings that would suggest a default starting place."

They studied the photo for a few more seconds and could identify no obvious markings that would indicate where a default position was. After a while, Winslow shrugged and said, "Let's go try it by spinning each wheel based on its current position."

All five of them geared up and climbed back into the mysterious grouping of trees. They activated their headlamps and once again, descended into the chamber. They took up position around the crystal wheels.

"All right," Winslow said when they had all quieted down and stood in place, "let's do this one at a time, since turning one wheel does not also turn the others. They move independently while the opposing crystals click past one another, so let's start with this one here that I'm in front of."

"It's closest to the entrance," Sal said, "so hopefully that means that's it's the first wheel."

Winslow nodded while consulting the image of the revealed 512 code on his camera. "If so, then this one should be '8 B'."

"The eighth white crystal from the current position," Santos clarified.

Winslow counted out the white crystals moving clockwise from the "top" of the wheel, which they identified as such because at the base of each wheel was a pedestal that came to a point, each facing in the same direction.

"That one there is number eight. Sal, would you do the honors, please?" Sal, who was already standing nearest to the eighth white crystal, put a hand on it and began to slowly turn the wheel. He stopped when the white crystal in his hand rested above the "starting position" above the point of the pedestal.

They all watched the wheels carefully for any sign of activity, even though only one wheel had been turned. When nothing happened, Winslow said, "Okay, let's do the second wheel." He checked the photo. "2 R."

"Second pink one," Santos said, moving in front of the second wheel and pointing to a crystal. "If this doesn't work, we could try it again counting from the counter-clockwise direction."

"Seems like clockwise would be the way to go, but I guess we'll have to try it if it comes to that. And God forbid there's a mix of clockwise and counter-clockwise," Winslow added, "but if there was you'd think that would be in the code."

Again, Sal grabbed the designated crystal and spun the wheel until that crystal was in position above the pedestal point. And again, they waited for a few seconds to make sure nothing would happen with only partial completion, and nothing did.

"Let's move onto the last one." Winslow walked over to the third wheel and stared down at it before checking his image. "3 V."

Sal counted out three green stones and then spun the wheel accordingly, this time stepping back away from it quickly when he was done. They all waited with baited breath, sure that something unexpected was about to happen, but once again, nothing actually did. The chamber remained silent, unmoving. Even the spiders continued their unceasing march up the walls and across the ceiling as if nothing special had happened.

"Looks like we got it wrong," Winslow said to break the silence.

"Wait a minute," Santos said, holding up a finger. "Counting out the crystals is completely dependent on what we assume the default position to be."

"I think the position we found them in, and with the point of the pedestals, which all face in the same direction, is a logical default," Sal said, receiving a concurring nod from Dr. Winslow.

Yet Santos pushed on. "But we spun the wheels already, before this session, when we first got here."

"We put them back the way they were," Winslow insisted.

Ruiz nodded to confirm this. "It's true, they were turned back the same number of crystal positions as they were turned forward. I made it a point to observe that."

"But," Santos continued, looking at Winslow, "what about the first time you encountered the wheels before we got here? Did you spin them then?"

Winslow and Sal looked at one another, then both slowly nodded. "We did," Winslow said.

"And did you spin them back into place that time?"

Again, Winslow and Sal exchanged glances, but this time neither had a confident response. But after a couple of seconds, Winslow held up the camera. "I took a picture of the wheels when I first got here, before I touched them at all. Here, wait..." He scrolled through the images on his camera before holding the screen out for the others to see. "This picture was taken *before* we ever touched the wheels at all."

"You are positive?" Santos asked.

"Yes," Winslow said, looking at Sal, who also nodded.

Sal scrutinized the image and let out an exasperated sigh. "They *were* in a different position. You're right," he said, turning to Santos. "We need to spin them back to how they were in this picture and *then* try it again based on the code."

After a round of head-shaking and deep breaths, the team regrouped around the first wheel while Winslow held up his camera with the first image of the wheels on the display. They turned each wheel back to the exact position they held in that image. That done, Winslow stepped back and again checked all three wheels against the picture.

He nodded. "*This* is exactly how we found them."

"So *now* we are ready to start again according to the code," Santos said.

"Okay," Winslow said, stepping into position in front of the first wheel. "Here we go again…"

They repeated the same process as before, using the code to adjust the crystal positions on the wheels one at a time, with Sal spinning the wheels. The jungle guide looked at the group as he dragged the specified crystal of the last wheel toward the pedestal point. "Here goes nothing…"

He pulled the crystal into position and hastily backed away from the wheel.

Nothing happened.

As defeated exclamations began to escape Winslow's lips, the grating of stone on stone rumbled beneath their feet, reverberating throughout the chamber.

CHAPTER TWENTY-SIX

"Something's happening!" Winslow yelled. All five men backed up to the walls of the crystal wheel chamber, terrified of the trembling beneath their feet. Winslow couldn't help but notice that even the spiders altered their usual activity by freezing in place. None of them were moving.

Then suddenly all three wheels dropped out of sight through the floor. A single cutout space resembling a figure eight was left in their place.

As the men stared at it in awe, the spiders came alive again and directed themselves toward the opening in the floor. They poured down into it at breakneck speed, no longer smoothly trundling along the surfaces of floors, walls and ceilings, but launching their bodies willy-nilly into the void in an avalanche of tiny bodies.

Thirty-seconds or so passed without further activity before any of the explorers dared speak or move. It was Santos who approached the opening first.

He peered down into it, standing in front of where the middle wheel used to be. "It's dark," was his first observation. That short utterance was enough to encourage the others to gather around, though, and soon all five of them stared down into the void they had unlocked.

"Let's set up a climbing rig," Sal suggested, already pulling a rope out of the small backpack he'd brought with him. Soon flashlights were shined down the hole.

"There's water down there!" Winslow said.

"I don't see the wheels. They must have sunk into the water," Sal observed.

"If there's water at the bottom," Santos wondered aloud, "what's the point of going down there?"

"We need to check it out," Winslow said. "Someone constructed those crystal wheels to guard the entrance to something. And there might only be water for the first part, or it could be shallow. I think one of us should go down there and see if it's navigable before we all go down there, though. Any volunteers?"

"I'll do it." Sal was already in the process of rigging a climbing harness for himself. "Need somewhere to tie this off," he said, holding up the free end of his climbing rope. They looked around the chamber but saw only smooth stone.

"I will belay you," Santos said, taking the rope from him and expertly tying a knot that allowed him to maintain good control over it while being able to let out slack. Sal held his gaze.

"I'm trusting you."

"Don't worry, I won't let you down," Santos said, eliciting laughter from the group at his pun.

With that, Sal flipped on a headlamp and poised himself with his back to the edge of the opening left by the crystal wheels. He began to walk backwards down the shaft the wheels fell into, which was shaped exactly like the cutout of the wheels all the way down. He proceeded slowly and carefully yet at a steady pace, noting nothing of interest on the walls on the way down.

When he was ten feet or so above the water, he paused and examined it with his headlamp. "It's not deep," he called up, his voice echoing in the well-like shaft. "I can see the crystal wheels just below the surface of the water!"

"Are they floating or on the bottom?" Winslow called down.

"Only one way to find out." Sal rappelled the rest of the way down and could see that a passage extended at least some distance off to his right, where one wall of the vertical shaft walls ended five feet before the other sides.

"Dropping down onto the wheels now," he shouted up.

"Ready," Santos returned.

Sal let himself fall onto the middle of the submerged crystal wheels with a splash. He steadied himself, balancing with both arms held out from his sides while waiting to see if his added weight would sink the wheels. It did not. He could feel the bottom of them grinding against whatever hard ground lay beneath the water, only a few feet below. Once he steadied himself on the wheels, he directed his headlamp into the opening to his right.

Sal sucked in his breath as he realized he was gazing into a wide tunnel that went on for a long way. Though it wasn't tall—he would have to stoop to walk through it—he could see that it had a slight incline, and that its floor became dry about a hundred feet in. He called up to the others that he was ready to be belayed back up and felt Santos take up the slack in the rope. He climbed back up the vertical shaft and was pulled out by two sets of arms at the top, back into the now empty crystal chamber.

He explained to everyone how the tunnel branched off, how the water was shallow, and that the new passage was completely dry a short distance in. Upon hearing this, both Winslow and Santos appeared so interested they practically foamed at the mouth. Recognizing they faced a potential trek into a vast unexplored territory, they decided to break for the night and then come back down at first light with more gear. After some discussion while they exited the chamber and climbed down from the trees, it was settled that they would bring their full packs with them, in case the new passage actually led somewhere. They wouldn't want to become too separated from their gear, Sal warned, and none of them argued against it, even though it would mean lugging their heavy frame backpacks down into the subterranean tunnel.

#

The next morning at sunrise, once the camp was dismantled and abandoned, the full expedition climbed up into the trees one more time and descended into the crystal chamber. They roped the heavy backpacks down first after wrapping them in tarps to guard against water intrusion. Then they took turns rappelling down to the bottom of the shaft. Sal went first since he was already familiar with the bottom and they wouldn't all be able to stand on the sunken wheels at once, so he wanted to be the first to reach the dry ground in the new passage.

This time, since the last person down would have no one to hold the rope for him, they came prepared by bringing pitons—metal stakes used in rock climbing that they possibly intended for use in trees—along with a rock hammer. Using these, Sal was able to drive a spike into the stone floor just outside the wheel shaft and tie the rope off to that. Santos, who was the last one down, was able to still use the rope to guide him, and it would still be there for them to use to get back up in case the new passage didn't lead anywhere.

Winslow was second to get down after Sal, and by the time he landed, Sal was already wading up onto the dry section of tunnel. The little rubber boat came in handy again here, to float across the water from the submerged wheels to the dry passage. Sal determined the water to be at least waist deep at the wheels. No one wanted to be sopping wet from the waist down while they explored the Amazonian underground.

When Ruiz rowed across to the new passage in the boat, the five of them donned their backpacks, adjusted their headlamps and flashlights, and began a cautious walk up the subterranean incline. The floor, walls and ceiling were all of the same smooth stone that the crystal chambers had been constructed from. They speculated who could have constructed such a marvel of engineering in the middle of the deepest Amazon without anyone knowing about it.

"It must have been done a long time ago," Sal suggested.

"The stone itself does look old and worn," Winslow said.

The slight incline of the passage eventually gave way to a level corridor that seemed to stretch on to infinity. They marched on for close to an hour with the unchanging scenery, pitch black if not for their artificial lights. It was then that Winslow noticed the spiders.

He wasn't sure how they had escaped all of their notice, but the train of spiders was here, perhaps a thinner line of them, but stretching out even longer as the arachnids moved along the ceiling in the same direction as the humans. When flashlights were pointed right at them, their eyes sparkled with white reflective light. Winslow pointed them out, but no one had a strong reaction.

"They've left us alone so far," Sal said, before adding, "They even kind of led us to this place in the first place, right?"

Winslow admitted that was true enough and soldiered on while casting a furtive glance at the eight-legged marchers. He unconsciously brought a hand up to his throbbing neck. The spider bite pulsed worse than ever now, a constant, rapid, distracting movement, and he even caught Ruiz staring in shock at his greenish neck. He felt all right, though, at least he thought he did. But maybe he was just being pushed along on the adrenaline of unlocking the crystal wheels into this strange portal?

For now, Winslow kept putting one foot in front of the other, glad to still be a few steps ahead of the law and maybe even one step closer to finding the lost city.

CHAPTER TWENTY-SEVEN

It was Santos who first noticed the change.

"I see light up ahead!"

The five explorers switched off their flashlights and immediately saw it, too. Up ahead, a faint, hazy light beckoned. The distance was still significant, but it served to spur them on as they trudged onward through the underground tunnel still made of the same smooth stone. Its construction was inexplicable, they all knew. There was no way that a construction project on such a massive scale could have gone unnoticed in the Amazon in recent times, which led them to believe that it must be leading them straight into the Lost City of Z.

This notion was both exciting and frightening, and the conflicting emotions served to physically drain Winslow as he battled his unknown neck malady. His shoulder hurt now, too, sore as though he'd been kicked yesterday by a UFC fighter, and when he rolled up his sleeve to have a look, he was mortified to see the terrifying mottled green pattern now covering one side of his neck, shoulder and upper arm. He didn't want to stop walking even long enough to get out his first aid kit and pop some aspirin or Tylenol or whatever pills he had that probably wouldn't do anything anyway, for fear of drawing attention to himself. So he ignored it and tried to block it from his mind, using the light ahead and the promise of discovery it portended to buoy his spirits and push him ever onward.

It grew gradually lighter as they walked on, the tunnel still more or less level, until one by one they shut off their flashlights until they could see using only the ambient light coming from straight ahead.

"Must be the end of the tunnel," Sal said.

"Great, the light at the end of the tunnel," Winslow quipped, feeling his neck. Was he dying? As a wanted man, he couldn't very well obtain medical help. He would just have to hope his body resolved the problem on its own.

The party was by now spread out in a single file line over a considerable distance, such that Sal, in the lead, was the first to reach the end of the passage and relay the news to the others. Ruiz, in the rear, caught up to Sal almost ten minutes later.

"Whoa," Winslow exclaimed when he caught up to Sal and witnessed the view from the end of the passage. They had come to a sudden drop-off of sorts, not a high one but perhaps a ten-foot drop down to soil that sloped downward. Sparse plant life occupied the slope, and they could see dimly outlined shapes far below.

The view above was equally stunning.

"Is…is that the ground up there?" Winslow asked. No one responded immediately while they all processed the strange sight. Perhaps ten stories up, a series of roughly circular holes emitted soft, filtered light. Sal shrugged off his pack and dug out a pair of binoculars. He trained them on the holes far above. "I think it is the ground," he said after focusing the glasses. "That's sunlight coming through holes in the ground, but they're covered with…" He fine-focused some more, "…with spiderwebs, I think, and maybe a layer of dead leaves."

Santos tried to make sense of it. "So if we were on the ground up there, we could fall through one of those holes and end up down here?" He looked around suspiciously as if afraid he might see the bodies or skeletons of those who had undergone just such an unsavory fate.

"I believe so," Sal said, "unless you got caught up in a spiderweb, that is."

"And what's down there?" Winslow asked, shifting their attention in the other direction. Sal retrained his binoculars so that he could examine the ground far below, at the bottom of the dirt slope.

"It's harder to make out detail down there—not enough light—but it's weird, I see shapes with straight lines, almost like structures."

This got all of them excited and they put their packs back on, adjusting their gear to be ready for the steep trek downhill into the unknown. They took tentative first steps to make certain the ground was solid enough to walk on. Once they found that it was, they increased their pace, now able to walk five abreast in the wide open, cavernous space. Winslow pointed out that the spiders split up here, half going off to the right, while the other half went left before disappearing from sight. Again, they ignored them and made their way down the slope. Scrubby ferns and wispy vines eked out a living in the dimly lit soil, and a host of flying insects, similar to those seen above ground, patrolled the air above the slope.

Winslow's mind was running a million miles an hour as he kept pondering if this could really be it—the gateway to the Lost City of Z—*I mean, why else would that elaborate construction be up there, and the code in 512 was accurate, so this must be it, right, this—*

His train of thought was shattered as his left boot encountered some spongy dirt, sinking deep enough into it to trip him and send him sprawling downhill. He came to rest against a clump of spiky ferns, his ankle in pain. Santos was the first to reach him and gave him a hand up. Winslow gingerly tested his ankle by putting weight on it, and found he was okay—it was not sprained. But the warning was clear: be careful, go slow, a serious injury like a broken or even sprained ankle down here could well prove fatal.

The group slowed their pace somewhat but continued slogging down the incline until they reached level terrain. The ground there was softer than the regular forest floor above, but still walkable. The plant life was different, with only a few skinny trees, and mostly ferns, mosses and scrubby ground cover. Moths, flies, and spiders abounded. The air was dank and smelled faintly of must and mold, like it didn't circulate much. Except for the occasional weak downdraft from the apertures far above, a lack of movement with almost no wind was the norm in this subterranean world.

Flashlights were still needed from time to time to examine specific areas, but their use was now only sporadic. The team picked their way across the spongy bottom, between circular shafts of light that illuminated swirling particles of dust and micro-particles.

Santos saw it first.

Some kind of structure, no doubt one of the ones they thought they had seen from above but weren't sure because of the great distance.

"I see a building up ahead!"

The group paused and looked where he was pointing. Indeed, it was shadowed, indistinct, but visible nonetheless: a flat-topped pyramid loomed in the remote dark.

"A ziggurat," Dr. Winslow said.

"What's a ziggurat doing underground?" Sal wondered aloud.

"I think we're going to find out." This from Santos, who started to walk in the direction of the stunning sight. After a moment, the others took after him.

When the ground beneath their feet transitioned from raw, muddy dirt to the same smooth stone they had seen in the crystal chamber, Winslow knew he had finally found it.

The Lost City of Z.

He walked on like a zombie, his body carrying out the necessary motor functions to effect forward motion, while his mind was completely elsewhere; a dangerous combination that he knew he should have avoided by taking heed from his previous lesson, yet the thoughts just wouldn't stop. The implications of this spellbinding find were simply too great to shove aside for a mundane task such as personal safety while trekking through an underground rainforest.

When his feet fell onto the stone floor of what could only be described as some sort of open plaza, all of them knew they had come across a lost civilization, something so extraordinary it would change their lives irrevocably and forever.

"I see another pyramid behind the first one," Sal said, pointing.

"Do you think this city used to be above ground?" Winslow wondered. "How could a people survive down here in the dark?"

"Maybe they had to periodically make trips to the ground above in order to collect food?" Santos suggested with a shrug.

"Maybe," Winslow conceded. "Or maybe the layout of the land was different centuries ago and it wasn't below ground then?" Everyone shrugged, entertaining the possibility, yet at the same time much more interested in what lay before them than in the academics of how it came to be. They walked toward the pyramids, the going much easier now that they were on solid, paved ground. Before they reached the first pyramid, they arrived at roads that branched off from the main pavement, leading left and right to smaller buildings.

"Most likely dwellings of some kind," Winslow said. "We should check them out before the pyramids, since those are large and will take time."

The group paused while they assessed their options. Roads led right and left, while the expansive plaza-like space continued on in front of them. "We could split up," Sal offered, "half of us go right, half left."

But Santos immediately shot this down. "No, I think it safest if we all stay together as a group. The last thing we need to worry about now is getting separated."

"We have walkie-talkies," Sal persisted.

"No, who knows what can happen. Batteries die, they get dropped, we go out of range. The risks are not worth it for saving a little time."

Sal shrugged while Winslow looked on. "Fine, just a suggestion. Which way do you want to go, then?"

They opted to take the right road. "Feels like walking up a city street, right?" Winslow joked as they walked along a pathway about the same width as a modern sidewalk.

"More like a village," Santos said. They walked on in silence until they reached the first dwelling, a small yet well-constructed hut made of stone. It featured no windows and only a single opening—a doorway on the far side.

Sal flicked on his flashlight and aimed it inside the building. "Empty," he announced without preamble, before walking inside. Santos went inside along with him, but the other three were content to look in from the doorway. Inside was nothing but a stone slab and empty walls, ceiling and floor, completely unadorned.

"I guess this could have been a bed," Sal speculated, eyeing the stone slab.

"Pretty simple accommodations. Very rustic," Santos joked. No one laughed.

They exited the dwelling and walked to another not far away on the same "road." It was constructed no differently than the last, but unlike the other, this one was not empty. A skeleton lay partially disarticulated on the stone shelf, and a pair of leather boots lay on the floor.

"Check it out," Sal called out. The others joined him, and they examined the skeleton without touching it.

"An adult male," Santos concluded after looking at the bones.

"Not a recent death," Ruiz added.

They searched amongst the bones for any kind of identifying articles but found nothing besides the boots. Exiting the hut, they looked up the road, where about a half a dozen more of the same huts stretched out into the distance.

"I think it's safe to split up here," Sal said, "so that we can each have a quick look into each one, and if any of them contains anything, then holler and we'll all check it out. But if they're all like this, we may as well find that out faster."

They agreed to the plan and went their separate ways, with Ruiz opting to scout the house that was farthest away. Winslow surveyed the next nearest one, while Sal, Steve and Santos took the three middle houses on the stone lane.

Winslow stood at the entrance to the abode and tried to imagine who had lived here, what their life was like. It seemed unfathomable to him that anyone would choose to live underground like this. Was there some reason for that choice? Did something or someone force them into a hidden existence?

He was hoping to find answers to these questions inside the stone walls, but he found the stone shack to be no different than the first one he'd entered. Essentially a smooth stone cube with a carved block for what looked, at any rate, like a bed, all of the same earth tone shade. He couldn't imagine more than two people living in here, he supposed a couple with a small child at most, but it was very sparse and confined for anything more than temporary accommodations. Maybe it was the equivalent of a weekend hunting shack? But then why the paved road set up almost like a suburban neighborhood, with orderly rows of houses?

He turned around to leave the former home, for it was certainly lived in no longer, and caught his breath when he saw what blocked the doorway.

A spider.

A single arachnid, not a flowing stream of them like he'd gotten used to, but an individual spider of proportions unlike any he'd ever had the misfortune to lay eyes on. Its eyes—however many of them there were in all their compound glory-stared back at him from about the same height as his own. Only some of its legs were visible—the two in front and two at thee back, while the others were splayed outside the width of the door frame. It looked like a gargantuan version of the little ones that had been "following" them—black and hairy, with each eyeball the size of a tennis ball.

Winslow froze in place, having no idea what to do, how to handle himself when facing off against such a creature. He'd heard at various times in his life, when facing off against different kinds of animals (usually bears, or big cats, or dangerous dogs and the like), that it was best to freeze in place, or else to make yourself appear big and threatening and make lots of noise. But a super-sized spider? He had no idea how to handle it. He felt fluid from his wound begin to flow freely down his neck, warm as it went.

And then it occurred to him that the safest place for him to be was right here, in this little stone house. The spider was far too big to fit through the doorway. Its legs would, he could see, but he didn't see how the bulbous body could fit, even by squeezing. Hopefully if he remained still, the beast would lose interest in him and wander off.

Then the spider turned around, and Winslow felt a brief sense of jubilation because he thought it was leaving. But the spider's next action took him completely by surprise. It raised its abdomen higher off the ground and began squirting a whitish substance out of somewhere on the rear part of its body. At first the historian thought it was squirting poison at him, but he soon saw that it didn't go very far, whatever it was. In fact, almost none of it reached beyond the doorway; it was all landing on the outside. As more of the substance piled up, Winslow was able to recognize what it was: silk. This spider was spinning a web.

That's when Winslow felt the numbing chill of terror. As he watched more of the whitish, ropy strands issue from the creature's silk gland, it dawned on him what was happening.

He was being trapped in here, hemmed inside a stone prison by a brainless arthropod, to be trapped like a fly in a spider's web. He was so mortified by the idea of his life ending in here, as a piece of meat in a spider's larder, that he screamed a bloodcurdling outburst unlike any he'd ever uttered in his life. He was sure that the others had to hear it, at least Sal and Santos in the next huts over.

They had to hear that, right?

That was when he remembered he had a walkie-talkie clipped to his waistband. He snatched it up and looked at it, annoyed and relieved at the same time to see that it was still powered on to the same channel they'd been using. Wasting batteries for a while, sure, but if he'd left his on, hopefully someone else did, too. As the massive spider continued to bar the doorway with multiple passes of spun silk, Winslow brought the radio to his lips.

CHAPTER TWENTY-EIGHT

Sal and Santos emerged from their respective huts. Sal was first to speak.

"Same as the other one in there—nothing in it. Yours?"

"Same. Say, did you hear something?"

"Like what?"

"I don't know, like—"

They were interrupted by the squawk of the walkie-talkie clipped to Sal's belt. Winslow's voice broke through it, sounding terrified.

"—help now, guys. I'm trapped in here with a giant one of those spiders!"

Sal began to laugh as he slowly raised the radio to his lips, but Santos appeared more concerned gazing up toward the hut Winslow went to investigate. "Look, I know that one spider did a number on you, but seriously, I'm sure you can manage to walk over one spider."

"It's trapping me inside here with its web, Sal! Come quick, have weapons ready!"

At this, Santos looked at Sal, shrugged, and then both of them ran off toward Winslow's hut. While they ran, Sal readied the most serious weapon at his immediate disposal—his machete. He didn't see how it applied to a spider, but Winslow could be stubborn and was used to being the boss, so he figured it was easier just to do what he asked and sort it out later.

Santos arrived a few feet ahead of Sal, turning the corner to the side of the hut with the doorway first. Sal had time to hear him mutter something about god, before he also got a look at the monstrosity that awaited them.

For that's what it was, Sal thought as he dug his boots into the ground to force a quick stop. *What is this monster?*

His walkie talkie blared again with Winslow's over-the-top voice. "Where are you? Help! Do you copy?"

Sal didn't bother with the radio, but instead shouted toward the doorway and the spider while raising his machete. He glanced at Santos, who now backpedaled while readying his own long blade.

"We're here, Winslow, outside the door. Holy crap, man, that is a *spider*! Never seen anything like it."

"It's throwing webs all over the doorway, trapping me in here!"

Suddenly the arachnid pivoted toward the newcomers, whether drawn by the noise or the motion, they didn't know. But it wasted no time in shooting a fresh salvo of silk rope in their direction. It passed over Santos's right shoulder, missing a direct impact but then draping over his shoulder and dragging the undercover *policía* down to the ground with it.

Sal saw the mega-spider turn its artillery toward him, but he was ready this time, and sidestepped right as another salvo of silk blasted in his direction. It missed, and while Santos struggled to his feet, Sal went on the offensive. Sensing the spider was preoccupied with rapidly spinning out its weaponized silk, he moved in with his machete, side-slashing the beast across its hairy, black side. He was rewarded with a curtain of greenish blood that fell from the creature like a fountain. The spider's web-spinning was interrupted mid-strand and it wobbled over to one side, in Sal's direction.

The wound apparently sapped it of its strength, however. It no longer moved with the quickness it had earlier displayed, but instead remained stationary while moving its various head appendages—antennae, feelers, pincers—Sal didn't know the proper zoological terms for them, but they were disgusting and all moving at once while the spider faced off against him.

Sal considered a final death blow against the eight-legged foe but decided against it since it seemed to be mortally injured; at least it was no longer moving. Winslow's cries for help wafted out of the hut and he and Santos shifted their attention to the doorway.

It was covered for nearly its entire height in thick, rope-like spiderwebs. Although he didn't want to touch them, they looked to Sal like they would be strong enough to bounce a man off of them who ran into them full speed.

"Dr. Winslow, are you okay in there?" Santos yelled through the cobwebs.

"What happened to the spider?" came his response.

"We killed it," Sal said, eyeing Santos. He wanted to let the man know that it had been a team effort, that he had taken a silk hit from the beast which had enabled Sal to move in for the kill. He might need backup himself at some point, so he didn't want to offend him by taking sole credit for the kill.

"Are you sure?" Winslow asked.

Sal eyed the arachnid, crumpled on the ground with a spreading pool of green beneath its unmoving body. "Positive. It's safe to come out now."

"Not sure I can get out with those webs across the door. I think it was going to trap me in here until I starved to death and then come back and eat me."

"That's quite a hypothesis, Dr. Winslow," Sal half-joked. Even he had to admit, it had a certain ring of truth to it. A very scary ring.

Santos broke him out of his dark thoughts by bringing up a more practical matter. "Stand back from the door, I'm going to cut through with my machete." He proceeded to hack away at the silken ropes, snapping one or two of the thick bio-strands at a time. "Stuff has some serious tensile strength," he huffed between machete strikes. After a few more cuts he opened up a hole large enough for Winslow to get out through.

He staggered out disbelievingly, untrusting that his foe—his captor—was dead. When he saw the spider dead on the ground, bled out, he put a hand to his gut, doubled over and vomited on the ground. While he was bent over, Sal made eye contact with Santos and silently pointed to Winslow's neck, which had taken on a dark green hue from the wound seepage. Winslow stood up and both men looked away quickly.

"Was it hard to kill?" the historian asked.

Santos nodded but Sal shrugged. "Not what I would call easy, but I'd rather face off against one of those—" he tipped his head toward the slayed arachnid—"than a tiger or something like that. But that's just me."

"Yeah, that is just you," Winslow said, leering at the kill. "I'd rather faceoff against a big pussycat than that alien thing."

Sal and Santos smiled. Santos entered the hut, was in there for a minute before reemerging. "All of the huts seem to be the same," he said. "This one is no different than the first one or the one I examined."

"Same here," Sal said.

Then Santos's radio crackled with Ruiz's voice. "Got something you should check out here in the hut I went into."

Santos picked up his radio. "Copy that, we're okay here. Be there in a few."

Winslow snapped a picture of his dead spider nemesis and then the three of them walked back to the beginning of the road where the house was that Ruiz had investigated. He was standing there at the doorway to greet them. After a recounting of the giant spider, he waved them inside. He walked to the back wall, where a series of crude scratch marks lined the stone.

But it was the skeleton that commanded their attention. This one was on the floor, most of the bones still in place, completely denuded of flesh. Like the other, a pair of leather boots covered the feet. Unlike the other, a machete lay nearby on the floor.

"Also an adult male," Santos said. "I am not enough of an expert to tell if it is the bones of a tribal person or a foreign explorer," he said, looking at Dr. Winslow, who shook his head.

"I'm not either. Need an anthropologist for that, not a historian, but I can tell you what these hash marks likely mean." He pointed to the crude lines hacked into the stone wall, probably with the machete.

"Looks like the classic prisoner's day tally," Sal said, brow furrowed. He looked at Winslow, who wore an expression of horror.

"I told you," he said, nodding to the skeleton. "This poor guy got webbed in here, and he counted out the days until he died, and then the spider came back for him…"

Santos stared intently at the markings, bobbing a finger in the air as he counted the hash lines indicating five. "Thirty-nine days, if that's what this represents."

They shuddered collectively as they imagined being stuck in this confined space for that long, dying of thirst and starvation until the mega-beast returned to haul them off for a meal.

"I think we should move on toward the pyramids," Winslow said, gazing off into the distance. "There's a lot more of this city to explore." But he was staring down at the ground as he spoke, at a long line of the same small spiders, marching toward the very same pyramids.

Then suddenly heard Steve Hoch's voice crackling through a walkie-talkie. "Everybody: got something here you're not going to believe. It's a corpse, but possibly identifiable. I'm three or four huts up on the left from your position, over."

They filed out of the hut with a last glance at the skeleton and ran up the road to the middle huts, where they saw Steve standing outside of one and waving. "This one," he said, before ducking back inside the stone structure. The other four explorers entered the hut and gathered around the bed ledge, on which rested another skeleton.

The bones of this person obviously belonged to a larger man, but it was what else was in the room that really caught their eye. Leather clothing of some type was still intact around the skeleton, although all flesh was gone, as well as a pair of leather boots. A silver object was clipped to the pocket of the garment. Winslow bent down and picked it up.

"It's a pocket watch, old, from the style common to the late 19th or early 20th centuries." He picked it up and noted that the time had stopped at 6:43, whether AM or PM there was no way to tell. "Needs to be wound." Then he flipped it over and caught his breath as he saw an inscription on the back:

To Colonel Percy Fawcett

With gratitude from: National Geographic Society
1921

"Looks like we found out what happened to the intrepid Colonel Fawcett," Sal said. "Consumed by one of those nasty spiders after being webbed in here until he became too weak to fight back."

Winslow's expression was one of disbelief and wonder. "Amazing! He was so close, so close to the Lost City of Z!"

"A lot of good it did him," Steve mumbled.

CHAPTER TWENTY-NINE

The expedition walked through the deserted subterranean town, marveling at how many stone huts there were, street after street just like the one they had just explored, each lined with the simple houses. The flat-topped pyramids loomed in the distance, at least two of them, with other indistinct shapes of similar size behind those.

The small spiders trailed them but exhibited a disturbing change in behavior. Now they began stopping to suck up the strange oozy, puss-like substance that dripped from Winslow's neck bite and ran down his body and clothes until some of it eventually ended up on the ground. When it did, the spiders nearest to it paused their forward march to sit on top of the greenish substance and soak it up.

"Whatever you're bleeding, they like it," Steve said, staring dubiously at the foul puddle on the ground rimmed with arachnids.

"It kind of looks like their own blood." Sal stooped down next to Steve to get a closer look at it. The spiders did not move from their feast. "How are you feeling, Hunter?" he asked.

Winslow passed his fingertips across his neck and looked at the smear of dull green. "I feel fine now that big Bertha's out of the way. But we found the lost city, so I'd be in high spirits anyway."

"Let's keep going, then." This from Santos, who was at the front of the pack, with Ruiz tailing everyone at the rear. The team resumed walking along the open stone plaza toward the pyramids. After a time, Steve pointed above their heads.

"Check it out!" About a hundred feet off to their right, another one of the massive spiders hung suspended from a single silk rope beneath one of the spiderweb-shrouded openings in the ground. It dangled there, high above the plaza floor, spinning sedately in circles.

Santos shook his head. "This place is some kind of den for extraordinary spiders."

"How many of those large ones do you think there are?" Winslow asked, unable to conceal the trepidation in his voice.

"That's two that we know of," Sal said, "so it's a safe bet there are more."

The huge spider seemed content to dangle in place rather than drop all the way to the ground, so the party continued their walk toward the pyramids under its watchful gaze. As they neared the structures, they could see that there were two ziggurats, one on each side of the plaza. But it wasn't the pyramids themselves that arrested their attention. It was what lay on the other side of them.

"These things are a gateway!" Winslow bellowed. "The true Lost City of Z is on the other side. We made it! We made it!"

More flashlights were switched on and aimed at the ground in front of them. In between the two pyramids, it transitioned from the earthen stone they'd been seeing, to a metallic gold substance.

"Is that…could it be…" Steve stammered.

"Z was rumored to have streets paved of gold, kind of like Atlantis," Sal said.

"Sure looks like gold. Let's check it out." They ran past the two pyramids to the new pavement, which was also smooth, with slight imperfections here and there, gleaming dully under the flashlights. Ruiz got down on one knee and unfolded the blade of a pocketknife. He gouged the material with the tip of the blade and examined the shavings carefully with his flashlight.

"It's gold," he pronounced. "I am sure of it."

Sal performed a similar test and came to the same conclusion. "I concur. I think we're looking at the real thing, boys."

Winslow stared ahead. He could not see an end to the expanse of gold-paved roadway. It was narrower than the stone plaza they had just traversed, but still about as wide as an eight-lane urban freeway, and it ran on as far as they could see in the limited light.

"Do we check the pyramids, or see where the road leads?"

"It'd be pretty hard to walk by a couple of pyramids without checking them out, don't you think?" Sal asked. After some discussion, they agreed to stick together this time in light of the giant spiders and investigate the pyramid on the right side of the gold thoroughfare. Each pyramid was set back a distance from the road, on unpaved earth.

Sal, Winslow and Steve started walking toward the ziggurat, but when they were about halfway there they realized Santos and his partner were still on the road, talking animatedly to one another, apparently in a heated argument.

"What's their problem?" Sal asked.

"Don't know," Winslow said, before looking to Steve. "You hooked up with these guys. Are they cool?"

Steve shrugged. "Far as I know. Not like I live with 'em or anything. They're hired guides who have a decent rep around town, that's all."

Santos looked over, saw them staring at him and immediately started walking in their direction. His partner followed suit. The others waited until they caught up.

"Sorry for the holdup," Santos said.

"Everything okay?" Sal asked.

Both Santos and his partner nodded with extra enthusiasm. "I thought he packed an extra flashlight, but he forgot," Ruiz said sheepishly.

Santos nodded, affirming the lie. "I told him before we left exactly what I was bringing…"

Ruiz shook his head. "You said—"

"All right, all right, break it up," Sal said. "You can go to marriage counseling when we get back. Right now it's time to see a pyramid. Let's go."

They set off again as a group, toward the ziggurat. "About the same size as the one I've been to at Chicehn Iza," Winslow remarked. "Similar construction, too, by the looks of it."

They continued on toward the amazing structure, which they could now see had hanging mosses and creeper vines festooning its upper levels. No one mentioned that the line of small spiders extended from the gold road across the dirt to that same pyramid.

Reaching the structure, they saw that each step was approximately ten feet high, and that there would be no way to climb it were it not for the stairwell hewn into the center of the large steps or blocks. Winslow suggested they first walk all the way around it to see if there were any openings, and they agreed. They walked counterclockwise around its perimeter, gazing up at the entire side of it, but found no openings by the time they got back to where they started.

"Let's go up there," Winslow suggested. "Maybe there's an opening on top."

"The spiders don't think so." Sal pointed to the line of spiders, which moved on the ground around the pyramid in a loop.

"Do the spiders also go to the other pyramid, or only this one?" Santos asked. No one had an answer.

"We forgot to check," Steve admitted.

"We'll find out when we go to look at that one." Santos watched the spiders crawl around the ziggurat. "For now, let's climb."

The steps were narrow, necessitating a single file line to the top. Santos led off, followed by Winslow, then Sal, Steve and Ruiz in the back. The steps were high for stairs, almost two feet high each, a few crumbling and overgrown with moss, all of which made for a tiresome ascent. About halfway up they encountered a bird's nest, with its occupant, a small black feathered creature, startled out of its nest in a flurry of feathers as it took to the air.

Other than that, the trip to the top was uneventful, and a few minutes later Santos called down that there was a lookout platform of sorts, but no opening. The rectangular space was just wide enough to accommodate all five of them. Looking up, they were beneath one of the cobweb-covered holes through which weak daylight filtered through to their subsurface world. Although the platform atop the ziggurat was itself featureless, the view from the top commanded their attention.

They could see the top of the other pyramid across the road, its viewing platform level with their own.

"What's the point of these pyramids if there's nothing inside them?" Sal wondered aloud. "Assuming that the other one there is exactly the same as this one."

"It sure looks like it is," Steve said.

Looking further down the gold road, two more identical pyramids straddled either side of the thoroughfare in the same configuration.

"I don't get it," Winslow said, gazing into the distance. "We'll have to actually check each pyramid to be certain, but if all four of these are empty, I don't see what their purpose is."

"Some sort of geographic markers?" Steve threw out. "They designate something special about this place?"

"I'd say a gold road is pretty special in and of itself," Sal said, eyeing the yellow ribbon leading off into the distance toward the other pair of pyramids. Santos and Ruiz smiled in agreement but said nothing.

"Before we start looking at the other pyramids, Dr. Winslow," Sal said, "you're the historian here. Did these ziggurats sometimes have hidden entrances? Is there anything we should look for?"

Winslow stared across the road at the twin pyramid and then back to the one they occupied. "I've heard of internal secret passages and chambers, but usually the main entrance is obvious, if there is one. Not all of them have internal chambers, either. Some of them, like the ones the Aztecs built, were simple platforms for the purpose of being closer to the heavens. They were merely elevated stages on which to perform their sacrificial rituals and the like."

"That's probably what this one is here," Steve said.

"Shall we take a look at the other pyramid?" Santos suggested, looking across the gold road. Everyone said yes right away except for Winslow, who was preoccupied with scratching his neck. He swatted at it a couple of times as if trying to kill a fly that had landed on him, stared at his fingers with a funny look and then wiped them off on his pants. Then he looked up at Steve like nothing was wrong.

"Sure, yeah. Let's go."

#

When they reached the base of the twin pyramid on the other side of the gold road, they walked around its base as they had done with the other one. Again, they found no obvious openings indicating that it offered an interior. It possessed the same hewn stairway cut into the broader steps, so they took those to the top, where once again, they stood on a small rectangular viewing platform.

Facing the direction the gold road went, they could see the second set of twin ziggurats in the distance. Behind those was the stone plaza area, while to the left was a wasteland of dark, soggy dirt, with fewer holes casting light from above. To the right lay the twin pyramid across the road, with more wasteland on the other side of that, also with less light. Above them was the ground pockmarked with spiderweb covered holes.

"Same as the other one," Sal remarked to a muted chorus of monosyllabic agreements.

"What, then, is the point of these things?" Steve stared in the direction of the other two ziggurats.

Winslow slowly shook his head while answering. "All I can think of that makes the slightest bit of sense is that they're marking off an area."

"The light holes are more common in the area marked off by the four pyramids, too," Sal said.

"We should probably check out the other two pyramids," Winslow said, and so they trooped back down the ziggurat on which they stood and continued down the road of gold. Winslow slapped at his neck and his hand came away with a tiny spider. He looked down at the golden ground and saw the line of them not far away. *Bastards are still attracted to me.* But this close to his goal, he wasn't about to let a little bug bite stand in his way.

About halfway to the second set of pyramids, though, and his neck began to itch uncontrollably, so much so that he had to stop walking in order to stand there in one place and concentrate on slapping and scratching it. Only Ruiz noticed it, as the others were up front in an animated discussion about conspiracy theories involving UFOs building ancient pyramids. Winslow slapped at his neck a few times, looked at the palm of his hand and saw seven or eight of the tiny little spiders smeared into the green stuff stuck to his hand. He looked down again at the ground, trying to see if they were climbing up his feet and legs even now, but he saw only an orderly, thick line of them on their left side, travelling toward the second set of ziggurats.

"Are you okay?" The simple question from Ruiz stunned Winslow. *Am I? Gee, I don't know...a bunch of spiders just crawled out of my neck...*

But he couldn't bring himself to say that, even though he believed it to be true. That bite he'd sustained earlier, he realized...that weird spider, the one the guides said was very bad luck...It must have laid eggs in him and now they were hatching, that was the only thing that made sense, unless they were dropping in on him from the air, but only onto that part of his neck, and no one else was affected? His neck twitched again and again he swiped at it. This time he could feel the grit of tiny spider bodies sticking to his palm. He stared at it and saw fifteen, perhaps twenty of them. *Oh Jesus...*he told himself to calm down. He'd seen his fair share of gruesome infections in the Amazon from drinking tainted water before—Malaria, Trypanosomiasis, the protozoan infection, Dengue fever-but this...this was so very unsettling.

"*Senhor*, are you all right?" Ruiz persisted.

"I...yes, these spiders seem to like bothering me, but I'm fine, thank you. I'll be all right."

The *polícia* eyed him dubiously but said, "Shall we catch up with the others?"

"Yes, yes, let's go."

They caught up with the rest of the group, where a conversation was already ongoing about how valuable the finds they had already made were—the gold road, the ziggurats—even with no additional treasure, Sal was saying, the worth was "damn near incalculable." At this, Winslow caught Steve's two guides exchange knowing glances. He was about to ask them what they thought when he felt the tickle start in his neck again. He slapped at it and his gooey green palm collected more smashed spiders.

"Hunter, let me take a look at that neck," Sal said, watching him slap at it.

"No, I'm okay, really. Let's press on for now. I'll take a look at it when we make camp."

Sal shot him a dubious look. "You sure you're okay?"

"I'm fine until tonight, sure."

"If you say so. But speak up if you want me to take another look at it," Sal said, before turning away and walking toward the new pyramids.

Winslow said thanks but no thanks again and then they resumed their hike to the pyramids.

Again, they repeated the process of circling the base and climbing the cutaway steps to the top, where there was a viewing platform and nothing more. After doing this on the second pyramid, they stood on the platform at its apex and surveyed the view.

Winslow's blood was pumping pretty good after all the exercise, and he now had a steady flow of greenish ick coursing down the left side of his body from his neck. It was flecked with black, the bodies of tiny spiders that issued from the wound. The worsening progression and free-flowing nature of the wound was disturbing the others to the point that it could no longer be ignored.

Sal waved an arm at the bleak and desolate landscape in front of them, the unknown territory into which they had not yet ventured. The gold road stopped at the second set of pyramids.

"This place is like an abandoned mining town or something. Yeah, the road is gold, yeah it's got pyramids and stone houses, but okay. We've seen it, we've documented it, we know where it is. Hunter, you've got to get serious medical attention for that bite. It's obviously become infected."

At this, Santos took on a serious expression and turned to face Winslow. "He is right. We have marked this site—above the ground— with GPS, and so we can return later to explore it more fully if we wish. As it is, you will go down in history as one of the explorers who discovered it. Why don't you accompany my partner and I back to Araçatuba, where you can get looked at?"

Winslow took on the expression of a child who was being asked to leave early from Disney World. "But, I'm here! There could be so much more to find out. So much more to—"

"Coming down, look out!" Sal's voice interrupted Winslow. They all turned to see him pointing up at one of the holes in the ground far above. Dangling below it from a single silken rope was one of the gigantic spiders, and this one was not hanging in place as the other one they had seen but descending fast on a course that would put it right on top of their pyramid.

Sal and Santos were the first two to act. Both of them drew their machetes. Ruiz was next to do the same, and then Steve. Winslow was too sick to do anything except stare up at the incoming arachnid and rely on the others for defense.

The giant spider continued its rapid descent without slowing. It dropped down onto the pyramid top like a living bomb, legs splayed wide except for one that was wrapped around the rope. Three machete blades were thrust upward to greet it. Sal swung first, connecting with the lower part of one leg, chopping it off. That wasn't enough resistance to slow his machete, however, and the sizable blade, which he had spent many an hour sharpening around a campfire, continued its arc under momentum that he could not stop in time before it lanced into his own right kneecap. It wedged there tightly, like a swung axe into a tree trunk. Sal went down instantly, shrieking in agony as the spider landed on all of them at once.

The blades of Steve and Santos hit each other with a clang reminiscent of a pirate sword fight, serving only glancing blows to the stout arachnid. The spider opened its mouth and gnashed its various oral appendages, pincers and the like as it searched for a meal.

Winslow and Sal were lowest on the deck, leaving Steve and the two *policía* to take the brunt of the eight-legged attacker's assault. All eight of its legs, even the severed one, flailed about with surprising strength. One of them lashed Steve in the face, knocking his headlamp away and giving him a gusher of a bloody nose. To his credit, he continued to battle the beast, bringing his machete around and swinging it again, this time connecting with the spider's abdomen in a piercing blow.

More of the now familiar greenish-hued blood or fluid or whatever it was issued from the gaping tear in its body, drenching Steve's pants and coating the stone floor of the viewing platform with the sticky, viscous liquid. The creature went ballistic, jumping around on the small platform like one who had stepped on something sharp, jerking its body up, landing back down on the humans and their blades, then spasmodically leaping into the air again.

Steve tried to duplicate the success of his last slice, but this time was not as lucky. As he swung the long blade, going for a thorax kill-shot, one of the spider's legs knocked it out of his hand, sending it clattering down the side of the ziggurat. He tried to retrieve it, but it was lost in the tangle of thrashing bodies.

Santos and Ruiz were left to tangle with the mega-spider. Santos shouted instructions in Portuguese, telling his partner to move left, to watch out—he had a clear shot—and then Santos thrust his machete straight into the face of the arachnid. The metal pierced through the head's exoskeleton into the bundle of nerves that served as the being's brain, and it was down, collapsed in a heap on top of Winslow and Steve.

"Get it off me!" Winslow bellowed. From a sitting position, Sal kicked out both of his legs and toppled the spider off of the two men.

Then the two *policia* joined in kicking it, and they toppled it over the edge of the platform. It tumbled down the pyramid steps, exploding in a mess of goop on the way down.

"Everybody okay?" Santos asked. He helped Steve to his feet while Sal got up on his own. Ruiz assisted Winslow, who was looking the worse for wear out of everyone. He lay contorted in a puddle of spider blood, that from the mega-crawler indistinguishable from what poured out of his own neck. A small army of normal-sized spiders now clung to his body from head to toe.

Ruiz scrunched up his face in consternation as he tried to make sense of the sloppy sight. He glanced around at the others, and at the platform itself, but by far the highest concentration of spiders was on Winslow's body. In fact, he was damned if they didn't somehow seem to be *coming out of* Winslow himself. The majority of the spiders were pasted to Winslow's skin and clothes in a quagmire of gummy blood, but those that did manage to get off of him were assembling into a line that now began to trail across the platform, over the side and down the ziggurat.

It was a thin, fragile line, and yet they moved with the same sense of purpose as the beefier congregations that had been with them for days now.

CHAPTER THIRTY

Santos and his associate huddled together in a corner of the pyramid platform in hushed conference while Sal and Steve did their best to tend to Winslow. That particular task was going to be anything but easy, it was plain to see.

In addition to the fact that his neck wound was now an open rift that oozed a continuous, slow-moving stream of green fluid merged with the black flecks of spider bodies, his mental condition had deteriorated accordingly. He bawled openly, lamenting the fact that he had finally discovered the Lost City of Z only to become incapacitated before being able to revel in and benefit from its discovery.

"Stay focused, Dr. Winslow," Sal told him. "Your health should be your main concern now. That spider bite has become infected, possibly the spider that bit you back before we got to Dead Horse Camp, it could have laid eggs in your body and they are now hatching out. I'm not sure, but we've got to evacuate you out of here now and get you to a proper hospital before your body goes into septic shock."

"But we have so much left to explore," Winslow whined. "We haven't seen hardly anything yet, I just know it."

Santos turned away from Ruiz and faced the stricken historian. "Actually, Dr. Winslow, I don't think there is much more to see here. Four pyramids, the gold road, the stone plazas and the stone huts. Outside of that appears to be nothing but undeveloped ground, so I don't know what else you're expecting to find down here, but I think it's safe to say that we have found the Lost City of Z. And now, in the interests of your longevity, it is time for you to seek professional medical treatment."

Winslow stared up at him, his face a mixture of confusion and regret. "Okay, well why don't we get back down off this pyramid and I'll see how I feel."

Santos shrugged. "*Can* you even get down off this pyramid without being carried?"

"Good question. Let's see." Winslow braced his hand against the deck to push himself up but slipped in the spider blood. Steve moved to him and held out an arm to grab, but it soon became apparent that Winslow wasn't the only one having physical problems.

"I might need a little help, too." Sal looked up from his sitting position on the floor, still clenching his sliced kneecap. Santos moved to him, noting the spreading pool of red blood beneath his leg, but having the discipline not to let his concern show on his face.

He bent down closer to Sal and said, "Move your hands please. I need to get a look at your injury."

"It's okay, just give me a hand." Sal reached up a hand, but Santos didn't take it. "Please, Mr. Torres, let me have a look so that we know what we are dealing with."

Reluctantly, Sal took his hand away from his knee. Santos swallowed to contain his revulsion, but Steve was the one who let out an exclamation of horror. The knee cap was split wide open, severed yellow ligaments falling outside the skin. Sal refused to look at it.

"How bad is it?" he asked.

Santos shook his head. "Bad. It will not support any weight. It's also susceptible to infection."

He moved over to Ruiz again, gently cajoling him to the farthest open corner of the platform, where they conversed again in hushed, conspiratorial tones. Meanwhile, Steve managed to help Winslow to his feet. He let him steady himself and then stepped back to see if he could stand on his own. He did, so he then turned his attention to Sal.

The jungle guide was now staring at his ruined kneecap, in a traumatic daze. "Don't leave me here! Okay? Just don't leave me here. I won't be able to fend off those things alone." He raised his head to look up at the faint light streaming down from the holes in the ground far above.

Steve stepped away from Winslow, who was steady enough on his feet without assistance. "Relax, nobody's getting left behind. We're all walking out of here together. I don't exactly know how yet, but we're going to find a way." He looked over at the two *policía*, still engaged in quiet talk. "Isn't that right?"

They continued their conversation.

"I said, *isn't that right?*" Steve repeated, louder this time.

Santos stepped over to them. "I think we are all in agreement that it is time for all of us to leave the jungle, yes?"

There were no disagreements, so Santos went on.

"We will have to take turns carrying Mr. Torres up to ground level. From there, I will place a sat-phone call to my pilot who will return to evacuate us by helicopter."

"Can you place the call now, so that he's ready by the time we get up there?" Winslow asked, one hand on his horrendous neck wound.

Santos held his hands up in a gesture of surrender. "I would do that if I could, but there is no reception here underground. Like GPS, it needs a clear line of sight to the sky."

Santos's associate dropped his pack and knelt down to unzip it. "The first thing is, we've got to do what we can for that knee," he said, pulling out a first aid kit. "We can wrap it to hopefully prevent it from becoming infected, and we have some pain killers," he said, looking over at Sal, who nodded.

He sterilized a roll of gauze with antibiotic and wrapped the knee so that it was no longer an open wound. Then he handed Sal a couple of pills along with some water and told him to take them, which he did.

"When we get down to the ground," Santos said, "we will need to fashion a brace out of tree branches, but the first step is to get him down off the pyramid."

Winslow slapped at his neck a couple of times while looking at Sal.

"Dr. Winslow, do you think you can climb down on your own?" Steve asked. "Because that way the three of us could carry Sal."

A small spider crawled across the historian's face as he answered. "I don't see why not. I'll just follow my little friends here down this way." He pointed down to the trail of spiders leaving his body and walking over the side of the pyramid.

"Are you sure you're okay?" Steve asked. "We could make two trips if we have to…"

"I can do it if I take it slow. I better get started." He put one leg over the edge of the platform and onto the first step leading down.

Steve leaned over to Ruiz and asked him if there was anything more that could be done for him. "He's already been given antibiotics. He seems to be in good enough spirits, though it may be due to going into shock. We really need to get him to a hospital, so if he can move on his own, that will speed things up."

They agreed to let Winslow proceed on his own after the trail of small spiders, while Steve and the two *policía* set about carrying Sal off the pyramid. Santos knelt next to Sal's head.

"My friend, you are going to feel some pain whenever your right leg moves. We will do our best to keep it still, but without a splint, it is inevitable that it will move some. You just need to bear with us until we get you down to the ground and we can work out a splint, all right?"

Sal gritted his teeth and nodded as Steve and Santos's partner also moved into position.

"On three," Santos said, and began the short countdown.

Santos had Sal by the shoulders and upper body, while his partner supported the left leg, and Steve had the unpleasant task of holding the right leg. He did his best to stabilize it, but Sal's piercing wail as they lifted told him that he wasn't able to do that entirely.

"Sorry, Sal, but we've got to get you down. Bear with me..." Steve said these kinds of things while they eased over to the steps and began their way down. Although they tried to minimize the shocks, with each step there was a jolt to his body and he let loose with another anguished moan. Santos tried to keep their spirits up.

"It's working," he kept saying. "Keep going."

Step by agonizing step, they carried Sal down the ziggurat. The going was precarious, and Santos was the first to lose his footing. He cried out in pain as his ankle bent at an unnatural angle, righting it just before doing serious damage that would have rendered him unable to walk as well. The move jolted Sal, who wailed in agony with the movement of his torn open kneecap. But they kept on with their descent until Steve's footing slipped, and he went down hard on both knees on the edge of a stone step. He lost his grip on Sal, which threw Santos and Ruiz off balance as well. Due to the incline and the fact that Steve had been supporting the lower leg—the one with the severed kneecap— gravity pulled Sal's body down and the two *policia* were unable to hold him.

Sal tumbled down ten or twelve steps, his wrapped kneecap banging squarely into them at least a couple of times, before he somehow managed to come to rest without sliding all the way down. Steve and Santos hopped down to him, noting the frozen grimace on his now unconscious face.

"He's out cold," Santos pronounced. He picked up a wrist and felt for a pulse. He nodded after a few seconds. "He is alive."

They heard Winslow's voice from out of sight down below. "You guys okay?"

Steve frowned at Santos before answering. "Give us a minute, Hunter. Dealing with something but we'll be okay."

They both bent back down to Sal's body to pick him back up, when Winslow's voice drifted back up to them again.

"I feel weird."

Steve rolled his eyes. "That's because you *are* weird, Hunter. What's up?"

"I feel lighter. More and more of them keep coming out."

Santos cupped a hand around his mouth and yelled down to him. "Sit down, take a rest. We'll be down soon."

Steve looked both *policía* in the eye when he turned back around, taking advantage of the fact that they were alone now. "So are you happy so far? I mean, I'm helping, right? We even found the city. I'm off the hook after this, right?"

The two *policía* exchanged a very brief glance that betrayed no information to Steve, and then Santos answered. "Your continued cooperation is very much appreciated, and you can be assured that it will be taken into consideration when this case is brought to justice."

Steve's mouth fell open. "*Taken into consideration*? I'm risking my life in some underground jungle hell with gigantic spiders!"

Santos fixed him a stern look. "We are not out of this yet, Mr. Hoch. After we return to Rio de Janeiro, the events that transpired will be taken into consideration. We know you are cooperating and it is working in your favor. That is all I can say at the moment."

"We still have a lot to do to get out of here safely," Ruiz added. "I suggest we get back to it. As you can see," he said, looking down at the comatose Sal, "Jail is not the only fate to be wary of."

Point taken, Steve nodded and assumed the position on Sal's damaged leg, noting that at least he was not crying out with every slight movement. They lifted him and stepped down the pyramid, proceeding slower this time to avoid a repeat mishap. About three-quarters of the way to the bottom, Winslow called out again from out of sight around another side of the ziggurat.

"Spider! Another big one, on the ground coming at us!"

On the pyramid, they set the still unconscious Sal down and looked down at the ground. At the base of the pyramid they saw nothing, but then Steve pointed farther away into the distance, into the dim murk of the undeveloped land. One of the massive spiders, even larger than the other two they'd seen, lumbered toward the ziggurat.

Sal was confused as Santos smiled.

"What are you so happy about?"

"This time, I've got enough time to be ready for it." He shrugged off his pack and removed from it a pistol in case. He took it from the case, checked its action, then cocked the hammer. Out of the corner of his eye, Steve saw Santos's partner watching him closely while Santos aimed the firearm at the approaching mega-spider.

It was not at all lost on Steve that the cops had not come out here unarmed. They were here to make an arrest after all. Or were they? They could have done it already…But his thoughts were blasted away by the report of the pistol. The spider kept moving after it was hit, a green spray of blood gushing out of an eye. But then it stopped its forward motion and stood in place, bobbing its head up and down.

Santos took the opportunity of having a stationary target to smash three more lead projectiles into the primitive assailant, all into the head and thorax area. Surprisingly, the arachnid charged toward them again, but right before it reached the base of the pyramid it collapsed in a tangled heap of hairy legs.

Steve let out a whooping holler of triumph, and then they heard Winslow join in from somewhere below. "Nice shootin', Tex," the historian shouted up to them. "I didn't even know you were packing heat!"

"Thanks," Santos yelled back before holstering his pistol and attaching it to his belt, rather than putting it back in his pack. "Let's get off this pyramid."

Sal was again carried by Steve and the two *policia,* and this time they were able to make it all the way to the base of the mystery structure without further mishaps. They set Sal down on the ground there, taking a breather. Steve called over to Winslow, who still remained out of sight around the other side of the pyramid, "Hunter, where you at?"

Silence. Steve called his name again. When he received no response that time either, he stood and told Santos and Ruiz that he would check on him. He was injured, too, after all.

He walked to the nearest corner of the ziggurat and around it to the other side. There was Dr. Winslow, standing there staring down at the ground.

"Hunter, hey, you all right?"

His reply was wordless; he pointed to the ground near his feet. "Watch them go."

"Watch who go?"

"The spiders. Watch them. They're going somewhere after they come out of me."

Steve stopped walking and observed Winslow more carefully. Was he going crazy? Had the stress of not only the expedition itself, but of being on the run finally gotten to him? *And to think he didn't even know that my "guides" are policia here to make an arrest,* Steve thought. And then he stared at the historian some more. *Or did he?* Could he have eavesdropped on them while they were talking in their tent or something like that?

After he had determined that Winslow wasn't an immediate threat to anyone, he followed his pointing finger and stared at the ground himself. A line of spiders moved along the dirt, like he'd seen before, trundling off as if they had some important purpose. But the difference here was in where they were coming from. He followed the line of arachnids with his gaze, back to....

Back to Winslow's neck.

He wasn't kidding, Steve thought. So many spiders now poured from Winslow's body that a good portion of his entire person was obscured by them. Steve had no idea how many eggs spiders hatch or how many spiders hatch from a single egg, what that life cycle was like, but it seemed to him that a ridiculous number of spiders was coming from Winslow's body, like they had turned him into a human incubator for their own species.

And they did seem to be going somewhere, Steve could see. They didn't meander off in random directions, but instead formed a tight line that was growing thicker by the minute and scurried off away from the ziggurat.

Sal's screaming took his attention away from the spiders. He ran back to Santos and his partner, who now held the conscious Sal between them. Santos fixed Steve with a no-nonsense stare.

"We need to get back above ground. Right now."

"I need something for the pain," Sal stammered, eyes glazed, muscles in his face slack. Ruiz rooted around in his pack for the first aid kit.

"You won't get any arguments from me." Steve pointed back to Winslow. "He's in bad, shape, too."

"Get him to come over here. The tunnel to get back up is this way." Santos pointed to their right, away from Winslow.

"Be right back." Steve jogged off back to Winslow to tell him they were leaving. "Hey Hunter," he said, rounding the corner of the pyramid. "Come on, they've got Sal awake and on his feet, and we're going to head back to the tunnel to get above ground now. So let's—"

He froze both in mid-sentence and in place as he looked around. He was positive this was where he had just spoken to Winslow.

But Winslow was not here.

Looking closely at the ground, he saw only a thick trail of spiders heading off into the woods.

CHAPTER THIRTY-ONE

"Hunter!" Steve yelled into the woods in the direction of the spiders. "Hunter, where are you?"

"He's probably taking a dump," came the reply from Sal.

"Find him," Santos's voice came from around the pyramid. "We need to get going."

Steve paused for just a moment and then said, "Maybe you should start toward the tunnel, and I'll find Dr. Winslow and catch up with you. We won't be as slow as you since Hunter can still walk."

A silence ensued. Steve knew the *policía* were considering the ramifications of allowing their suspects—both of them—to walk away unsupervised.

"One of us will stay here with Sal, and one of us will go with you. It is important that we do not get separated." Santos was resolute.

Steve smiled to himself. *Yep, not going to let us out of your sight.* "Okay, I'm going to look for him now. Radio channel 17 if we get separated too long."

"Copy that," Santos returned.

Steve set off away from Santos and Sal in search of Winslow. Not knowing what else to do, he followed the trail of spiders. Winslow couldn't have gone all that far by now, so he wasn't too worried. He kept after the arachnids easily enough until they snaked off into the dark, unpaved part of the landscape, where uneven mounds of dirt were dotted with scrubby ferns and mosses. Here he had to slow down in order to find the trail of spiders, but they were still a solid line. He would move after them a few yards before losing sight of them behind clumps of tangled foliage before picking up the trial again a few yards further on.

The next time he lost sight of the spiders he called out for Winslow and was surprised to hear a response. "Over here!"

He turned in the direction of the voice and vaulted over a mound of rocks before trotting through a waist-high sea of ferns. When he emerged in a muddy clearing, there was Winslow, standing there almost completely covered in spiders, but pointing up at a tree that somehow managed to grow rooted into the ground in this almost lightless place.

Looking at the tree, Steve could see that it was long dead. It had no bark, no leaves, although its trunk and branches were still intact. The spiders scurried up the tree, which passed through one of the openings in the ground far above. Unlike the other openings, however, this one had no light penetrating through it whatsoever. If it weren't for Steve's flashlight, he wouldn't be able to see that it was an opening at all. And yet the tree passed right through it. There must have been light for this tree to grow at one time, Sal reasoned. He was ripped from his thoughts by the sound of Winslow's voice, which now sounded higher and thinner than usual.

"They're telling us to go this way." He pointed up into the tree.

"Hunter, listen. That's interesting, it really is. But the guides want to get back topside right now. Sal's in a really bad way with his leg, and, honestly…" He paused to gaze in wonder at Winslow's arachnid covered body, almost completely obscured now with spiders except for his face. "And frankly. Dr. Winslow, you're not looking much better. Doesn't it bother you having all those spiders on you? Coming *out of* you?"

Winslow shrugged, a jerky little movement that knocked a clump of spiders off his shoulder, only to assimilate with the herd of them lower down on his body. "Not really. They're helping me!"

Steve was worried that Winslow had suffered some kind of brain infection. "How are they helping you, Hunter? We really need to get you to a hospital."

"They're showing us the way. Look: we can get up above ground right here, without going all the way back to the other trees where we came down from."

Steve stared up at the top of the tree again, where it passed through the opening in the ground above. "But it's dark up there."

"Could just mean it's getting dark outside. What time is it?"

Steve shook his head. "It's late afternoon, but that's not it. There's still light streaming down from the other holes back there." To confirm his own statement, he turned around and looked at them. Yes, circular shafts of light, still there. And then his radio crackled with Santos's voice, brimming over with irritation.

"Steve, where are you? Do you copy?"

Steve unclipped the walkie-talkie from his belt and brought it to his mouth. "I copy. I found Dr. Winslow."

"Good. How long before you get back here. We've run out of painkillers for Sal."

Steve could hear the jungle guide caterwauling in the background during Santos's transmission. He pushed the talk button, but it was Winslow who spoke, shouting in the direction of the radio. "Tell him I found another way up right here that's much closer than going back. Tell him!"

Steve sighed while Santos came back with, "What did he say?"

Steve depressed the transmitter again. "He thinks we should climb this tree that he found—that the spiders are crawling up—that goes above ground, because it's a lot closer than going all the way back the way we came, over."

Brief pause, and then, "What do you think?"

"It's dark up there is the only thing. There is a hole that leads above ground, like the others, but there's no light coming through like with the others."

"How easy is it to climb? We have to drag Sal up with us, remember."

Steve studied the branches for a few moments. "We'd still have to get him up the other tree, too, but not as high. With this one, we could rig a harness for him out of the climbing ropes. The rest of us could climb it without ropes, it doesn't look like a difficult climb."

Then he turned away from the historian and spoke in a lower voice into the radio's mic. "I'm worried about Dr. Winslow. I think he might be losing his mind, succumbing to shock from his injuries, maybe even a brain infection. I'm surprised he's still in as good physical shape as he is. Not sure how much longer that's going to last, over."

"I feel great with my new spider friends," Winslow said before Steve let go of the transmit button, his voice high-pitched and cheery.

"You hear that?"

"Yes," Santos returned. "Medical attention is a priority for more than one of our party. All right, we will come to you, hoping that a shorter route to get above ground, even though it is dark up there, proves to be the right decision. Can you guide us?"

Steve gave him directions to the best of his ability and told Santos he'd started rigging a harness for Sal out of his climbing gear. Fifteen minutes later, Steve had a rope rigged through the lower branches of the tree and was hooked to the harness.

"I'll go first," he said, as Santos and Ruiz staggered into camp holding the whimpering Sal. They set down the maimed man and studied the tree, and then Winslow, still covered in moving spiders.

"These spiders," Ruiz said, staring wide-eyed at Winslow, "they come out of your body and then run in formation up this tree?"

Winslow nodded, a gleeful expression on his face. "My spirit animals!"

"He's lost his fucking mind!" Sal wailed, without looking up.

"Oh no, I've found a higher consciousness!" Winslow declared. "These spiders are leading us to somewhere important. We must follow them."

"How come their bigger brothers try to kill us?" Steve queried. "Did they tell you that?"

Winslow was silent as the sea of arachnids washed down his body like a wave.

Santos nodded to Steve and his climbing apparatus. "Let's get on with it."

Steve stepped up to the tree and started to climb with the aid of the ropes and harness. The going was not difficult for a single, able-bodied man and inside of a minute he was about halfway up. "I'll see what's up there, make sure it goes somewhere we can get out from."

Santos responded over the walkie-talkie, signifying his agreement, and Steve responded by clicking the transmitter button two times. He ascended higher into the darkened upper reaches of the tree, moving at a deliberate yet careful pace. He knew their team could not afford any more serious injuries, and so that sense of caution tempered his every move. As he neared the top of the tree, where it passed through the opening in the ground above, he saw that there was weak light filtering down.

Where the tree passed through the ground opening, there was little space on the sides, but the trunk bifurcated into two large branches, making it possible to slip in between the two and to move up between them by placing a foot on each one. Steve poked his head up through the opening and quickly ducked back down again, as if seeing something he wasn't supposed to see.

Excited, he brought the radio to his lips and pressed the transmitter. "You're not going to believe this!"

CHAPTER THIRTY-TWO

"Does it look like it offers a way out?" Santos was to the point over the radio.

In the tree, Steve pondered the question. "I…I can't really say just yet. But this is incredible."

The exasperation in Santos's tone was evident. "What is incredible? We are in dire need of medical attention here. We found what we came to find and now it is time –"

"Oh, *now* we have!" Winslow's excited voice drifted up from below. "*Now* we've found it! That stuff down there? That's nothing. It must be some kind of underworld, some kind of offering…oh my God, I think I get it now!"

"Are there some meds you can give him?" Steve intoned softly into the radio.

"Negative," came Santos's reply through the speaker. "Sal's far worse off. We used everything we had on him."

"It's okay. He might just have a point," Steve said, trailing off as he stared up into a new world.

"Mr. Hoch, I ask you again: does it look like we can get out from up there? Over."

"It's a forested area that appears to be…inside a hollowed-out mountain, would be my best guess. Some type of enclosed natural area. But this is definitely the Lost City of Z. The real city. There is daylight here, but it's filtered through a heavy forest canopy and lots of cobwebs. I guess you two could take Sal back the way we came in and Dr. Winslow and I could check this out and meet you back at our last camp?"

Santos pressed the transmit button and Steve heard Winslow's voice through the radio. "We should all just follow the spiders." Then Santos said, "We will go with you, but we would like you to come back down first and assist us with getting Sal up the tree."

"Copy that." Reluctantly, with a last glance at the strange, alluring world through the opening, Steve descended the tree until his feet hit the ground in between the *poliicia*, Sal and Winslow.

Steve rigged a special harness for Sal so that he could be lifted up the tree and then he, Santos and his partner began the ascent with only Sal in the actual web harness, while the rest of them utilized crude rope harnesses created with carefully arranged knots.

"What about me?" Winslow said. His entire body was covered in spiders. His speech was slurred now, more difficult to understand. "I guess I can climb without ropes. The spiders will show me how, maybe even carry me."

"Just wait until we get Sal to the top," Santos said. "Then we'll come back down for you. Okay?"

"Sounds terrific!" Winslow gushed. Steve glanced at him and almost vomited, so revolting a sight did he make with his horrendous, gangrenous neck wound, or whatever it was, hatching out a river of spiders that all proceeded to run in the same direction; the same direction in which the humans wanted to go, no less. He was eager to get away from Winslow, so he started up the tree again, spurring Santos and his associate into action.

The arboreal ascent with Sal's broken body proved to be much more taxing than getting him down the pyramid, although it was easier on Sal himself, a low impact affair, since they managed to avoid banging his knee into any branches. Steve was in the lead position, and so was the first to step from the tree onto the new land. Head on a swivel, he checked his immediate surroundings for threats, but saw none. He hauled Sal up out of the tree and untied his harness from the climbing ropes.

The two undercover *policía* stepped up onto the firm ground with wonder in their eyes, for they, too, could now see that they had truly found the lost city.

"You guys stay here with Sal. I'll go back down for Dr. Winslow." Santos nodded absentmindedly without taking his eyes off the view while Steve descended the tree again. On the ground, he found Winslow on his feet, covered in a thick menagerie of spiders from head to toe, staring up at the tree, where the line of spiders ascending also grew heavier.

"Hunter, step into this harness, and you'll be able to pull yourself right up the tree." Steve tossed him the climbing rig, not wanting to get close to the mess of spiders. He had no idea what was happening to the man, but it was beyond his understanding or experience and wanted only to return to civilization at this point, lost city of treasures or not. The entire experience was affecting his psyche.

"No problem! Lost City of Z, here I come!" Somehow Winslow stepped into the harness and began climbing the tree, great masses of arachnids cleaving off his body when the rope would pass through them. Steve stood far back from the tree to avoid the avalanche of falling spiders that rained down from Winslow as he made his way up the tree. The spiders from his body merged with the stream flowing up the tree into one massive river of arachnids, and Steve found that he could actually see Winslow's body for the first time in a long while.

The sight did not inspire confidence. He told himself that he couldn't be sure from down here on the ground at this distance, that maybe he was seeing things. Yet it appeared that the historian's clothing had been eaten away by the spiders, exposing the flesh underneath— which was a gangrenous green, discolored mass of mottled, oozing sores. Zombie-like, was the best description Steve could come up with in his shocked brain. He didn't see how the man's body could still function normally, but Winslow kept pumping his legs against the tree trunk and using his arms to pull himself up the branches. Still, Steve pondered, it didn't take a medical doctor to know that something was very wrong with Winslow's body, and although he seemed all right now, they were in no position to help him should his condition worsen and render him unable to move.

Steve smiled as he watched Winslow haul himself up through the hole, without assistance from the two *policía*, who were no doubt afraid of his odd, spidery condition.

And then it was Steve's turn to climb. "Never mind the harness," he radioed up. It would be riddled with spiders, anyway. He used a single, plain rope to loop over the first branch, and bracing his feet against the trunk was able to "walk" up to it. From there, he proceeded very slowly and carefully without clipping himself into anything, using the branches like a ladder to ascend the tree to the hole in the ground where the rest of the team waited.

He jumped off the tree onto the ground, noting that the tree itself continued up for another fifty feet or so, dwarfed by many other trees around it since it started from sub-ground level. The forest was thick here, but that wasn't the only reason the light was so dim. Looking around and up, it was evident that they were contained within a kind of natural amphitheater, trapped within a steep bowl formed by tree-covered mountains. Running water could be heard but not seen nearby.

But it was the gleaming spires of gold that truly arrested his attention. Jutting up amongst the canopy trees, they were partially covered in creeping vines, but enough of the dully gleaming metal shone through the plant life to make their construction unmistakable. *The fabled golden towers of the Lost City of Z.*

Before he could take his first step away from the tree, his walkie-talkie crackled on his belt. Santos's voiced hissed through the speaker.

"Get down! Someone's coming!"

CHAPTER THIRTY-THREE

The animals' calls were disorienting to Steve. They seemed to come from everywhere, and yet it also became clear that they weren't animals. Steve had heard the vocalizations of native tribespeople before, and while these particular sounds were new to him, he recognized them as human. And although he didn't understand the language, it didn't sound all that friendly. Worse, they were spread out all over, surrounding Steve, and he supposed the rest of his team, too, even though he couldn't see them.

He whispered into his walkie-talkie. "Where you at? I'm at the entrance."

Santos's shaky voice came back through the radio. "We are about a hundred feet straight in from the entrance."

"What's making that noise? Animals, or—"

"No, not animals. Tribesmen. They're—" Santos cut off abruptly with a grunt. A few seconds later Steve heard something unintelligible, followed by clatter of the radio being roughly handled, and then: "Try and help us if you—"

A gunshot echoed throughout the semi-enclosed space and then all was silent.

"Gabriel? Gabriel?"

No reply came. Steve heard the rustle of foliage off to his left and instinctively hunkered down amidst the tall grass surrounding the tree. He glanced around but could not see anyone. Yet he still heard the voices—war cries, they sounded like. Little percussive whoops alternating with guttural growls, coming from both near and farther afield. If they were a native tribe, they would know where the entrance from below was to this place, so Steve decided to move out. He set off at a low, ambling crouch, straight ahead away from the tree that had brought him here.

Where there were clumps of ferns and spiky palm trees, he moved through those for the cover they afforded. In the open spaces, he dropped to his belly and low-crawled, even though he imagined a war club crushing his skull from above at any moment. A thin black snake slithered under his belly as he crawled, passing beneath him without striking. He continued on, the strange tribal yells still emanating from around the bush. Raising his head to glance ahead, he saw the bases of one of the golden spires perhaps fifty feet away.

A cluster of feet were grouped around it. He brought the radio to his lips. "Is that you at the base of the tower?"

The reply was Santos's and it came back immediately in the affirmative. "Yes, we're under attack, they've—"

But no sooner did be begin his sentence than his words were strangled to a close with a breathy gasp, followed by a loud CLACK and then radio silence. All was not quiet, however. Steve could hear the fracas taking place a few yards away. When he heard, "Get him off me!" he got up and ran toward them.

At the base of the tower he found the others—the two "tour guides," Winslow and Sal being accosted by a tribe of nude, body-painted tribal men, all of whom carried a weapon of some sort, weather bow, club or spear. Physically, none of the tribal men were that tall or particularly well-muscled, but there were at least six of them in the fight with more all around. He watched as one of them easily batted Santos's gun out of his hand with a long spear, sending the firearm splashing into a small stream bubbling a few yards away.

Steve cursed himself for not having drawn his machete in advance. He made a move for it now, as a tribesman leapt toward him, mouth open in a menacing war cry. Steve loosed the long blade from its sheath and raised it cross-ways over his head as the tribal man descended on him. Steve had to roll his head to one side to avoid his own blade as his foe's body landed on the weapon, seemingly without care to his own self, knocking it toward Steve.

The dull part of the blade caught the bridge of his nose and he felt the blood flood out over his face as he rolled over into the dirt. The tribal warrior stayed right on top of him, easily flipping the machete from both of them. He somehow wrapped his elbow around Steve's neck in a choke hold that wasn't part of any wrestling program he'd ever seen. His neck was bent sharply upward until he felt a vertebrae crack—not severely, but as if a chiropractor had done it or like cracking a knuckle. Not knowing what would come next, though, he tapped on the ground, hoping the tap-out signal was universal enough to get through to this savage combatant.

It was, but not because his opponent was showing any mercy. Suddenly, he saw four bare feet stomp up next to him, and a moment later, knees bending and then tribal, painted faces eyeing him sideways on the ground. Tusks of some sort pierced noses and cheeks. Nearby he heard Sal howling about something he couldn't see. It was hard to hear because the pulse of tribal drums reverberated throughout the area. He suspected Sal was now receiving the same treatment.

Steve felt something rough wrap around his ankles and realized he was being tied up with vines, backpack still on. He was pulled to his feet by his wrists, and then his arms, too, were bound, in front of him. The man he had wrestled with stared him in the eyes for a moment and then grunted while pointing up at the golden spire that towered above them. Steve glanced up at it but didn't see anything special about it, other than it was a golden spire. He looked to the tribal man, hoping to convey an "I don't get it" expression, but the warrior had his attention focused on Sal.

The scuffle still played out around them, with Santos and Ruiz providing some resistance, but soon even they were overcome by the tribal forces that seriously outnumbered them. Recognizing they would be beaten to death if they did not surrender, Santos told Ruiz to stand down.

"What do you want?" Santos spat in Portuguese, and then Spanish. But if any of the words were understood, the tribal men gave no indication. They ignored the captives completely as they were bound with vines as Steve had been. With one exception: Winslow. Although clearly he was not permitted to leave, he was not bound as the others were. At first Steve imagined it was because the natives were afraid of his spider-filled condition, and yet, as Santos, Ruiz and Sal were led off bound hand and foot, Winslow was chair-carried by four tribesmen as if he were the coach of a football team who had just won the Rose Bowl. Steve, although bound, was not led anywhere.

"What's happening?" Steve asked in three languages. His answer was given not in words, but in action. Trussed like a pig with his pack still on, three men hoisted him and easily began to climb the tower with him, which, as far as Steve could tell, somehow appeared to be constructed entirely out of gold. The tribal men ascended this golden ladder while Steve remained helplessly bound. He stopped yelling about halfway up, resigning himself to his fate. He tried to think of why they hadn't just killed him already. He supposed they were going to throw him off the top in some kind of tribal sacrifice.

And what of the others? Looking down at the ground, he could see the other parties had reached the bases of the other golden spires and had begun to climb those as well, also with trussed captives. And then, craning his neck to look in a completely different direction, he found Winslow, still being chair-carried. His procession had reached the base of a dirt trail that sloped upward to what looked like a cavern of some sort, its entrance partially obscured by hanging vines. He saw no golden towers that way so wasn't sure what they were doing with the historian.

He was sure what they were doing with him, however. Reaching the top of the spire, he saw there was a simple but stout wooden platform beneath a golden framework of cables that formed a steeple of sorts, like a tent over a hunter's tree blind. Any hopes Steve had of being untied upon reaching this lofty perch were quickly dashed as his captors not only left him tied, but in fact lashed him in place, in a standing position, to the framework of spires. He could now only stand in place looking out on the natural amphitheater where his fate would play out.

The tribal men knelt around him and performed some kind of ceremony, lighting a cluster of leaves by rubbing two sticks together. For a moment he thought maybe this place was to be his funeral pyre, but they left the burning material on a flat rock rather than on the wood platform itself. *Well that's not it*, he thought. *Maybe they just want to keep the bugs away*...But his attempts at self-humor were short-lived, for his captors then filed back down the spire, the last one of them grunting something unintelligible at him before disappearing down the outside of the spire.

"Why are you leaving me here?" Steve bellowed. To his surprise, he received an answer, though not from one of the tribal people.

"I think it's a sacrifice!" Santos's voice echoed at a height equivalent to Steve's own. The lab tech glanced off to his right and saw a silhouetted figure standing there against the side of another one of the golden spires. No doubt Santos was tied in place, too. Looking down from the undercover *policia*, Steve could see three men scaling down the tower. No doubt the same scene was playing out on other spires with Sal and Ruiz. He looked about and found one more he could see with his limited mobility. He couldn't tell who was tied there—either Ruiz or Sal—but he'd seen enough to know what was happening. They were being left up here as some kind of sacrifice, possibly to simply perish from starvation, thirst and exposure to the elements, like the fate of a pirate in Colonial times, left to rot in a hanging cage in a public place until he died.

And then, fainter than Santos's voice, but audible just the same, Steve heard Winslow's eerie cackle. He was actually laughing, Steve thought, though he knew the man was probably delusional. But then he started to speak actual words. "I am the spider king! Dr. Hunter Winslow, King of the Spiders! I am the ruler!"

His pitchy, wavering voice echoed out across the natural amphitheater. Steve cringed at the thought of the historian having gone mad. At the same time, he wondered where exactly he had been taken, since he wasn't atop one of the golden spires like the rest of them. He recalled the cavern or cave entrance but couldn't see how it was that he could hear him if he was inside that.

Steve inhaled deeply and turned his head toward Winslow's voice. "Hunter, what did they do with you? Where are you?"

Another off-kilter cackle emanated from somewhere below and behind Steve. Then Winslow said, "They have installed me into my rightful throne, as king of the arachnids!"

"Are you crazy?" It was Santos's turn to yell over to Winslow.

"Hunter, are you free to move or did they tie you up? Are they still with you?"

A pause, and then Winslow's voice tumbled out over the bowl-like space. "They left me alone in peace to rule over my subjects."

"What about us? Can you help us?" Steve shouted, his throat growing sore from shouting so much.

"Yes. You *are* being helped."

Steve breathed a sigh of relief, but then realized he should seek clarification. Winslow wasn't all there, after all. "How are we being helped?"

"You will be delivered to your ultimate peace by the Sacred Ones."

Steve shook his head in disgust as he strained against his bonds. "Shut up, Dr. Winslow! You've lost your mind. You need help. We all need help. How do we get out of here?"

The historian's voice came on a light breeze, faint and warbling. "I will never get out of here. This is my destiny. The rest of you will be delivered unto the next realm."

"When?" Steve wasn't sure what he meant, but he was ready to go just about anywhere rather than here.

Nevertheless, Winslow's response was anything but what he wanted to hear. "I hear them coming. It won't be long now."

Steve was ready to pass this off as delusional nonsense, when his peripheral vision caught movement far down and to his right, where a procession of the monstrously-sized spiders marched into view. He wasn't sure where they had come from—if they were already in the amphitheater and woke up all of a sudden, or if they had come up from underground the same way he had—but it didn't matter. They marched along relentlessly until they were deeper into the amphitheater, closer to the cluster of spires. At that point, they split up, with one each of the monstrosities making a beeline for one of the spires with a sacrificial human tied up top.

Steve strained harder than before at his bonds.

CHAPTER THIRTY-FOUR

Steve yelled at the top of his lungs as the mega-spider drew near. "Dr. Winslow, can you make the spiders stop?"

The reply came, faint yet audible, from the same place as before, wherever that was. "You don't want them to stop. They are here to deliver you to the ultimate realm."

Santos's voice joined the pleas for sanity. "Dr. Winslow, please! If you can do anything to stop them, you must act, or we will all die!"

Winslow's voice warbled out again. "To go against them would be tantamount to sabotaging myself. This is the natural order of things. It might seem scary, but it will all be over in a few minutes and then your place in the universe will be as it should."

"Screw you, Winslow!" This from Sal.

Steve took up their case again in front of Judge Winslow. "It's almost to the base of my tower, Hunter. I'm begging you, please call it off, or climb up here and untie me. Untie any one of us, and we'll handle the rest, okay? Can you—*will* you-please do that?"

"I cannot do that, Steve. We are here for a reason."

"Forget him. Slide the rope against the strut they tied it to, to weaken it," Santos's voice carried across the air between the spires. "We've got to get ourselves out of here."

Resigning himself to this truth, Steve began to work his rope across the tower itself, back and forth in a sawing motion. He couldn't see if it was having any effect, but at the same time he could think of nothing better to try, so he kept at it.

He paused his rope sawing when he felt the tower sway a little as the mega-spider jumped onto the structure. Looking down, Steve could see it, frozen on the side of the lattice-like framework. After a few seconds it began to crawl straight up.

Realizing he had only a couple of minutes before the monster would reach his platform, Steve started to saw even faster than before, straining his arms, shoulders and back to move the rope over the tower strut in the hopes it was fraying his bonds. He couldn't look directly at it to see, so he just had to hope it was having an effect.

Meanwhile, Winslow's weird-sounding voice carried up to his ears yet again. "Welcome them, for they are your friends!"

"Shut the hell up, Winslow!" Steve spat as he frenetically sawed the rope across the strut. Then his upper arm cramped viciously, and he had to stop the motion while he cried out in pain. He looked down, hoping to see the tribal people looking up at him, as if they might change their minds about leaving him up here. But they were nowhere in sight.

"Keep at it, Mr. Hoch," Santos yelled over. "We mustn't give up!"

"Not…giving…up," Steve shouted back. He glanced down at the spider and was shocked to see it had made it nearly halfway up the tower. Its progress was erratic; it would scramble rapidly up ten or twenty feet, then pause to rest for a few seconds, or whatever it did, before scrambling upwards again. Steve tore his gaze away from the approaching horror and went back to sawing the rope.

He felt the tide of hopelessness rising in his soul when suddenly he felt the rope binding his wrists catch on the cable of the tower. He stopped for a second, moved it up an inch and back again…and sure enough—it caught again! It had to mean that he had cut a notch in the rope, that the cutting was working.

Spirits buoyed by this revelation, he doubled down on his efforts to free himself, working the rope even faster over the notched section. He worked some more until he could actually feel that the cut was deeper.

"It's working!" he called over to Santos. "I can feel it cutting the rope!"

"Same here. Keep going!" Santos encouraged. "Your spider is three-quarters of the way up. Don't look at it, just keep cutting!"

Steve managed to turn his head without interrupting his work and glimpsed the spider on Santos's tower. "Yours is about halfway up!" he relayed to him.

"Thanks."

They went back to working in silence while the mega-spiders ascended the golden spires.

"This place has been awaiting my arrival forever!" Winslow bellowed. "It drew me here like a siren, like a moth to a flame."

This time Santos told Winslow to shut up, before calling out more loudly than before. "Listen up, everybody! There is something I want you to know about me and my associate, Filipe."

"If you're gay, save it. I don't care how other people live their lives as long as they leave me out of it," Sal yelled out. None of the levity caused any of them to slow their attempts to release themselves in the slightest.

Steve smiled at hearing Santos actually laugh, despite the grave situation. "No, we're not gay. But both of us are police officers with

Polícia Civil do Estado do Rio de Janeiro. We came here to arrest Dr. Winslow for the theft of a national treasure from the library of Brazil—Manuscript 512-and possibly Mr. Hoch as well, depending on his level of cooperation. Which has been good, I might add."

Steve tensed as he glanced down at the spider while processing Santos's words. He could now make out individual hairs on the arachnid's hideous head. *Funny how matters of the law now seem trivial by comparison to my current predicament*, Steve thought. He yelled over at Santos while hectically sawing at his wrist rope.

"Who cares about that now?"

Santos's reply was immediate enough that it was clear Steve had taken his bait. "Dr. Winslow might care. Hey, Hunter: You led us to a place containing a Brazilian national treasure you intended to exploit for your own personal gain, willfully and with extensive planning and deliberate preparation. It was our intent—that of Filipe and I, to arrest you before returning to Rio de Janeiro for the crime of stealing Manuscript 512 from the National Library."

"You will be delivered!" Winslow's thin voice somehow projected up to them.

"Dr. Winslow, here is my point: if you help us now, I am offering you a one-time deal of amnesty—the country officially absolves you of all charges and you are free to go on about your life how you choose. If you do not help us and we survive, I can assure you that you will spend a very long time in a Brazilian prison."

"I corroborate and affirm his statements," Ruiz shouted.

"What is your response, Dr. Winslow?" Santos pressed.

The warbly, thin voice echoed across the amphitheater. "You have already helped me! I cannot ask for more. My ascension is complete! Thank you!"

"Is that a 'no', Dr. Winslow?" Santos hollered.

Steve felt something bristly brush against one of his elbows as it sawed back and forth on the rope. He looked down without pausing his sawing movements and saw that one of the mega-spider's antenna was brushing against him. He let out an involuntary scream and the creature dropped back a little, freezing in place just below the platform. Steve could feel that the notch in the rope had grown bigger and judging by the thickness of the rope binding his wrists, he knew he had to be close. He was cutting through his rope with renewed vigor while trying to ignore the elephant-sized spider in his midst when Sal's triumphant cry echoed throughout the amphitheater.

"I'm free! I cut the rope! It worked!"

"Help me!" Santos yelled, while both Ruiz and Steve also cried out simultaneously for assistance.

"I'm closest to you!" Santos shouted.

But as Steve could see from his perch, the spider climbing Sal's tower had already reached him. It topped over the platform with eight-legged ease, enveloping the injured Sal like a Bison sitting on a prairie dog. Sal's anguished cry was smothered mid-breath as the arachnid cradled him in a death-embrace. Then, as the rest of them looked on, the mega-spider jumped off the tower with Sal in its clutches, falling all the way to the ground such that Sal was on bottom. The spider bounced off of the amphitheater floor and scuttled away while Sal lay in a pool of blood and crushed, broken bones.

"Sal?" Steven shouted even as he continued to saw away. The spider right below him, whether sensing that its brethren was locked in battle, or else by chance, had still not moved from its last position immediately below the platform. "Sal, say something!"

But no words came from Sal.

"Sal, seriously—say something to let us—" But Steve never got to finish his sentence, for at that moment the spider on his tower climbed up and heaved itself onto the platform. "Help! Somebody do something!" Steve went into a blind panic, but without stopping his attempt to saw through his rope. He thrashed and kicked out at the mega-spider, which had positioned itself opposite the human on the platform but did not yet make a move toward him.

To make matters worse, Steve could hear the battle cries of Santos and Ruiz on their respective towers. From the sound of things, it didn't seem like they were fighting a winning battle. But he had his own fight to deal with.

His right arm was numb from the elbow down, a result of bending it at an unnatural angle for a prolonged period while attempting to cut through the rope binding his wrists. But he knew his efforts were paying off; he could feel the rope loosening as it was cut nearly all the way through now. He let loose a guttural scream as the gigantic spider twitched its mandibles and various mouth appendages in anticipation of coming into contact with its prey.

As his body tensed with the vocal outburst, he was suddenly pitched forward as the rope finally snapped. He was thrown into the spider's head area, and the arachnid reared back on its rear legs to make itself taller. Steve had been relieved of his machete by the natives and so had no weapon with which to confront his beastly opponent. He knew that he couldn't allow the oversized critter to get a good grip on him with its array of various appendages, or he would be finished, so he made sure to keep his body in motion.

He used his momentum from breaking the rope to spin off to one side, bounding off the spider while twirling about rapidly. He reached the side of the platform and was barred by the tower cables. To hell with it, Steve thought; he planted his feet on one of the support cables and flung himself up and over, keeping one hand on the cables, knowing that a fall from this height would be fatal. As soon as he could, he latched onto the tower supports, and by the time he managed to do that, he glanced up to see the spider's twitchy head peering down at him from ten feet up on the edge of the platform.

He had survived a face-to-face encounter with the beastly menace and was still alive for now. But the lab tech was under no illusions that he was out of danger. He dangled precariously from the tower scaffolding with one numb arm, seeking purchase with swinging feet. His right foot found a support strut and soon after that he stabilized himself by latching the fingers of his left hand around a cable of some sort. But immediately after he had gotten situated, the ginormous spider head appeared over the top of the platform.

Even as he saw the threat materializing again, his mind registered the fact that the screams from Santos's associate had ceased. He could still hear Santos fighting for his life, screaming and spitting Portuguese at the spider and at Winslow, who for now remained silent. Steve glanced down at the tower to try and pick out his next hand and footholds with which to make a safe rapid descent. The construction did not feature as regular a pattern as something in a modern city, however, which made it more difficult to choose his holds. But the spider wasn't waiting for him to figure it out.

The big arachnid charged over the side of the tower head first and vertically charged at its quarry. Steve released his hands and dropped until his feet hit the next support, quickly latching his hands around the nearest crossbar. But the spider kept coming, its eight long legs easily able to always grip a hold somewhere. Steve had no choice but to become more reckless in his descent. He let himself drop without looking down for the next hold, bracing himself for when his feet would next contact a support strut. It worked for the next couple of drops. He was able to outpace the hunter-spider, but on the third drop, when his feet hit a crossbar, his hands missed the nearest cable to grab and he fell backwards straight out from the tower. He thought he was dead as the ground came into view upside-down and far, far below. But as his body became vertically oriented, albeit upside-down, he saw the blur of the tower structure next to him and instinctively reached out with his arms.

He was able to hook an elbow around a support post after falling nearly thirty feet. He felt something snap and realized that he'd dislocated the shoulder of his right arm, the one which he had hooked around the tower. He screamed out in agony, adding his wails to those of Santos, who still struggled with his own gigantic spider on the platform of his own tower.

Steve looked up and saw that his unplanned fall had bought him a little time, but not much. The massive arachnid steadily made its way down the tower. Steve recalled with a shudder how the other spider had simply leapt from the top with Sal in its clutches and lived to tell about it, so he was under no illusion that this one had any particular fear of falling. It was simply doing what it thought it had to do in order to capture its prey.

So what to do? Down, he demanded of himself. He mentally cajoled himself into releasing his grip on the tower cables once again, and this time let himself freefall as the golden cables flashed by in a blurry rush. He didn't think he would die if he hit the ground, but he didn't need to be any worse off than he was already. So he extended his arms and braced himself to grip something sturdy and abruptly arrest his fall. It worked. Again, he grimaced and cried out in pain as he locked onto the structure after a hefty fall, but also again, he was able to stop himself before hitting the ground. Looking down, he saw that he had less than twenty feet to go. Looking up, he saw the spider was now high above him, although on the way down with its usual speedy gait.

"Heeeeelp!" Santos's anguished cry rang out across the amphitheater.

"Almost down!" Steve managed to call back. And he was, although with a hundred-pound spider barreling down on you, he surmised, nothing was certain. He winced as his shins banged into a crossbar but kept moving down until he was about ten feet off the ground. There, he looked up and saw the spider drop off the bars and freefall toward him. With a gasp, Steve pushed out and away from the tower so that he landed on the ground some distance from the structure.

The spider gave him no time to get his bearings, but dropped ten feet at a time, falling down the tower until it jumped onto the grassy amphitheater floor, landing a mere ten feet from Steve, who leapt to his feet and ran toward Santos's tower. The *policia* was still screaming, but his cries were noticeably weaker now. Gabriel! Steve called out as he half-ran, half-staggered toward the tower. He ran the rest of the way to it in a sensory blur—the ground rushing by under his feet, the sound of Santos's screams assaulting his ears like a kaleidoscopic nightmare.

He reached the base of the tower and looked behind him. The mega-spider galloped toward him on all eight legs, only a handful of seconds away. Steve whirled back around and prepared to ascend the tower. He wanted to help Santos, for one thing, but for another, he didn't think he had anywhere else to go. He wouldn't last but a minute at the most on this open ground. He glanced up at the tower as he prepared to step onto it.

A dark shape fell toward him, and with a start, he realized it was going to land right on him. It happened so fast that he had no time to hope it was Santos's spider. Steve jumped to the left and then the object hit the ground exactly where he'd been standing with a startling thud.

The lifeless eyes of Santos stared up at him while trickles of blood drained from his cracked head.

CHAPTER THIRTY-FIVE

Steve stood at the base of the golden tower, hunched over with his hands on his knees, knowing he didn't have time to take a breather with the mega-spider bearing down on him. *Sal's gone. Santos's gone. What about Ruiz?* He recalled hearing his screams halt mid-struggle atop his tower, but, looking over at it now, he didn't see a body on the ground, which meant he might still be up there.

Steve put himself into motion, changing course and running toward the tower where Santos's associate was fighting his own mega-spider. Behind Steve, a disconcerting screech sprang...from the spider itself? Steve didn't know spiders to make noise, but this one certainly was: an ethereal, high-pitched whine, very grating on the nerves, Steve thought. But he had no time to listen to it carefully, for the mega-beast was on the move again, scuttling rapidly over the uneven ground.

He didn't relish the thought of climbing another tower, but if Ruiz was alive up there, he had to help him*; even better, maybe he can help me*, Steve allowed himself to hope. He got to the tower and leapt from a sprint without stopping to the highest cable he could grab. Started climbing. The spider reached the tower and jumped right up, almost to the height Steve had gotten to by sheer exertion and luck. He felt one of the raspy antenna brush against his ankle and forced himself to climb even faster.

"Are you up there? I'm coming up!" he yelled. But no reply came. He continued to hoist himself up the tower, scared to think about what he might find when he got up there. He couldn't hear anything. Couldn't see anything when he looked up, but he couldn't do that for very long while climbing as fast as he needed to in order to outpace the spider. The only thing in his favor was that the construction of the tower was top notch. At first he'd worried that in his haste one of the crossbars might snap under his weight, but the materials and design were the least of his problems.

He found it impossible not to glance down at the giant spider every few seconds. What if it was about to pounce on him and drag him off the tower to his death, like the others? All he could do was to keep climbing, and yet he couldn't resist the urge to slow himself just a bit and crane his neck to look down. And there it was. The enormous beast, closing in on him, looking like it was taking a leisurely stroll up the side of the tower, and yet still outpacing him. For a split second he saw his own reflection in one of the creature's two big eyes, each the size of a pizza dish. Two smaller eyes, below those and out to the sides, were the size of dinner plates. Not wishing to watch himself be devoured in the reflection of the monster's eye, Steve jolted himself back into upward motion.

He reached and pulled, scrambled and jumped his way up the side of the tower while feeling the monster's antenna tickle his ankles. "I'm coming up!" he shouted up to Ruiz. He had no idea if the man was still alive, but if he was, he needed his help. "Almost there! Come to the side, pull me up if you can!" Still no response, but still he kept climbing. So did the arachnid, but for some reason it chose to move out laterally so that it was below him and to his right rather than directly under him. For some reason this made Steve even more nervous. What was it up to?

He was sure he would find out, but for now, at least, he had other things on his mind, for the tower platform was coming into view a few feet above his head. Still no sign of Ruiz or another spider on top. He did not relish the idea of being sandwiched between two mega-beasts, one on the platform and one below him, but on an expedition, the team members had to look out for one another. He had to know the status of his team.

He found solid purchase with his right foot on a strut, placed his right hand on the edge of the wooden platform, and hauled himself up. As soon as his eyes cleared the platform he saw the hairy body of one of the mega-spiders. He ducked back down, hyper-aware that another of the beasts was coming for him just below and to his right. It moved up rather than toward him, and with a sickening jolt, Steve realized what it was up to. It would reach the platform first and then, from up there, be able to easily prevent him from topping over.

Now or never. Steve stuck his head up over the platform once again, warily eyeing the other spider, but he saw that it was in the exact same position. Unmoving. Looking around the platform, he saw that it was empty—no sign of Ruiz. And then, as he swept his gaze across the platform to see two of the other spider's hairy appendages seeking purchase on the platform floor, he spotted it.

A black leather boot, sticking out from under the platform spider's body. Also unmoving.

Steve hauled himself up and over the platform with the realization that the mega-beast up here appeared to be already dead. Lucky break! But what of the man pinned beneath it?

He pulled himself all the way up, got to his feet and moved to the fallen super-beast just as the spider that was on his tail during the climb up also made its way onto the platform. The fallen spider remained unmoving. Steve jumped over it to put a physical barrier between himself and the other spider which now sat on the edge of the platform, appendages twitching as its sensory organs interpreted what lay before it.

The lab tech reached out and put a hand on the big spider's body, though it disgusted him. He called out Santos's associate by name, but the man gave no answer of any kind, including movement. Steve shoved the spider to one side, terrified that it would awaken and then he would have to face two of the giga-beasts at once. The arachnid was much heavier than he anticipated, but he nudged it just enough to be able to drag Ruiz's body out from under it. His entire head and neck were an unrecognizable pulpy mass, as though they had been partially digested. He took the man's pulse at the wrist and was not surprised to feel absolutely nothing. Ruiz was gone.

So was the spider, and now he could see why. A machete was wedged up to the hilt in the arthropod's abdomen, green slimy fluid—which likely partially cooked the human's face—spilling onto the platform and dead human.

Steve lifted his head to stare at his remaining opponent on the platform. The massive mega-spider raised its body high on its legs, so that its eyes were almost level with Steve's own. Even though he faced off with a deadly giant, he still couldn't stop thinking of the implications wrought by the death of both *poliícia*. Was his deal with the Brazilian police still valid now that Santos and Ruiz were dead? He had no idea. He suspected that Santos and his partner might have been operating as rogues, that they had told no one of their case, perhaps because they felt they didn't have enough evidence yet, or else because they wanted to find the lost city's riches for themselves. But of course he had no proof of this.

Steve almost laughed out loud as he looked around at the city of Z. A lot of gold—towers, roads—evidence of a past civilization in the form of buildings, but not much else. Was it worth all the death and pain and suffering, not only by their own party, but by the innumerable expeditions that had come before them in the quest to find Z? He still hadn't concluded anything when Winslow's shaky voice reached his ears from wherever he was below.

"Steve, it's just you and me now! Come on down."

Steve didn't take his eyes off the mega-arachnid. "There's a giant spider up here with me, Dr. Winslow."

"He won't hurt you."

"What makes you say that? Look what his friends did to Sal and the two *policia*." He realized his slip as soon as the words escaped his lips. But maybe Winslow was too far gone to notice, or care.

"Two *policia*. Bad men coming to steal the treasure of this place, and to take both of us to jail. Now they have been taken care of. Anyone who tries to harm the true keepers of this place will be taken care of."

Steve stared at the spider's face. Its antenna and mandibles or whatever the hell they were continued to twitch and bounce around, but the animal made no moves with its legs. He doubted it was under Winslow's control, but perhaps the historian somehow knew something about it, enough to predict its behavior in this situation, anyway. He shouted over toward the direction Winslow's voice came from.

"Everyone is dead but you and I, Dr. Winslow. I'm going to climb down now and come to you, okay?"

The reply was forthcoming and in a surprisingly strong voice. "It's not only 'okay', it is destiny!"

Steve shook his head in wonder. The academic's mind seemed to be all but gone. He would check in on him, see if he could get him to function well enough to leave with him, and then they would get the heck out of here. If he wouldn't leave, then Steve would be forced to trek out on his own and come back for him later with help once he reached a town.

"Okay, I'm coming down," Steve bellowed, one eye still on the one living mega-spider atop the platform. Winslow had no response to this, but Steve had no reason to stay up here, so he positioned himself away from the living spider so that he could slowly lower himself without taking his eyes off the predator. It stayed in place, not moving while Steve slid himself below the outside of the platform until he could no longer see the animal.

Steve began his descent down the tower. Strangely, he felt no sense of urgency, no stress that he was being chased. He kept a watchful gaze above him, half-expecting to see the multi-jointed behemoth scrambling from around the corner or flopping itself down from the platform at any second. But when he reached the halfway point to the ground, he knew the mega-spider had simply opted not to pursue its former prey. *Had Dr. Winslow somehow communicated with it? Impossible...*He had no other explanation, but refused to accept that one, even through the fog of his battle-weary fatigue.

He continued climbing down the golden tower, any curiosity over the lost city's structures having long since vanished with the wave of death that had washed over the place. With a kind of single-mindedness seen in marathon runners deep into the race, Steve kept putting one foot lower down than the other, kept seeking out new hand and footholds in order to facilitate his descent. After a while he stopped looking for the mega-spider. His brain still tried to feed a fresh fear to him: what about the spiders on the ground? Would they leave him alone also? He had no idea, but at the same time he had the attitude that there's only one way to find out. He was too exhausted, mentally and physically, for anything else.

So he kept working his way down until he was within jumping range of the ground. He performed a visual scan of the immediate surroundings, checking to see if the big spiders were nearby. He expected to find one lumbering along in the distance, perhaps, or maybe lurking behind a clump of bushes. But he was not prepared at all for what he saw.

Like a parade. That was Steve's initial reaction as he gazed at the astounding sight from his perch not far above the ground on the side of the golden tower. A line of colossal mega-spiders stretched from near the base of the tower over to the edge of the amphitheater where the steep side rose to a mist-shrouded mountain top. Winslow's voice called out from the base of it.

"Follow my brethren, Steve. They will lead you to salvation. Let them lead you to me."

Steve closed his eyes for a moment and shook his head. He was sure he must be experiencing some kind of hallucination, perhaps brought on by tainted water or something he ate. The jungle harbored many toxins. And yet when he opened his eyes again he saw the same sight. Heard the same voice.

"Do not be afraid. You are a disciple now. Come toward my voice. If they wanted to kill you, they would have already done so, isn't that obvious?"

He had a point there, Steve had to admit as he looked down on the gauntlet of super-beasts that awaited his presence. Deciding Winslow was right, and that he couldn't hang around on the tower forever, Steve prepared to jump.

Here goes nothing...

CHAPTER THIRTY-SIX

Steve looked down the long row of twitching spider appendages to the base of the mountain that formed one side of the natural amphitheater. There was nothing left to do, nowhere else to go. It had all come down to this, he thought, as he started to walk. A gauntlet of gigantic arachnids. Their movements became more pronounced as he passed, but still they remained in place, not attacking. At first he cursed the fact that he had lost his machete to the fight with the tribesmen who had tied him to the golden tower, and that he had the chance to take the one Ruiz had buried to the hilt in the spider atop his tower. But then Steve realized how futile it would have been wielding it as he marched down the line of mega-spiders toward the base of the mountain.

As he moved, he saw that the little spiders, the ones that had followed them for days now, from deep in the jungle, had formed a thick line opposite their oversized cousins, so that the man now walked down a road delineated by spiders large and small.

"Walk the path of the righteous one!" Winslow called out as he neared the base of the cliff, where he could now see the entrance to a large cave or cavern. No doubt Winslow was inside.

"I'm on my way, Dr. Winslow. Are you okay?" He didn't know what else to ask, and he definitely knew he wasn't okay, but wanted to keep him talking so that he had something to home in on.

"I am neither okay nor not okay. I simply *am*."

"Well that explains a lot, Dr. Winslow. Thanks for that." Steve kept trudging on down the line of hideous monsters. He tried not to look directly at the four-eyed beasts, but it was hard to avoid and when he did, they usually had some kind of green viscous substance dripping from their disgusting, bacteria-ridden maws. Then a tiny rogue spider that for some reason had gone astray from the river of its cousins ran out in front of Steve, and he squashed it under his left foot. He froze in mid-step after lifting his foot from the crushed beasty, tensing as he realized the gravity of his error. Three of the big spiders immediately took steps toward him to his right, but then they halted as Steve kept walking.

"I'm sorry!" he called out. "I didn't mean to, it just…it just…" He found himself breaking down as he walked on, starting to sob. "It just ran out in front of me. I'm sorry, I'm so sorry…"

Winslow had no response to this, nor did the spiders react further. He continued to trudge toward the cave. To keep his mind off the arachnids, he thought about what he was going to do when he reached Winslow. He recalled the historian's physical condition with a shudder. He was very bad off and wasn't sure he would be able to walk the kind of distances they would need to get back to any kind of civilization. He himself was certainly in no condition to carry him any appreciable distance. He may have to leave and come back for him, he had decided when the mouth of the cave came into view.

"Winslow, I'm here—are you in there?" Steve stood at the mouth of the cave, waiting for his eyes to adjust to the darkness beyond. The small spiders continued into the cave, while the large ones remained outside. "Dr. Winslow?"

"Yes, I am here. I will always be here. I have always been here."

An awkward pause ensued while Steve waited for him to elaborate. He did not.

"May I come in?"

"Please enter."

Steve took a deep breath and looked back at the giant spiders, which had gathered near the entrance of the cave without blocking it. He wondered if they intended to block the exit after he went inside, but then he figured they could kill him anytime they wanted to anyway, so he saw no reason to worry about it.

He walked into the cave.

"Welcome. Come back this way," Winslow's voice said. It sounded high and feeble, and yet was somehow quite audible in the cavern. "This way," it said again, but sounded so close to him that he jumped, startled. "Right this way, come on!"

And then Steve looked down at the cave floor, by his boots, and saw a cluster of little spiders. "This way!" His nerve endings tingled from head to toe as his brain struggled to process the fact that Winslow's voice was coming from these spiders.

He tried to stammer out a coherent question. "Are you…are you talking…?"

"Yes, Steve, I am talking."

"But…the spiders…" Steve trailed off in disbelief as he looked down to where Winslow's voice issued from.

"I am them and they are me, Steve. I talk through them, they deliver my messages throughout the forest."

Steve carefully lifted his foot over the gaggle of spiders that delivered Winslow's voice and began walking deeper into the cave. The interior was so dark that he could not see how far back it went.

"How...." Instead of trying to figure it out, Steve decided it was best to go see for himself.

"It is better that you see for yourself, Steve. Come see for yourself!" The train of little spiders squealed at him as he put one foot in front of the other toward the rear of the cavern. While he walked he told himself that he must be hallucinating, that all the stress was affecting his mind. The light became dimmer and dimmer the further back he walked, even as his eyesight adjusted. He brushed copicus cobwebs out of his way as he made his way back.

"Why do you have to be all the way back in this cave?" Steve called out to a still unseen Winslow.

When his voice came it was clearer and louder than before. Steve realized with a start it was because he was hearing from Winslow directly, and not through the spiders. "It has always been this way. Come forward."

Steve took a few tentative steps deeper into the cave. "How do you know it's always been this, way, Dr. Winslow? You've never even been to this place before this trip."

"Oh but I have. I realize that now. I have always been a part of this place. And now you are a part of it too, and you always will be."

Steve shook his head slowly in the dark. "You're scaring me, Dr. Winslow. I want to go home now. I want you to come with me. Otherwise I will have to leave you here, but I can come back with more people—"

Suddenly two of the massive mega-spiders dropped from the ceiling and stood in place in front of Steve. Winslow's voice boomed with great anger. "People from the outside are not welcome in this sanctuary!"

Steve backed up a step from the mega-beasts while a throng of tiny spiders ran around his ankles, Winslow's voice emanating from their collective mass; "Not welcome, not welcome!"

The lab tech felt like he had been detached from reality, like he was perhaps on drugs or in some sort of dream world. And yet his body, racked with pain and an assortment of injuries…it was all too real.

"You're from the outside, Dr. Winslow. Before today, you lived in America, do you remember that? You were a respected professor of history at a major university."

The professor's voice echoed throughout the cavern, with spiders large and small somehow reproducing his sound, like a speaker system with woofers and tweeters strategically placed around the room. "It was my understanding of history that led me to my current position here. This is my ultimate destiny, Steve. Come and see for yourself now. Step forward. Just a few more steps and you will see. You will understand. You will realize."

Somehow, Steve doubted this, but he was tired of the games, and so he took a step forward. A gaggle of tiny arachnids scuttled out in front of him as he stepped. "This way! This way," they squeaked while he walked. "This way!"

Winslow's voice came again. "Do not be alarmed at the sight of me. I am all right. Take three more steps if you are ready to see me. Three more steps."

"I'm ready to go home, Dr. Winslow. But yes, I want to see you first, to try to take you with me if I can."

"No one can take me away from this place ever again, Steve. One more step."

Steve Hoch took one more step and felt himself plunge.

CHAPTER THIRTY-SEVEN

The feel of coarse silk strands passing over his face, neck and hands was what keyed Steve into the fact that he was falling through an extensive network of dense cobwebs. He braced himself for a hard impact, or possibly a splash into water, so he was surprised to feel the silk strands themselves break his fall. He bounced around as if he had jumped from a burning building into a fire net. When his movements settled down he clutched the strands that were supporting his body; *strands* wasn't really the proper term in this case, he realized—they were more like ropes, at least the diameter of the 550 paracord so many guides liked to use on their expeditions. Thick, unbreakable stuff.

Looking down, he could see only darkness. He felt around on his belt for the pocket flashlight, hoping it was still clipped there. Found it, aimed it down and clicked it on. The sight below was disorienting to the point he didn't trust what he was seeing. Winslow's voice only added to his confusion.

"Congratulations, you found me!"

Steve was surprised to see Winslow's face staring up at him. It was odd-looking, somehow puffy and distorted, like his entire neck had abscessed and billowed out around his head, surrounding it in a puss-filled flesh pillow.

"Wh-wh-wh-where is the rest of your body, Dr. Winslow? What…I can't tell what I'm looking at."

"I don't need it anymore."

His voice was very high-pitched, lacking any real resonance. "What do you mean, you don't need it anymore?" Steve tried to shift his body position, but the thick, springy webs made any kind of controlled movement exceedingly difficult.

"My destiny is here. Everything I need to do, I can do from here, just by thinking."

Steve adjusted the aim of his flashlight and realized with a violent shudder that the reason Winslow's voice was so thin was because he was missing most of his body, including the diaphragm. He must have vocal cords to produce the sounds, and a mouth to modulate them into words, but as far as Steve could see, that was it. Below the abscessed billow of flesh enveloping his head, there was nothing but a black, pulpy mass that spread out amorphously in all directions. Looking closely at parts of it as he aimed his light beam around, he could see areas that pulsated, like a beating heart or a pulse of some kind.

"Dr. Winslow, your body...is it underneath that black mass that's below your...your head?"

"No!" He said it with the incredulous tone of a child who was asked something silly, like pointing at a dog and asking, "Is that a cat?"

Steve felt a chill so pervasive as to be almost paralyzing. To fight against it he twisted his body yet again within the silken cords, but found that the more he struggled, the more entangled he became.

"Well then, wh-what is it?"

"My body has been assimilated."

"Assimilated into what, Dr. Winslow? What is going on here?"

"Into the network of my destiny. You heard me talking to you out there, right?"

"Yes."

"I am part of the hive mind now. I am the main brain of the hive mind. I have always been a thinker, you know."

"Yes, I know, Professor Winslow." He used his full title so as to hopefully trigger some kind of recognition as to who he was, although he doubted it would have much effect at this point, at any rate, mental condition or not, his body was not simply incapacitated, it was...gone. There was no way in hell Steve was going to be able to get this guy, this...*being*... out of here, to extricate him from whatever he'd been...*assimilated* into. The best Steve could figure out was that the spiders had co-opted his brain to use as their central hive mind, like a bunch of hackers who came across a supercomputer and connected it to their own distributed machines.

"Winslow, I cannot get you out of here myself. I will have to leave and come back for you with serious help to do the heavy work of extracting you out of this place." *What's left of you, anyway.*

"No one can get me out of here, anymore. I *am* this place, and this place is me." Winslow adopted the matter-of-fact tone once more, even though the voice delivering it was disembodied and frail.

Steve began to yell in anger. "Well I am *not* this place, Hunter, and this place is *not* me! I am going to leave now and get help for you."

"Don't be silly, Steve. I don't require help. I have always valued your services over the years as one of my technicians, but honestly, if we're being frank, one of your shortcomings has always been impatience. You remember that time on the Magna Carta project, when I told you we needed another pass on the data?"

Steve let out an exasperated sigh. "Yes, yes, I told you I thought we were done, but you insisted there was more to be gleaned by doing another pass, and you turned out to be right. Fine. But this is nothing like that, Dr. Winslow. No one in the world would disagree with me now when I say that I need to bring back some kind of team to get you out of here for some prompt and thorough medical—and psychiatric—evaluation and treatment."

"I have a better idea."

Steve peered down at the apparently disembodied head that was his former boss and colleague. "Do tell."

"Why don't you stay here and work with me?"

Despite the grim situation, Steve was barely able to suppress a laugh. "*Work* with you? Doing what, pray tell? Besides working to get the hell out of here, that is."

"To uphold the sacred permanence of this place, the heart of the jungle, the lost city."

Steve shook his head. "Look, I know you're very into the history of this place, but I can help you with that from home. It's time to leave, Dr. Winslow. Do you want to come with me or not?"

When a couple of seconds passed with no response, Steve continued. "Because if not, as soon as I get out of this confounded web, I'm going to make my way back to the nearest town, any town, and come back with a rescue team to get you and recover the bodies of the rest of our expedition. After that, you and I can work together to tell the story about this place, of what happened here through the centuries right up to this very expedition."

When Winslow's voice came, his words were very precise, very measured, as though he had put a lot of thought into them. "No one needs to know about this place any more than they already do."

And that was it. No elaboration.

Steve managed to stick one hand through the strands of silk and began pulling them apart. "Well that doesn't sound like you, Dr. Winslow. A man of history, a professional scholar with a distinguished career educating others about places like this and communicating their value to the public at large—until very recently, that is."

"I served the public for decades with my so-called career, and then they went and turned their backs on me. I don't need them, and they don't need me. This is my domain now, this is where I will dwell."

"How do you eat? Get sustenance?"

"I am well taken care of. As long as I keep everyone away from this place. And you will be, too, as long as you take care of it also, that is."

"We can work on that once we get out of here, Winslow. I'll go now and get help, then I'll come back and—"

"NO! YOU WILL NOT TELL OTHERS ABOUT THIS PLACE." The voice was booming and loud this time, if somewhat processed sounding. Steve wondered how Winslow had suddenly gotten his voice to have so much body, such a deep, full tone to it compared to the high, screechy drone he had going before, when a large silhouette descended through the air and came to rest a few feet above him. One of the massive mega-spiders twirled at the end of a silken cord, and Steve knew with a start that Winslow was somehow projecting his voice through it, as he had done with the mass of tiny spiders before.

Steve forced himself to contain his emotions, lest he let anger get the better of him, so he concentrated on the meaning of the words themselves, rather than the delivery. When a second mega-spider dropped down next to the first, he found that to be difficult.

"I'm getting out of here, Hunter. With or without you. I'm not going to stay here with you and be *assimilated* into whatever this is."

At that moment an army of little spiders flowed down into Steve's web, circling around him. When Winslow next spoke, his voice carried a high, shimmering component as well as the deep bass of the mega-spiders.

"You're either with us or against us, Steve. If you're with us, you stay here, and this is where you live from now on. You become one of us. If you're against us, your aim is to return to civilization and expose this place to others in return for personal accolades and material gain. If you're against us, we will have to end your existence. This place is sacred. It must be protected."

Rage and frustration boiled up inside Steve as he shrunk back from the two immense beasts dangling on silk ropes a few feet from his head. His urge to rebel was so strong that he didn't trust himself to speak, for he knew it would not take much to sign his own death warrant. He bit down on one of the silk ropes, not because he thought he would be able to chew through it, but to have something to bite down on and vent his screams into, like a wartime soldier having a bullet removed in the field. When he felt that enough of the rage had passed, he lifted his head and turned toward Winslow.

"Okay. You are right. I could never make it out of here now, anyway. Who am I kidding? I do belong here." Not convincing enough, his inner voice told him. *Add some more personal stuff.* "This is where my life has led me, after all, my professional career supporting research as a lab tech, and then my expeditions to the Amazon…it's all led me to right here. And what do I have back at home, anyways? No wife, no kids, don't even own my own house…"

"Here, you do not need a house. We are your house." The big and small spiders boomed and whined Winslow's words.

"Okay," Steve yelled down to Winslow's head. "How do I become a permanent part of this place, like you?" He was afraid to hear the answer, but at the same time, he wanted an idea of what to expect. He needed to buy time until he could make a move to escape. Right now it felt hopeless, though.

"Stay where you are, and my disciples will do the rest." Winslow's voice boomed throughout the chamber, and the two mega-spiders latched onto the edge of the web that held Steve prisoner.

"Wh—what are they going to do to me, Dr. Winslow?"

His answer came without hesitation. "They will make you part of us."

"But what exactly does that entail, Hunter?" Steve's eyes were wide with near-panic as the first of the two super-spiders drew near. At the same time, a clap of thunder resonated with booming clarity up above and down into the cave.

"It is raining outside," Winslow uttered through his network of arachnids. "Won't be easy to leave. It's going to rain for weeks. The rivers will overflow."

"What does that have to do with what I just asked you, Hunter?" Steve watched the oversized spider open and close its mouth rapidly, many times in succession as it perched next to him. Was Winslow lying to him, just lulling him into being easy prey for his minions? Or was there really some process to be assimilated into the bio-network, something that involved being bitten or worse?

"I'm simply stating a fact, that's all. I do hope you choose to stay, but the process of integration may seem a bit scary at first."

Steve lamented the lack of any serious weapon, but knew he had a folding blade pocketknife in his front right pants pocket, if he could only reach it. He twisted his arm uncomfortably until he thought his shoulder might pop out of the socket. The mega-spider drew near with its open maw while the second giant arachnid crawled onto the web on the other side of Steve's body, so that he was in between the two super-predators.

"I wish you would elaborate on what exactly that process is," Steve called out in a voice almost as shaky as Winslow's disembodied vocalizations. "Give me an idea of what to expect."

"Expect the unexpected, my old friend."

CHAPTER THIRTY-EIGHT

Steve's fingers were inside the pocket with the knife when the first mega-spider's head appeared directly above his own. Its feelers and antenna and various mandibles twitched and jerked as it stood over the human.

"What's happening, Dr. Winslow? What's it's going to do to me?" The panic in his voice was genuine, but he didn't stop reaching for the knife, the muscles of his arm and wrist straining with the effort.

"The assimilation process requires you to be injected with the spider's special biochemical. Don't worry, it doesn't hurt. Feels kind of good, actually. Just lay back and enjoy it."

Steve had the errant thought that Dr. Winslow had probably said that very phrase before to one of his female interns but held his tongue. His life was in Winslow's hands at this point, not that he had hands any longer, but in his spiders' mandibles, he supposed. Even worse.

"And it's going to do what—melt away my insides, like what happened to you?" The fright in his voice was almost uncontrollable as he watched the mega-beast lower its head toward his own.

"It will melt away your preconceived notions of what a meaningful existence really is, Steve. Now just relax. Just close your eyes and think of a peaceful scene, think of…"

Steve tuned out the rest of whatever drivel Dr. Winslow was spewing when his fingers curled around the knife in his pocket. His panic was still increasing, though, since he didn't see how the small blade was going to help him against the pair of mega-monsters slavering over him now, not to mention he was still ensnared in the industrial strength cobweb. One thing at a time, he told himself. *Focus on getting control of the knife.* Fortunately it was a type that could be opened one-handed; if not for that, he wouldn't even try.

"…standing in a meadow with butterflies all around, a light breeze in your hair…" Winslow was blathering on. Steve slipped the knife from his pocket. He placed the thumbnail of his right hand on the blade's indentation and forced it open, smiling as he heard it lock into the open position. He went to work cutting through a particularly thick strand of webbing that was severely restricting the movement of his left arm. The spider jostled the web at the same moment as the blade snapped through the web strand confining his left arm.

The unpredictable movement combined with the sudden acceleration of the knife blade after it severed the silk caused his arm to move quicker than anticipated. The knife fell from his hand and dropped below his web trap out of sight far below. He didn't even hear a sound when it impacted, wherever that was.

Steve felt as though the wind had been knocked out of him, a crushing mental blow that instantly deflated his spirits. His only weapon, and tool, was now gone. The second huge spider clamored over to him as the first began to drool a viscous grayish-green fluid from its mouth onto Steve's head. He turned his head so that he faced down and saw Winslow's misshapen head staring back up at him, expressionless and yet somehow interested at the same time.

"Dr. Winslow, I am not ready to be assimilated. I am begging you to please call off the creatures. Please!"

"Why would I do that, Steve? Rest assured, once you undergo the transformation, you will love life here like I do."

"I beg your pardon, Dr. Winslow, but you've only been here in this capacity for one day."

"Time is meaningless at this point."

"Not for me it isn't." Steve kicked and thrashed as he felt the second spider start to walk on his legs.

"It's about to be, old friend. You'll see."

"I don't want to see, Dr. Winslow! I want to return home. I will not divulge the location of the lost city, you have my word."

The sight of Dr. Winslow's putrid neck folds shaking and billowing with his ensuing laughter was almost enough to make Steve vomit.

"Don't worry, soon you will no longer wish to leave this wondrous place. The lost city is lost no more, Steve. We found it, and now we are home."

Something in the words triggered an idea for the lab tech, who was only moments away from being—devoured, penetrated, injected?—by the mega-spiders. He yelled down to Winslow, his voice cracking with emotion and desperation.

"There's something you don't know about the Lost City of Z, Dr. Winslow."

Steve could hear the smugness in Winslow's voice when he replied. "I know everything there is to know about this place. I *am* this place."

"There's another section of Manuscript 512 that I decoded but never gave you."

Almost instantaneously, both giant spiders lifted their dripping maws from Steve's head and body before retreating. Not far, only a couple of steps, but still, he was no longer in direct contact with them.

"How can there be another section-I counted the pages myself. I've been working with that document for the better part of my career, Steve, you know that."

Steve had a hard time processing the fact that this near formless blob below him had a distinguished, if ruined, career, and that he himself had worked with him. "It's not a separate page, Dr. Winslow, but a hidden section of the document that is only revealed by parsing the known text on the physical pages with an algorithm that I first identified, and then applied."

"AND YOU KEPT THIS FROM ME UNTIL NOW?" The enormous spider closest to Steve's head crawled up over him again, its maw somehow moving to articulate the vowels so that Winslow's words were synthesized from the arachnid. Thin strings of clear fluid dripped onto him as the spider "spoke."

"I started to sense I might be in danger, Dr. Winslow, when I was sequestered in the basement of a Rio de Janeiro house with a couple of *policía* watching my every move in the lab. That's when it first occurred to me, *Hey—Dr. Winslow has led me to a situation that isn't all that safe for me.* So pardon me for taking precautions which might lead to saving my own life!"

"Your life is not in danger, Steve. It is simply going to undergo a transformation—a most wonderful transformation that will make you a part of this incredible place, the Lost City of Z, forevermore!"

The mega-spiders twitched and bobbed while Winslow's words echoed around the cave. The train of little spiders was somewhere nearby, because a high-pitched component was now audible in the voice.

"I'm sorry, Dr. Winslow, but the situation you now find yourself in is not the life for me. So I am offering you a deal…"

He was interrupted by more of Winslow's ethereal-sounding laughter, delivered by a host of arachnids, large and small, near and far. "*You* are offering *me* a deal? I'm not sure you comprehend the gravity of your situation, Steve. The only thing keeping your fate from being the same as that the rest of our expedition have already suffered, is my kindness. And now you're trying my patience."

A trickle of little spiders ran up and over his neck, tickling and stinging him. He made a move to swipe them off but the massive beast of a spider near his head stepped on his arm with two of its legs, effectively pinning him down. His skin itched and burned where the contact was made.

"I guess you don't want to know where the real Lost City of Z is, then, do you, Dr. Winslow? The knowledge is going to die with me."

A pause ensued, and then the large spider stepped off Steve's arm. Winslow's voice, a shade calmer, emanated from that same beast as well as all the others. "You're not going to die, Steve, you're going to live on forever, here with us in the most sacred part of the Amazon!"

"No thanks. I signed up to help you find the lost city, not to live in it forever. And guess what? This isn't even it. Why do you think there are so many spiders here, Dr. Winslow?"

"To guard this sacred realm."

"Guard it from whom?"

The silence that passed told Steve that he was making progress. "From those who would seek to destroy it for their own personal gain. You know this."

"You're right!" Steve surprised even his own self with his boldness as he smirked down through the web at his former collaborator.

"Of course I'm right! Now, let us proceed with—"

"You don't understand why you're right, though. Dr. Winslow."

"Come again?"

"You don't know why you're right. You think you're guarding the treasures and splendor of Z from the greedy world, when in reality, this place—these spiders, and the uncontacted tribal people—are guarding the city of Z from the likes of *you*! Think about it. You're stuck here, down in this subterranean pit, turned into some kind of pseudo-sentient blob! The real Z and its treasure, meanwhile, sits safe, away from you, the one who came to take it over."

"Prove it!"

"You have to release me for me to be able to show you. I will never tell you where I hid the manuscript unless I am free."

"All right, so if you climb up out of here, back to the entrance to the cave, will you then tell me?"

Steve shook his head, jostling the net of webs as he did so. "Oh no, Dr. Winslow. You think I don't know you can sic your big spiders on me as long as I'm anywhere near here? Look at the rest of our team. No, I need to be out of the crater and in the regular jungle, away from this giant spider nest. Then, you can have one spider there, and I will tell it the information. At that point you will know the truth and I will be free."

The truth shall make you free, he recalled seeing on some academic institution's letterhead somewhere, sometime far away. Make *me* free, he silently hoped.

"How can the lost city be anywhere else?" Winslow asked. "We saw the houses, the roads paved with gold, the towers of gold…if that's not the city of Z, then what is?"

"It's part of it, Winslow, but not the bulk of the treasure. These are but mere outskirts, designed to trap and trick those who are unworthy."

"YOU LIE! LIE LIE LIE LIE LIE!"

"Where's the actual *treasure*, then Winslow? Okay, golden roads and towers, it's pretty impressive and worth more than a man needs for the rest of his life, I give you that. But a city, a true thriving civilization like the one Z was, has cultural artifacts, true treasures, works of art, valuables beyond compare. Where are they all?"

"TELL ME! WHERE!"

"You're getting angry, Dr. Winslow, because you know it's true. You have been turned into a spineless jelly blob incapable of moving, because this place, as you guessed, is indeed very powerful. But it has trapped you into working for it, into being a hive mind for its army of spiders, who protect the real treasure."

"NO!"

"I'm afraid it's true, Dr. Winslow, and I can prove it. The manuscript is in my pack up top by one of the towers. But you need me to decipher it," Steve was quick to add. "You won't be able to see anything new in it yourself. I almost didn't see it either, but once I did…" he trailed off as if lost in the wonderment of a new discovery all over again.

"Fine. Tell me what it says."

"I can't recall it from memory, Hunter. I need the document in my hands to read the code. It has some complexity, a series of coordinates, really. At the time, back in the lab, it didn't make as much sense as it does now that I've already found this place and seen it with my own eyes."

"You have thirty minutes."

Steve was stunned by the change in direction, and it took him a moment to respond. "Pardon?"

"Thirty minutes to get the manuscript and come right back down here. If you are not within my sight in thirty minutes, your fate will be the same as the others."

"You have a deal, Dr. Winslow. I will go now."

"Twenty-nine minutes and counting…"

CHAPTER THIRTY-NINE

Steve extricated himself from the giant cobweb while the mega-spiders retreated to the walls of the pit, where they kept their multiple compound eyes on him while maintaining their distance. One thing Steve hadn't counted on as he eyed the vertical distance to the top of the rocky chute in which he found himself, was how much of a real climb it would be. On the way down, he'd basically fallen into the net of cobwebs, like a stuntman dropping into a prepared cushion. But on the way up, he'd have to actually rock climb without the benefit of rock climbing equipment. There were plenty of nooks and crannies to use as hand and footholds, but still, the light was low, and it was difficult and slow going. With Winslow's time limit ticking, it only added to the pressure.

Spiders crawled everywhere, too—large and small, escorting him, as it were, out of the lair. Winslow's voice echoed around the chamber, delivered by the arachnids. "Don't fall Steve. Time is of the essence." He broadcast various taunts as the lab technician climbed, slowly but surely towards the top of the pit. When he got there, he was happy to pull himself up and out of the hellish chute. It was brighter on the floor of the amphitheater, and that lifted his spirits even though he knew he was still under arachnid escort and could be killed at any second according to Winslow's whims.

It took him a second to get his bearings and locate the golden tower where his pack still lay at the base from where it had fallen from the top platform. Once he got the lay of the land again, he set off in the direction of that tower, the procession of spiders both large and small never leaving his side. Something was different, and it took him a minute to realize that a wind had cropped up in the basin, kicking up leaves and various debris. A steady rain also fell.

"Don't take too long, Steve!" the beasties wailed at him. "Don't waste time or we'll eat you!" Winslow's cackling filtered through the spiders' bodies and resonated throughout the natural amphitheater. Steve started to jog. He passed by the body of Ruiz, crumpled and bloody at the base of one of the towers. *Whatever your goal was*, he thought, *it wasn't this*. He was sorry for all that had gone wrong, the lives lost, all in pursuit of a legend. But now that he had seen it, although wondrous in its own way, he couldn't understand how it justified the death toll. He thought of the lives lost over the centuries in pursuit of this "lost" city. Should have let the spiders keep it, he thought. If they were even spiders. Things had gotten so strange he wasn't even sure what was what anymore.

Until he saw his backpack, that is, lying on the ground. Even the spiders made screeching noises when he made eye contact with it. Could Winslow see through their eyes? He didn't know, but somehow there was a strong sensory connection, that was for sure. Winslow had truly been wired into the arachnid hive mind. But Steve knew only one thing. As strong a leash as they had on him now, he sure didn't want to end up like Winslow. This was as much freedom as he could hope to have. He had to make an escape now, or meet his end trying.

He ran to the backpack and scooped it up. Made a show of opening it and looking inside, tossing out items-a canteen, a paper map, a compass....

"It's not in here!" he screamed to the massive arachnid acting as nearest sentry. Then he looked up and saw another spider—a super-spider—actually take to the air from the top of a different tower. He had seen it before—they weave a type of crude parachute from silken threads and, if the winds are sufficient, can go airborne for reasonable distances. He recalled fighting the mega-beasts atop the tower and how they were very light for their impressive size. So when he saw this spider seeming to glide through the air over the majority of the amphitheater floor, he knew how it was made possible even though the silken parachute was invisible from the ground.

The airborne spider dropped onto the ground ten feet from Steve with a barely audible thud. Then, in unison, it and the first mega-spider vocally projected Winslow's words: "You lied to me!"

"I did not. It must have fallen out at the top of the tower. I know where it is. I'll climb it now and get it. You said I had thirty minutes. Let me look for it."

Steve didn't wait for a reply. It occurred to him that the spiders could climb much faster than he could, and that Winslow could simply send one up to see if the manuscript 512 transport tube was up there. Before he could think of that Steve wanted to be underway, so he started to run for the tower while yelling "Just a couple of minutes—if it's not up here, I'll come right back down and admit that I lost the manuscript, but I am positive it's up here. It's got to be!"

He reached the base of the tower and started to climb while a line of small spiders called over to him: "You better be right, Steve! You better be right!"

"I am right!" he called back over his shoulder without pausing his climb. "I have to be right!"

"Yes you do!" The mega-spiders bcomed out in unison. "You are right that you have to be right!"

Steve climbed faster than he knew was safe, without taking the time to rig any kind of safety harness or other climbing equipment. He free-climbed up the golden tower, one thought racing around his head, screaming at him from within: there is no secret manuscript code left to reveal. This *is* the lost city. He had completely fabricated the whole business about the real lost city having revealed itself in the manuscript's coded language. Not a wise move, he knew, but at the time, down in the pit, he was so revolted, frightened and uncomfortable at the same time that he was willing to say anything to get out of it. And that's what he had done, made something up.

And now here he was, approaching the top of the tower, where the manuscript might or might not be, but it didn't even matter, since it contained nothing new (that he was aware of, anyway), that hadn't already been revealed. But if he wanted to live, he had to get out of here, and the barest kernel of a plan that he had sown in his fragile mind was now the only hope he had left.

And it was a faint hope at best. So many ways to die, he thought. So few ways to live.

"Don't fall, don't fall or you'll die!" The small spiders screeched over to him as they marched up the tower with him.

"I won't! I'm not going to fall!" Steve had tears streaming down his cheeks from the sheer emotion of it all, the realization that the plan he had in his mind was the scariest thing he'd ever thought of, that if all those other people on his expedition had died, why should he be any different. Even Winslow had died, in a way, he thought, taking his mind off the dangerous climb as he moved upward. He was physically still alive in some strange capacity, sure, but he was no long Professor Winslow, a real three-dimensional, fully functioning human, that was for sure.

Steve reached the top of the tower and wasted no time scrambling onto the platform. He could see right away that there was no manuscript here. He looked up into the spires above the platform to see if it might have been tossed up there in the fighting, but he couldn't see it.

Manuscript 512 is not here!

No sooner than he thought it did one of the mega-spiders land on the platform—from the sky—a billowing parachute of silk draping around the tower spires. Its voice boomed Winslow's message at him.

"It's not there!"

Steve knew there would be no argument that could save his life. He was weaponless, facing off against a giant spider the size of a small car, with untold more on the ground below. Making matters worse, a shadow passed over the platform and he looked up to see another mega-spider parachuting down to the platform.

The wind intensified, knocking the spider already on the platform off balance for a moment before it recovered.

Then it began to come for Steve.

CHAPTER FORTY

Steve thought about ending it all by jumping. It was a much preferable way to go than to be devoured by a ginormous spider. Just launch himself off the tower...it would all be over in a few quick seconds. He certainly didn't want to be alive enough to be *assimilated* into whatever godforsaken reality Winslow now lived in, if that was Winslow's plan for him rather than be eaten alive.

He turned to face the edge of the platform just as the second, airborne, spider came in for a landing. Looking up at the parajumping spider, he saw that its silken 'chute wrapped around the struts of the tower as it glided in over the platform. Fortunately for Steve, that spider landed on the first, temporarily impeding it from reaching Steve, who had been about to spring himself off the tower to certain death.

This gave him a few seconds to think about the end of his life. This was it. This is how it all ends, jumping from a tower in the deepest possible reaches of the Amazon rainforest. And you did it to yourself, he thought. *You signed up for this, your greed to discover a lost city has brought you straight to this point.*

"Go ahead and jump, Steve! Jump if you don't want to be assimilated. I thought a couple of old work buddies might like to hang out for eternity, but perhaps anything more than a little shop talk at the water cooler would strain our relationship." Winslow laughed through his mega-spiders. Steve could even hear peals of laughter coming all the way from the ground. It made him ill.

And then the second spider negotiated its way off the first-mega-beast's back, and it was lumbering toward Steve with a vengeance. Coming to consume him. Steve turned and ran, seeking the quick death of the high fall.

As he launched into his jump, a gust of wind whipped up a trail of silk. He realized it was one of the severed parachute cords that had gotten tangled in the tower's golden support bars, but that had now come unraveled in the wind with the spider no longer attached to it.

As Steve launched himself from the platform, without really knowing why, he reached out and grabbed the nearly invisible rope. He was surprised to feel its thickness fill his palm and clutched his fingers greedily around it.

Then he was off the platform and into the air, Winslow's voice screeching after him: "Goodbyyyyye, Steve! Hahahahahahahaha!" Like some kind of maniac. "Have a nice trip! See you next fall!"

And Steve was falling, at least it felt like it, but after a couple of seconds it became clear that he was falling in the wrong direction—he was falling *up*. Enough of the spider's silken parachute was still intact and untangled from the tower and the spider, that it was supporting his weight in the air, and actually carrying him up in a strong updraft of wind swirling around the bottom of the natural bowl. Steve felt another silk rope brush against his free arm and grabbed it too, so that he had one cord in each hand. He held on with absolutely no idea of what to expect. He figured he was only delaying the inevitable, but when he opened his eyes and looked down, he sucked in his breath as he gazed *down* at the top of the tower's spire.

It took Steve a moment to realize what had happened, and when he did, he felt a stab of both wonder and fear. He was now firmly aloft in the spider's own parachute. The steady winds were enough to keep him airborne. He knew that without the gusts, he'd drop fast to the ground, possibly enough to be fatal. But even if he survived the drop, he knew what awaited him down there. That was where the fear part came in. The 'chute could simply fail—fall apart under stress—or the wind could die—and that was if he didn't simply screw up and lose his hold on the 'chute. So many ways to die, and yet…

…he was alive. Against all odds, Steve Hoch, humble lab technician, was still drawing breath! The exhilaration and improbability of it all gave him a spark for life that Winslow's strange regime had all but sucked out of him. Suddenly he wanted to live again, if that was possible. Yet at the same time he was under no illusion that things were not still firmly beyond his control. He was now at the mercy of the winds and a spider's spun construction.

His thoughts were spectacularly interrupted by a chaotic crosswind that sent him tumbling literally straight up. When he levelled out, he was overcome by a wave of vertigo as he gazed down upon the entire natural amphitheater—on the whole of the Lost City of Z. He eyed the waterfalls and mountains and trees and the golden towers. Spider predation was the last thing he'd have to worry about if he fell from this lofty height, he thought. The view didn't look much different from the helicopter rides he'd taken over the jungle.

He flexed his fingers on the silken ropes, making sure his grip was solid. As soon as he made the adjustment, there was a pause in the wind and he plummeted a good 100 feet before being blown sideways by a fresh gust. He passed over the tower where Santos had battled and lost his fight against the mega-spider that had taken his life. Then he saw the tower where Ruiz had made his last stand recede into the distance. As he passed the last of the golden towers, he saw the green-shrouded walls of the amphitheater approaching.

He tensed as another eddy of wind—like a mini-tornado—sent him spiraling downward. When he stabilized on a level track after the wind died down, he could hear Winslow's army of spiders cursing up to him: "Death to you, Steve! Death to you!"

And it did look like the end could be near. With the rim of the mountain wall that defined the hidden amphitheater fast approaching his eye level, Steve knew that it was going to be extremely close. If he was to hit the mountain or have the silken 'chute snag on the tree tops festooning its summit, Winslow's arachnid army would make short work of him. Of this he had zero doubt.

With three additional passing seconds he could see that he was going to hit the trunks on top of the crater if he didn't do something, so he yanked on one of the parachute cords, knowing it would alter the way air passed through the parachute system. He'd seen videos of skydivers controlling their movements in the air by pulling the cord to bend the 'chute left or right. He had no idea if that would be applicable here, but he pulled on the left rope, and was rewarded with a slowing of movement accompanied by a slight lift in altitude.

He lifted his legs to avoid an outcropping of rock on the top of the mountain, but still a cluster of treetops stood in his way. He repeated the same maneuver, jerking the cord in his left hand and holding it down, but for some reason, this time it had the opposite effect. He plummeted down. Steve let go of the left silk cord and instead yanked down hard on the right one and was immediately pulled upwards in a near-upside-down position. Leaves brushed over his face and he closed his eyes as he was dragged through the treetops.

Out of his peripheral vision and upside down, he saw one of the flying mega-spiders parachuting toward his general direction from behind in the amphitheater, probably after launching itself from the nearest golden tower.

"It is over for you, Steve!" the spider bellowed. "You have betrayed us and chosen your path."

I've chosen my path all right, Steve thought as he felt a thin tree branch whip against his backside, slowing his momentum until he cleared it and suddenly felt the freedom of open air. He yanked on one of the cords, knowing he needed a little more altitude, and let loose a holler of joy when his body was rocketed upward a good twenty-five feet. By the time his tumbling slowed, and he stabilized to an upright position, once again dangling from the silken parachute, Steve sucked in his breath with wonder at his new view.

He was now looking back at the entire bowl-shaped amphitheater— at the heart of the Lost City of Z, the golden spires slick with rain, sparkling in the weak sunlight that filtered through wind-whipped clouds. Looking behind him, he could see the vast flatness of the mighty Amazon rainforest stretching to the horizon, and he was airborne over it all.

Steve dangled from the mega-spider's parachute, watching the protected crater housing Dr. Winslow's final resting place, if his fate could be called rest, recede into the distance. A couple of mega-spiders that managed to stay aloft over the mountain's rim were still visible in the air, but they quickly fell away into the canopy below, unable to sustain flight long or high enough to catch up with Steve.

He had done it, escaped from the Lost City of Z. But as a fresh updraft of wind drove him almost a hundred feet higher, he realized that his outcome was still far from certain. He needed to somehow land his silken paragliding rig safely. He looked around for a suitable flat spot. Besides a large river, gleaming silver in the distance, he saw nothing but green treetops. And then he felt the cord his left hand had been gripping onto snap. The parachute was starting to fall apart.

Land now! He screamed at himself, the urge to live blaring with renewed vigor inside him. He put both hands on the remaining rope, praying it would not break as he yanked it down, hoping it would vent air from the roughly bell-shaped yet invisible parachute somewhere above him. At first he noticed no difference in his course, but after about ten seconds, he felt himself begin to slowly descend. He continued to drop until he could make out individual leaves on the treetops, and then he let the rope back up. He wanted to stay aloft as long as possible, since he travelled much faster like this than he would on the ground, and he knew that Winslow's spiders would be coming for him. He was free for now, and he wanted to keep it that way. And yet the parachute was already starting to fail, so he wanted to be at a height that was survivable if he did fall.

Steve caught a lucky break when the wind died down a bit, or maybe it was just that being closer to the trees prevented upwellings and eddies, because his vector became more predictable and stable. He was able to lower his distance above the canopy to a mere ten feet and stay there while he drifted across the Amazon basin.

He floated that way for an unknown amount of time, hours, until the sun began to set. He passed over many rivers and streams, even a couple of small clearings, but kept flying. He didn't think it wise to fly at night, though, since he could easily lose track of his altitude, so he began to look for a landing spot. He would just have to take his chances with whatever was on the ground from here on out, but he felt reasonably sure that he had outpaced the mega- spiders for the time being.

Where to land? He didn't see any other way but to risk a treetop landing, yet wanted to avoid doing it at speed. If he had to guess, he was travelling at a good twenty miles per hour now, and at times upward of thirty. Steve experimented with pulling the single remaining cord to see how it would affect the 'chute, which, all things considered, had held up remarkably well to this point. After some stops and starts, he arrived at a technique where he would pull the cord, hold it down for a few seconds, and then allow it to reset to resting position before repeating the process. In this manner he was able to gradually slow his forward progress until he was essentially hovering over the canopy, descending very slowly from ten feet above the treetops.

Steve let himself drop onto the tree below his feet. He grabbed for its thin branches, clutching at them to slow his fall until they snapped. When he fell far enough, the chute itself tangled in the branches and that slowed his fall even more. By the time he had fallen perhaps thirty feet, he was grasping a tree branch with both hands thick enough to stand on, no longer connected to the 'chute which had been separated and no doubt shredded to pieces somewhere in the branches above. He pulled himself up onto the tree branch and hugged it while crawling slowly over to the main tree trunk. Once there, he sat in place, catching his breath for a few minutes until he was ready to begin his final descent. He could see nothing of his surroundings at this height, shrouded in foliage.

When he felt sufficiently rested, Steve carefully climbed down the tree, one branch at a time, knowing that darkness was rapidly approaching. He dropped to the forest floor while it was still twilight, extensive shadows marking the ground, strange fireflies and lightning bugs twinkling here and there in the lower reaches of the canopy.

He slowly looked around the forest floor in a 360, awareness heightened for signs of arachnids. But he saw none, not even the little ones. Steve lamented the fact that he was essentially gearless other than the clothes on his back and his boots. But it was a small price to pay for being alive. He had not expected that at all

And so it was that Steve Hoch began to walk out of the Amazon rainforest as night fell, unafraid, looking forward to contacting civilization again. The moon was full, at least he had that going for him, and it gave him barely enough light to navigate by if he walked slowly. He broke off a stout tree branch and used a rock to fashion it into a crude machete.

Steve smiled to himself as he forded a small stream, walking stick / machete in hand. He spotted a rotten log and flipped it over, grabbing a handful of the white grubs he saw scurrying there. Popped a few in his mouth and swallowed them without even chewing. He would need sustenance for the journey out of here. But it was nothing to him now. He could feel it in his bones that he would make it. He could do anything.

He had discovered the lost city of Z.

EPILOGUE

27 days later
Rio de Janeiro

Steve Hoch paused at the foot of the concrete steps leading up to the *Policia Civil do Estado do Rio de Janeiro* police station. He'd had a couple of days to reacclimate to civilization, starting with a hotel where he'd showered, shaved and eaten a real meal for the first time in nearly a month. Getting out of the jungle had been predictably difficult, but as he knew he would, he made it. First to a remote tribal village where they fed him bush meat—mostly monkey and sloth-gave him a few supplies, and from there on out he absolutely knew he would make it.

His first stop was to return to the rental house where he'd retrieved what belongings he'd had, including some cash and his passport, which he never took into the jungle. From there he'd gone to the city, checked into his hotel and convalesced for a couple of days while thinking about what to do. That night in a bar he'd tried to relay to various acquaintances that he'd just come back from an expedition—even after cleaning himself up his appearance was still haggard. He had deep scratches visible on his face, neck and hands, he was very thin, was covered in various insect and spider bites, and something about his eyes lacked spark. But the conversation always fizzled when he realized there was no way he could describe it. He couldn't divulge that he'd found the lost city, people would dismiss him as a wacko, or worse—go looking for it based on his information.

So he'd simply let everyone think he'd gone on a routine trek, roughing it for a few weeks while being guided around on a sightseeing trip. The next day when he woke up in the hotel, he decided he was going to fly back home to the States and retire. He had enough with his university pension, even with early retirement, to live a simple, frugal life until he died. And that was all he wanted.

As for his fellow expedition mates, he knew there would be questions, so he decided to address them head-on rather than leave for the States and risk appearances that he was fleeing in the wake of mysterious circumstances. So it was that he found himself striding into the police station.

He walked up to the public reception desk. He asked to speak with the supervisor of officers Santos and Ruiz. After a look of consternation from the receptionist, he was told that no such officers worked at this location. When he told her he wanted to speak with whoever was in charge of the Manuscript 512 case, a detective appeared within a few minutes, studied him coolly from a distance, and then introduced himself before asking him to join him in his office.

Steve followed the Brazilian man into a small, undecorated office and sat in a metal folding chair in front of the desk. Without preamble, Steve gave him a highly edited verbal account of how he, the wanted Dr. Hunter Winslow, and the two *policía* from this station, along with jungle guide Sal Torres, went looking for the lost city of Z. Steve became separated from the group and did not know what happened to the rest of them. He urged that perhaps a search party was in order, since, as far as he knew, they had not yet returned. He left out the actual discovery of Z completely. Saying they died looking for it was plenty.

The detective eyed him intently and then asked to see his ID. Steve slid his passport across the desk. The detective squinted at him and leaned forward in his chair to made direct eye contact. "Mr. Hoch, we never assigned any officers to go into the Amazon. We have a case open for the manuscript theft, but…" He reached for some folders and pulled out a piece of paper, "…Officer Rodrigo was the lead detective on that case. And he was never sent into the jungle. That is not something we would normally do."

Steve sat there, stunned, trying to process what it all meant. He pictured Santos and Ruiz, ordering him to complete the lab work on the manuscript in the house…trekking through the jungle with them…*they were just two criminals posing as cops in order to find out where the lost city of Z was so that they could steal the treasures for themselves!*

"Are you all right, Mr. Hoch? Would you like some water?"

Steve cleared his throat. "I'm fine, thank you. I…"

The detective appeared to relax and leaned back in his chair, placing both hands behind his head. "Look, Mr. Hoch, as you may know, Brazil has its fair share of crime, including crimes of a very serious nature. If we interrupted those kinds of investigations to pursue…goose chases like lost cities and jungle treasures, we'd never solve any crimes. Dr. Winslow is wanted in connection with the library theft, and I will pass your information on to the officer in charge of that case. But there is nothing actionable here for me. Leave me your contact information, and you are free to go."

Steve eyeballed him for a moment before getting up from the chair and nodding. "I thank you for your time, detective."

The detective nodded and as Steve turned for the door, he caught movement out of his peripheral vision on the desk. He focused on it just long enough to see a small, perfectly ordinary looking spider scuttle from beneath one piece of paper to the next.

END

CPSIA information can be obtained
at www.ICGtesting.com
Printed in the USA
BVHW031205240121
598599BV00031B/479